Fractured Crystal

Margaret Manchester

First published in the United Kingdom in 2020 by
Mosaic (Teesdale) Ltd, Snaisgill, Middleton-in-Teesdale,
County Durham DL12 0RP

ISBN 978 1 9164327 6 5

Design, layout and typesetting by
Mosaic Design and Print, Middleton-in-Teesdale

About the Author

Margaret Manchester lives in County Durham,
England, with her husband and two sons. She was born
in Weardale and spent her childhood there. Research
into Margaret's family history discovered that many
branches of her family had lived and worked in the area
for centuries, either as lead miners, smelters or farmers.
While she studied local history and archaeology,
Margaret worked as a guide at Killhope Lead Mining

Museum. She was awarded a Masters degree in Archaeology from the University of Durham and then taught archaeology, local history and genealogy. As well as writing, Margaret is currently the managing director of an award-winning business; she is the chair of a charity that supports industrial heritage, and she enjoys spending time in her garden and with her dogs.

http://www.margaretmanchester.com

https://twitter.com/m_r_manchester

https://www.facebook.com/margaretmanchesterauthor

Dedication

This book is dedicated to
my husband and best friend,
Alec Manchester,
with love.

Acknowledgements

I would like to thank my husband, Alec, for his patience and understanding while I was writing this book, and for reading and commenting on my early drafts. I could not have completed it without his support.

I am very grateful to my sister, Linda Brown, my father-in-law, Leslie Manchester, and my friend and former solicitor, Tony Turnbull, for providing feedback prior to publication.

The photograph of fluorite crystals used on the front cover was taken by Andy Hopkirk.

The sunset photograph on the back cover shows a view of Weardale from Crawleyside, Stanhope and was taken by Linda Brown.

Finally, thank you to Judith Mashiter at Mosaic Publishing for transforming my manuscript into a book.

Chapter 1

St John's Chapel, Weardale
July 1895

Josie climbed the steps of the town hall and gasped when she entered the large room full of glistening minerals. She moved from table to table, asking collectors about their exhibits. As she examined an unusual piece of yellow fluorite, she noticed that she was being studied from across the room. A dark-haired young man was watching her, and when their eyes met, he smiled.

She worked her way around the room until, eventually, she reached his table, which held some beautiful specimens of fluorite. There were several clusters of purple crystals, and a large, single crystal that was so clear she could almost see through it.

'Good morning,' he said. 'What brings you to the Grand Mineral Exhibition?'

'I love minerals,' replied Josie. 'I collect them. Just pieces that I've found, you know, on spoil heaps and in the river. They're nowhere near as nice as these.'

She looked enviously at his collection.

'I'm surprised, that's all. I've never known a lass show much interest in spar before, never mind come to an event like this.'

'My family tease me about it.' Josie blushed. 'They say I'd have made a good miner.'

The man laughed, and said, 'Well, that'll never happen, with you being a lass. You'd not be allowed to set foot in a mine around here.'

'I know,' said Josie wistfully. Gesturing towards the table, she asked, 'Where did you find these?'

'Boltsburn mine over at Rookhope. Some of the best pieces have come out of there. I look for them after our shift's finished and take them out in me bait bag. And sometimes I go in at weekends when there's nobody about.'

'Isn't that stealing?'

'No. Not really. Spar and quartz aren't worth enough for the bosses to be bothered with it. They only want lead ore — galena; that's where the big money is. The rest is just waste as far as they're concerned. They turn a blind eye to us miners taking the crystals out to make a few extra shillings on the side. And collectors will pay decent money for good bits.'

'I don't have any money to buy anything from you,' Josie said regretfully, 'and for obvious reasons, I can't collect them from the mines like you do, so I suppose I'll just have to keep searching the spoil heaps.'

She sighed as her gaze swept around the room at the beautiful array of sparkling minerals. Realising that she had sounded petulant, she said, 'I'm sorry, it's not your fault. It's just the way it is.'

He smiled sadly, and hesitated slightly before asking, 'Have you seen where a river cuts through a mineral vein?'

'No, I don't think so.'

'If you know where to look, you can see the vein in the bank sides, and sometimes you can find decent pieces in them. If you'd like to come for a walk with me next Sunday, I'd be happy to show you.'

'Aye, I'd like that. Thank you.'

Josie noticed the way the man raised his eyebrows when he smiled, and she couldn't decide whether it made him look cheeky or happy, but whichever it was, she liked it.

'I'm Josie Milburn,' she said. 'I live near Westgate.'

He held out his hand for her to shake, and said, 'Elliott Dawson, from Rookhope. I'm very pleased to meet you, Miss Milburn.' He held her hand firmly and, when he seemed reluctant to let go of it, she looked up into his dark blue eyes.

'We could meet at the bridge in the village, at about 2 o'clock?' he suggested.

'That would be perfect,' she replied.

He released her hand, and she moved away, heading for the last table in the room. While she'd been talking to

Elliott, she hadn't been aware that the hall had filled with people. The sound of voices bounced off the walls, the heat was almost unbearable, and the pungent smell of tobacco smoke filled the air. She wanted to leave. Glancing back at Elliott, she saw that he was chatting with an older man. He waved farewell to her, and she smiled at him, blushing slightly, before stepping out into the warm sunshine.

On the walk back to High House Farm, a mile or so beyond the village of Westgate, Josie had only one thing on her mind. Elliott Dawson. Nobody had ever asked her out before, and she was flattered that such a good-looking lad wanted to spend his day off with her. He hadn't been put off by her interest in minerals either; he'd seemed to like that.

As a horse and cart approached, she stepped off the road and stood with her back against the dry-stone wall until it passed. The driver inclined his head in greeting, and she recognised him as a boy called Johnny from her schooldays. Her memories of that time stirred up mixed feelings. She had loved classes and reading and learning about new things, but she had been teased mercilessly by the other children. To this day, she didn't know the reason. Perhaps it had been because she liked school, or because she lived outside of the village, or because she'd been a tomboy back then, preferring to work on the farm rather than in the house. She had mostly ignored their name-calling, but once or twice she'd retaliated with her fists. It was all in the past now, but she couldn't forget their harsh words.

Josie had felt different from other girls. She didn't understand why they were eager to get married and have children and seemed content to devote their childhood to honing the skills required to be a housewife and mother. They followed the same path without question — a life of bearing children, cooking, cleaning, making and mending clothes, knitting and matting. Josie sighed. Surely there must be more to life?

Walking up the farm track, she glanced towards the old, stone-built farmhouse perched on the hillside, where she lived with her family. It was surrounded by hay fields, most of which were full of long grass and colourful meadow flowers that swayed gently in the breeze. In the others, the grass had been cut and lay in lines on the ground to dry. Men formed a row across the field bordering the track, swinging their scythes in front of them, cutting the long grass as they walked.

When Josie drew closer, her father, Tom Milburn, shouted over, 'What was it like, love?'

'Fantastic!' Josie enthused. 'Even better than I imagined. You should have seen them — they were beautiful!'

'I'm pleased you enjoyed it, lass, but you've been a long time. I thought you were coming back to help your mother make tea.'

'There's still plenty of time,' she said, looking to see

where the sun was in the sky.

'Well, you'd better get up there quickly. There's a lot of mouths to feed today with your Uncle Joe and his lads helping us with the hay.'

'I'm on my way,' she said, and she turned and ran up the hill to the farmhouse.

Time slowed down for Josie from the moment that she met Elliott Dawson. The week dragged. When Sunday morning eventually arrived, she went to the chapel at Westgate with her family. During the service, her mind drifted away from the sermon, and she daydreamed about her meeting with Elliott. She was shocked out of her reverie by her mother, Mary Milburn, who nudged her when it was time to stand for the final hymn.

When they returned home, Josie went straight into the kitchen to help her mother prepare Sunday dinner. While Mary took a joint of roast beef from the oven, Josie washed the vegetables in the kitchen sink. Her mother took them from her and peeled and chopped them, and then dropped them into pans of boiling water.

As they worked, Mary asked, 'What are you planning to do today?'

'Not much,' said Josie. 'It's a lovely day. I might go down to the river for a walk after dinner.'

'That's nice,' said Mary, not showing any surprise at her daughter's reply, and they lapsed into a comfortable silence while Josie mixed the batter for Yorkshire puddings and Mary made the gravy.

Josie felt a little guilty because she hadn't mentioned that she'd arranged to meet Elliott Dawson, and walk by the river with him. She wondered why she'd neglected to tell her mother that. Perhaps she was worried that her parents might stop her from going, or that they might insist on meeting Elliott before they'd allow her to go out with him.

Her parents were less strict with her now than they'd ever been. She often went out walking or riding by herself when she had time to spare, although that was usually just on Sunday afternoons as there was always something to do, either in the house or out on the farm. Her parents only worked on Sundays when absolutely necessary, with it being a day of rest, and Josie was grateful for that; it gave her time to explore and collect her minerals.

As Josie set the table, her younger brothers, Tommy and Matt, having heard the clinking of cutlery, barged into the kitchen and sat down at the table ready for their dinners, scraping the heavy chairs on the flagstone floor.

Tom sat in an armchair by the unlit fire, reading a newspaper. Although he hadn't travelled far from the county of Durham, her father liked to know what was happening in the world.

'Well, I never!' he chuckled to himself. 'There's been an automobile race in France, from Paris to Bordeaux and back. The winner took nearly forty-nine hours to drive seven hundred and thirty-two miles. That's a lot faster than a horse-drawn carriage, but a train can travel that distance in less than half that time.' Shaking his head, he said, 'I cannot see them automobiles catching on.'

'I'd have one,' said Tommy. 'You get off a train at the station, and then you have to make your way home from there. With a car, you could drive right up to your front door.'

'It's only a short walk back from the station — a mile and a half at most — that's hardly an inconvenience,' countered Tom.

Josie saw Tommy roll his eyes, before saying, 'Aye, maybe. But I'd still have one. I'd be able to go anywhere I wanted, and see places I've only ever heard of. By meself. I hate being in a crowded carriage with people sitting in silence staring at me, or even worse, talking to me when they haven't got anything to say.'

His words struck a chord with Josie; they echoed her secret desire to travel. She'd read widely about other countries and cultures, and she would love to see more of the world. The thought of Tommy owning a car so that he could explore the places he longed to visit made her smile.

When the meal was ready, Mary served out and carried the plates to the table, where all of the family sat waiting. Tom said grace before they began to eat. Watching her brothers wolf down their dinners, Josie had to agree with her mother, who often said the lads' stomachs were like bottomless pits. Hard work and fresh air certainly gave them an appetite.

This Sunday dinner was no different to any other really, but to Josie, it felt like it lasted for such a long time. She was anxious for it to be over so that she could get ready to see Elliott. Her thoughts drifted to the afternoon ahead. She barely registered the conversation about Uncle Joe and his farmhands coming to cut the last of the fields tomorrow, or that her father and brothers would return the favour by going to Springbank Farm to help her uncle cut his grass later in the week. She desperately wanted them to stop talking and finish their food.

When the meal was finally over, Josie cleared the table and quickly washed the dishes, while her mother dried them and put away. As soon as they had finished, she rushed to her bedroom and checked her reflection in the dressing table mirror. The dark auburn hair that she had prepared so carefully that morning had come loose, and several strands were hanging down. She pulled out the hairpins and brushed it thoroughly before tying it back up neatly in a bun. Her face looked a little pale, so she rubbed her cheeks — that would have to do. As Josie passed the tall clock on the way out, it read a quarter to two; she didn't want to be late. Grabbing her bonnet from a hook on the door, she rushed out of the house.

The warm, summer air hit Josie as soon as she went outside. Walking briskly down the farm track and along the main road into the village of Westgate, she didn't notice the butterflies that fluttered around the cornflowers and knapweed, or the fledgeling wagtails bobbing on the wall top. She was worried that she wouldn't know what to say to Elliott, or that he mightn't like her when he got to know her better. When she reached the bridge, Elliott was already there, and his smile made her feel more at ease.

'Hello, Mr Dawson,' she said.

'Please, call me Elliott,' he said, still smiling. 'Would you mind if I call you Josie? It's a lovely name.'

'Thank you, Elliott. I'd rather you did. I don't like being called Miss Milburn.'

He was looking at her intently, and she started to feel a little uncomfortable.

'Which way are we going?' she asked.

'Downstream. There are a few veins that cross the river between here and Eastgate.'

They walked side by side through the woodland that lined the riverbank, and it wasn't long before Elliott pointed to the river, and said, 'Look here. This is the first one. This is Dawson's vein.' He laughed. 'It's got nothing to do with me, though!'

'Maybe an ancestor of yours discovered it, or worked it, or maybe even owned it!'

'That'll be the day when a Dawson owns a mine,' he said cynically. 'All my family has ever managed to do is scrape a living out of them. That's why I sell bits of spar on the side — the extra money helps us out.'

'You never know,' Josie said optimistically, 'it might happen one day.'

Elliott laughed. 'Aye, we can live in hope. Anyway, let me show you this vein, and then we can have a look for bonny bits.'

He jumped over the bank and landed in the shallow running water. Smooth stones, polished by the river, protruded from the surface. Josie took the hand Elliott offered to help her down, and she lifted her skirts with the other so they wouldn't get wet. She wondered why Elliott was looking away, and then it dawned on her that, with the height difference, he could see her bare legs.

'I'm sorry,' she said blushing. 'It's too warm to wear stockings today.'

'Nothing to be sorry for,' he replied, smiling and raising his eyebrows in that way he had. If he'd been one of her brothers, she would have pushed him into the water for being cheeky, but instead, her cheeks reddened even more.

When she'd climbed down safely and was standing on the riverbed, Elliott pointed out the band of minerals showing in the riverbank on each side, and he explained how rivers cut through veins. They looked for spar in the bank side, but couldn't see any good bits, so they climbed back up and continued their walk downstream to the next vein.

Josie could make out the second vein much more clearly. A piece of green spar under the water caught her eye and, although it was in the river, its five crystals were still sharp-edged.

'That's not been in the water long,' said Elliott. 'There's no sign of wear. It's nice.' He examined the lower bank. 'The water's not often this low. I don't think I've seen this bit before.'

He took a small hammer from his jacket pocket and chipped off a few pieces of vein material, and then wrapped them in a cotton handkerchief before putting them in his pocket.

When they'd finished, Elliott helped Josie climb up from the riverbed, and they strolled back to Westgate through the trees, chatting about vein formations and mining methods. As they neared the bridge, Elliott stopped suddenly and turned to Josie.

'Can I see you again?' he asked.

'Yes, I'd like that.'

'Same time, next Sunday?'

'Yes, that would be good,' said Josie. 'Where do you want to meet?'

'How about up at Middlehope? There are some interesting old workings up there.'

'Alright, I'll walk up and meet you at the Middlehope turn-off.'

'Great,' he said, smiling. 'I'm looking forward to it already.'

Elliott leaned forward and kissed her gently on her lips, and then he turned quickly and walked away, leaving Josie standing there in surprise. She touched her lips and smiled to herself as she set off for home, holding the spar in her hand. It would always remind her of her first kiss.

Chapter 2

Westgate, Weardale
July 1895

The following Sunday, Josie walked up the fields and across the fell past West Rigg quarry and waited by the Middlehope road for Elliott. She rested against a dry-stone wall and watched a line of lapwing chicks follow their mother across the track.

It wasn't long before Elliott appeared at the brow of the hill and made his way down to meet her.

'Hello, Josie, I'm pleased you could make it,' he said.

'You too,' she replied.

He smiled at her, before pointing westwards and saying, 'We should go this way. There are a lot of old mines over yonder.'

They walked over coarse fell grasses, avoiding rough patches of heather, bracken and rushes, until Josie stopped suddenly at a small pond.

'Look at the frogs!' she said. 'They're tiny. And some of

them still have tails!'

As she stepped forward to get a better look, Elliott grabbed her arm and said, 'Stop! Don't go any closer. That's a fall.'

Josie stopped awkwardly. Elliott held her arm until she regained her balance, and when she had both feet firmly on the ground, she asked, 'What do you mean — a fall?'

'Imagine an abandoned mine tunnel running underneath the fell. A fall is when the roof of that tunnel collapses in. The ground above it gives way and falls into the mine, and you get a hollow like this on the surface. When it fills up with water, it looks just like a pond, but I know that a mine runs under here, so this is a fall. And there's a strong likelihood that the ground on either side of it will be unstable an' all.'

'Thank you,' she said. 'You might have saved my life.' She moved away from him, smiling at him over her shoulder.

Elliott quickly caught up with her, and said, 'The first shaft's over here.'

He led the way to a mound. The grass appeared to be a brighter green than the grass around it, and there was a dip in the top. Josie thought it looked like a miniature volcano. She'd never seen an actual volcano, but she'd read about them, and this is what she imagined one would look like — only larger. She began to climb up the small hill to get a better look, with Elliott right by her side, and he took hold of her hand when they reached the top.

'Don't step down into the hole,' he said.

'Why not? It looks safe.'

'Well, appearances can be deceptive. There's a shaft under there that's probably about thirty foot deep. They back-filled some of them properly with rocks, but they just covered some over with timbers. You can't tell which is which until it's too late — the rotten wood has given way and you're lying at the bottom of a deep shaft.'

'Sorry,' Josie said, 'I didn't know.'

He looked at their joined hands, and said, 'I think I'd better keep hold of this to keep you out of danger, young lady.' He smiled his cheeky smile, and she simply nodded. He'd opened her eyes to the potential dangers on the fells.

As they strolled along a narrow path, Josie couldn't believe that she was walking hand in hand with a man. She never thought that would happen. She'd recently turned twenty-two years of age, and nobody had shown much interest in her before. That's why her parents weren't concerned about her going out alone — they were no longer worried about lads chasing her. It wasn't that she was plain; she could look nice when she made an effort. It's just that most men seemed to want a homey woman for a wife, and Josie would never consider herself to be homey.

Being so close to Elliott, she couldn't help but notice that he was about four inches taller than her, and he looked strong and healthy with his broad shoulders and lean waist. She'd been acutely aware of how attractive he was the first time they'd met, especially when he smiled his boyish smile and his eyes twinkled. Thinking about his age, she guessed that he would be a little older than her but not by much.

She wondered why someone like him would want to be with her. There were plenty of pretty girls in the dale. Why hadn't he been snapped up by one of them? Was there a reason he wasn't married already? Maybe he was! She shook her head as if to clear it of her wayward thoughts. Why was she even thinking about marriage?

With a sudden compulsion to know more about him, she asked, 'Do you still live at home — with your parents?'

'Aye, with me mother. Me father died a few years back.'

'I'm sorry.'

'Thank you,' he said. 'It's just the two of us now. I would have liked to have a brother or a sister, but it never happened. Me parents married late in life. They used to call me their 'little surprise'. I suppose they didn't expect to have bairns. What about you?'

'I live with my mother and father, and my brothers, Tommy and Matt. They're younger than me. We live at High House Farm, about a mile from Westgate.'

'If you don't mind me asking, how old are you?' he asked.

She smiled as she realised that he'd been wondering about her too. 'I've just turned twenty-two,' she replied.

He stopped and turned to her. 'Really!' he said. 'You're twenty-two. And you're not promised to anyone?'

'No, I'm not promised to anyone.'

'I find that hard to believe, you know, that you're still single. A bonny lass with a head on her shoulders is a rare find.'

Josie blushed. 'How old are you?'

'Twenty-five. I'll be twenty-six on Sunday.'

Josie's face fell.

'What's the matter?' asked Elliott.

'If it's your birthday next Sunday, you'll not want to go for a walk with me.'

'Why should that matter? I'd love to see you again next week.' He leaned forward and kissed her lightly on her lips. 'That's if you'd like to go out with me again?'

Reassured, she returned his smile. 'Aye, I would.'

'Is there any chance that you could come over to Rookhope?' asked Elliott. 'There's something I'd like to show you.'

Josie noticed a glint in his eye.

'And what would that be?' she asked, bewildered.

'Well, you know the spar that I took to the exhibition...'

'Yes, of course. How could I forget? Those pieces were beautiful.'

'It's the place that they came from.'

As his meaning sunk in, Josie's eyes widened. 'You mean you'll take me into Boltsburn mine?'

'Aye, I'll take you into the mine. I'd love to show you the mineral flats.'

As much as Josie had wanted to go into a mine, she'd

never expected that she would. She was so excited to think that at this time next week she could be underground with Elliott. She couldn't stop grinning as they continued their walk, although the smile fell from her face when the words that she'd heard many times over the years came into her head, and she spoke them out loud, 'But it's unlucky for women to go in the mines.'

'I don't believe any of that old superstitious nonsense,' said Elliott. 'People make their own luck.'

Josie raised her eyebrows in surprise. 'You really believe that?' she asked.

'Aye, I do.'

She hesitated only for a moment before she said, 'In that case, I'll meet you at Rookhope. What time should I be there?'

'How about 3 o'clock?'

'Yes, that would give me time to ride over after dinner.'

As they walked down the slope, Elliott stopped next to a small hole in the ground that Josie would have passed by without noticing.

'This is an old mine as well,' he said, pushing the grasses aside so she could see it better. 'It's not as old as the pit you tried your best to fall down, but old enough to be forgotten about.'

He took a candle from his pocket and lit it, and then he lay down on the ground and put his arm down the hole; the flickering flame illuminated the dark tunnel. He said, 'Lie down and look inside.'

Josie did as he said.

'See those bits of wood? The old miners used them for climbing in and out of the mine, before ladders.'

She looked through the small opening and could see a narrow tunnel lined with dressed stone, with what looked like wooden rungs fastened into the stonework. She couldn't see the bottom.

'How deep is it?' she asked.

He picked up a stone and dropped it down the hole, and they listened for the sound of a splash as the rock hit the water at the bottom. From the time it took, Elliott estimated its depth and said, 'It's not that deep — no more than about twenty-five feet. It'll go down onto a level that drains the water from the workings in the vein further up.'

Josie was genuinely impressed by his knowledge; she sat up and asked, 'How come you know so much about mines?'

Elliott sat up too and blew out the candle before saying, 'Me father trained as a surveyor for the mines, and he used to love to tell me about them when we went for walks.'

Looking back at the hole, she said, 'Can we... '

'No! I'm not taking you into this one. I don't know if it's safe.'

'Oh, alright then,' she said, pretending to sulk. 'I suppose I'll just have to wait until next week.'

Elliott laughed loudly. He stood up and took her hand

to help her up, and they walked back to the road. When they reached it, he wrapped her in his arms and kissed her. Loosening his hold, he stepped back and said, 'See you on Sunday.'

Then, he climbed back up the hill towards Rookhope, stopping at the brow of the hill to turn around and wave.

Chapter 3

When Sunday came around again, Josie told her mother that she was going for a ride, but omitted to mention where she was going or who she was meeting. She tacked up her father's chestnut mare, Nutmeg, and set off for Rookhope.

It was a warm day with just a slight hint of a breeze. The road over the fell was quiet apart from the clip-clop of the horse's hoofs and the call of curlews overhead. Rabbits raced to their burrows when Josie passed them, their little white tails bobbing as they ran. As she headed down the steep, winding road towards Redburn smelt mill, her eyes were drawn to the opposite hillside where the long line of the flue stretched right up to the chimney at the summit.

Families and couples walked along the road and the railway line that ran in parallel along the valley floor, and as she crossed the stone-arched bridge, she spotted children paddling in the burn. She continued down the Rookhope road until she reached the village, and then she turned onto the track that led to Boltsburn mine. The horse splashed through the ford and snorted, clearly pleased to cool down in the slow-flowing water.

Josie let Nutmeg take a drink from the river before she dismounted and tethered her to a tree in the shade, where the horse put down its head and began to nibble at the sparse grass.

For some reason, Josie's heart was beating faster than usual. She wasn't sure whether it was apprehension at going underground for the first time or excitement at seeing Elliott again. The entrance to the mine was only a hundred yards away, just out of sight. She slowly walked towards it and, when she turned the corner, she saw Elliott waiting for her by the adit. He grinned when he saw her.

'Good afternoon!' he said. 'I'm pleased you've come.'

'Hello,' she said brightly. 'And happy birthday!'

'Thank you.' He reached forward and hugged her, kissing her gently on the cheek before releasing her from his arms.

'I didn't know what to get you, so I brought you a bag of sweets. I hope you like them. It's what my brothers like best on their birthdays.'

'Thank you,' he said sincerely, taking the packet from her. 'I love bullets. I don't know anyone who doesn't.'

Elliott leaned towards her, and his lips brushed lightly

against hers, and when she thought he was about to move away, he surprised her by putting his arms around her and pulling her closer, kissing her more passionately.

'I'm sorry,' he said, looking down at the ground, 'I got a bit carried away. It's just...'

'What's wrong?' asked Josie.

'I'm pleased you remembered my birthday, that's all. You're the only one who did.'

'What about your mother? Did she forget about it?'

'Aye, but it's not her fault. She's old, and she forgets things.'

Josie noticed a pained look in his eyes, and then he added, 'She forgets most things. Sometimes she doesn't even know who I am.'

'Oh, I'm sorry.' Josie didn't know what else to say.

'Anyway, we'd better get a move on,' said Elliott. 'If you haven't changed your mind about going in? Are you ready?'

'Aye, I'm ready.'

Elliott took a tallow candle from his pocket and lit it with a match. 'I'll go first. Keep close behind me so you can see where you're going. Alright?'

Josie nodded.

Water a few inches deep flowed out of the horse level. She bowed her head and stepped between the tracks to follow Elliott, and water seeped into her boots. It was cold, but she didn't complain. She wanted to experience everything about the mine and commit it to memory. She listened to the strange noises, felt the damp stone walls with her fingertips, smelt the stale air and the pungent smoke from the tallow candle, and shivered. Still, she ignored the discomfort because for the first time, and probably the only time in her life, she was about to see the treasures hidden deep underground.

It felt as though they'd walked for about ten minutes when they reached a fork in the tunnel, where they veered off to the left. Elliott turned, and said, 'It's not much further. Are you warm enough?'

'It's a lot colder in here than it was outside.'

'Here, take my jacket.' He slipped off his jacket and placed it around her shoulders. 'Put it on.'

'Thank you.'

She slipped her arms into the sleeves. The jacket was warm from Elliott's body, and she wrapped it around her, thankful for his kindness.

They continued for about five more minutes, and then she was surprised to step out from the narrow tunnel and into a cavernous chamber.

'Excuse me,' said Elliott, his voice sounding strange as it echoed around the void. 'I need some more candles. They're in me jacket pocket.'

Before she had time to reach into his pocket to retrieve the candles, Elliott's hand was already there, and through the thin lining of the jacket, Josie could feel his hand move slowly over the contour of her waist and rest briefly on her hip. Her eyes widened in surprise at his forwardness.

Smiling his cheeky smile, Elliott said, 'I know they're in here somewhere.' He pulled out several candles from his jacket pocket, and then said, 'Stay here.' He moved away and placed lighted candles at various spots around the cavern.

As light filled the space, Josie was awestruck. The walls and ceiling were covered with streaks of different coloured minerals and patches of crystals. It looked like a vast grotto, and she thought that it could have been one of the Seven Wonders of the World. A spar box that took pride of place in the parlour at home came to mind; filled with crystals and strategically placed mirrors, candles lit up a mining scene complete with small lead figures of miners and their ponies and tubs. Looking up at the crystals that sparkled in the flickering candlelight, Josie felt as though she was one of those tiny figurines in a spar box; it was so unreal.

'It's beautiful!' is all she could think of to say.

'I knew you'd love it.' He said with a smile. 'Minerals are found in vertical seams, like a wall buried into the ground, but sometimes they spread out like they have here into the surrounding rock.'

'I can't believe how much you know about mines. I used to ask my father about them all the time. He must have been sick of me asking questions. Did I tell you he was a miner before we moved to the farm?'

'No, I didn't know that. Why did he move into

farming?'

'He had an accident at the mine when I was a baby. My mother said he was lucky to survive it.'

Seeing Elliott's look of concern, she quickly added, 'Oh, he's alright now.'

Josie noticed a spectacular piece of purple fluorite above them. It looked like it consisted of two perfectly formed cubic crystals. They were simply beautiful.

Elliott saw what she was looking at, and said, 'Very nice! Stand back.'

He took the hammer out of his pocket and tapped the rock around the spar to loosen it. He tried to move it with his fingers, but it was stuck firmly to the rock. Again, he tapped around the edges, a little harder this time, and tried to dislodge it. It moved a little. After being in that place for millions of years, Josie thought the crystals were resisting Elliott's attempt to remove them. Eventually, he managed to loosen them, and they dropped into his left hand, which he held out in front of Josie and slowly opened his fingers. Josie gasped. Two almost identical crystals sat in his palm.

'It broke!' she exclaimed. 'They looked so beautiful together.'

'Aye, they did. But at least this way we can have one each.' He smiled, and asked, 'Which one do you want?'

Josie held them both up to the light and was amazed to see that they looked identical. She placed them together where they had fractured, and they fitted together perfectly. She took one and handed the other to Elliott. He wrapped it carefully in a handkerchief and placed it in his waistcoat pocket.

Patting his waistcoat, he said, 'I'll treasure this. It will always remind me of today — and of you.'

He leaned forward, wrapped his arms around her and then he kissed her.

The privacy, the candlelight, or the special moment that they'd just shared, Josie didn't know what it was that made her move closer to him and return his kiss, but she did. They stood together in that enchanted place for the longest time, holding each other close and kissing lovingly before he eventually broke away.

Looking into her eyes, Elliott said, 'Josie, you've made this the best birthday I've ever had — just by being here with me. I'll never forget it.'

Josie heard the emotion in his voice and could see that his eyes were glassy.

'It's been a magical day. Thank you for bringing me down here,' she said, and she hugged him tightly.

'We'd better get back,' he said. 'We've been down here ages.'

Josie stepped back from Elliott's embrace and watched as he blew out the candles and gathered them up, before walking over to her and placing them in the pocket of the jacket that she still wore. This time she anticipated his touch, but his hand didn't linger. Instead, he reached for her hand and walked her back to the tunnel and through the level. They'd just passed the fork in the tunnel when he stopped suddenly and blew out his candle.

'Shh! Someone's coming,' he whispered.

Josie looked straight ahead, to the light at the end of the tunnel, and in it, she saw the silhouette of a man.

'We need to hide,' said Elliott quietly.

Silently, she followed him back through the pitch-black tunnel. She could hear his feet moving through the water; that was the only sign of him being so close to her. She couldn't see anything at all, and in fear, she reached out and grabbed his shirt and clung to it as they ventured deeper into the mine, this time taking the tunnel that bore right at the fork. They walked another thirty yards or so before Elliott stopped and whispered in her ear, 'Stand with your back against the wall so he can't see us.'

They stood in silence, side by side. Josie felt Elliott's hand reaching for hers, and she took it gratefully. She knew that they couldn't risk being found there together; the consequences didn't bear thinking about. Two single people alone in a place where they shouldn't be; everybody would jump to the same conclusion — that they were lovers. That was bad enough, but it wasn't the only problem. Elliott's colleagues would never forgive him for taking a woman into their place of work, tempting fate. She surmised that they'd wait until something terrible happened and then blame him for it. Poor Elliott! He'd never live it down. And he'd only taken her in because he knew how desperate she'd been to see inside a mine.

She shifted uncomfortably and felt Elliott's grip tighten on her hand, a silent warning to be still. It seemed like an inordinate amount of time had passed before the light from the man's candle disappeared into the other tunnel. They waited a while longer until they thought it would be safe to leave the mine.

With every step, the fear of discovery diminished. As Josie and Elliott neared the adit, she noticed the air was warmer, and she had to shield her eyes from the brightness of the sunlight when she stepped out of the mine. As much as she'd enjoyed the experience, she was pleased to be back outside in the late afternoon sunshine. She took off Elliott's jacket and gave it to him, and he slipped it on.

'Thank you, Elliott. I'll always remember today too — it's been very special.'

'You're welcome. And I hope we can do it again sometime.'

'What! You'd take me underground again?' Josie asked. Despite how close they'd just come to being caught, she heard herself say, 'That would be great!'

'Perhaps we could meet at Grove Rake next week. Same time?'

She nodded.

Elliott leaned forward and whispered, 'See you then,' and gently kissed her ear.

Blushing as she remembered the passionate kiss they'd

shared inside the mine, she said, 'Aye, I'll see you then.'

Josie wandered back to the river and mounted her horse. Aware that Elliott was still watching her, she turned and waved at him before heading for home.

Chapter 4

Elliott stood by the mine entrance and watched Josie ride away until she was out of sight. He couldn't wait to see her again next Sunday, and the realisation that he was falling for her disturbed him because he'd been hurt by a woman before. Betty Jackson. He'd first set eyes on Betty when she'd been hanging out washing in a garden in the village, and he'd admired her from a distance for weeks before plucking up the courage to ask her out. He'd been delighted when she'd agreed, and they'd started to meet regularly at weekends. A few months later, when they'd been walking down the woods one Sunday afternoon, he'd almost asked her to marry him — the words had been on the tip of his tongue — and he wasn't sure why he hadn't spoken them. But he thanked God that he hadn't, for that same week he'd seen her in the arms of another man. Her infidelity had hurt him deeply, and since then he'd had no interest in women until Josie

Milburn had walked into his life.

Josie was unlike any girl he'd ever met, and he liked that. He'd never known a lass to be so interested in mining and minerals — unless they were set in jewellery, he thought cynically. Taking Josie underground had felt great; in fact, it was probably one of the best things he'd ever done. Seeing her eyes fill with wonder when he'd lit the candles had been great, and he felt proud that he'd helped her to achieve her dream. And when they'd kissed, he knew that she'd enjoyed it as much as he had. He was sure that Josie had feelings for him too.

As Elliott turned to follow the railway line back home, he noticed a group of lads walking down the tracks towards him. One of them raised an arm in the air in greeting, and shouted, 'How do, Ell?' It was Jimmy Lonsdale, a large man with a voice to match his stature.

Elliott waved back.

When their paths crossed, Jimmy said, 'We've been up to Rispey for a swim. You should have come with us. A dip in the pool is just what you need to cool off on a day like today. So, what have you been up to?'

Elliott looked away.

'Howay man, you can tell us. We saw you standin' outside the mine so you must have been gettin' some more of your bonny bits. You can't stay out of that place! Six days a week not enough for you?' Jimmy laughed loudly, and the other lads joined in.

'Ah well, it keeps a man out of mischief,' said Elliott, as

he passed them and walked away.

Jimmy's suggestion that he should have gone with them was surprising because he'd never done anything outside of work with them; he'd never been to the river for a dip, or to the pub for a drink, or played cricket or football, or joined the village band.

The Dawson family had always kept themselves to themselves. He remembered the day that they'd moved from Allenheads to Rookhope when he was seven years old. He didn't know it at the time, but his father had told him that he'd been lured to Redburn mine by a promise that he'd be surveying, for at least some of the time, and would get a surveyor's wage in return. The promise had turned out to be false, and he'd ended up spending the rest of his days as a miner, taking home a miner's wage. He'd gone to his grave disappointed with his lot.

Elliott couldn't remember much about living at Allenheads, whether he'd liked it there or not, but he'd never felt that he belonged at Rookhope. Perhaps it was because he'd lived on the outskirts of the village, or because he'd started school a few years later than the rest of his class.

These days, he worked six days a week at the mine and attended chapel on Sunday mornings. He knew most of the people in the village by sight, and a few by name, but there was none he could call his friend. The Dawsons didn't mix much.

He reached the row of stone cottages where he lived

with his mother. It was a pleasant spot surrounded by mature trees, about half a mile from the village. Theirs was the end cottage on a row of three, which overlooked the railway to the back and the river to the front. He took off his boots at the door and stood them neatly to one side and then took a key from his pocket and unlocked the door.

'Mother, I'm back.'

'Where've you been?' said Mrs Dawson, walking into the kitchen. 'School finished hours ago.'

'It's alright. I'm home now.'

'Your father's not back either. I thought he would have been here by now. His tea will be cold if he's not back soon.'

Elliott took a deep breath and went to wash his hands. His mother had always been a bit forgetful for as long as he could remember, but her memory had worsened steadily after the death of her husband. On her good days, she knew who Elliott was and remembered that her husband was dead. On her bad days, she thought her son was an intruder and shouted for help.

A few months earlier, she'd started to wander. The first time it happened, a lady from the chapel had met Mrs Dawson on the path to Blue Row. She'd soon realised that his mother was confused and had taken her home. Since then, her disappearances had become more frequent, and it didn't seem to matter to her if it was day or night. The last time she'd gone missing, Elliott had found her walking into the village wearing just a nightgown. Thankfully, he'd found her before anyone had seen her, and he'd wrapped her in his jacket to walk her home.

He hated to keep her locked in the house when he was out, but he had no choice. If she went outside when he was at work, she could walk miles before he even knew she was gone. He worried about her crossing the boggy peat fells that surrounded Weardale, which could be treacherous at any time of year, about her falling into old mine workings, and about the changeable weather and her being lost outdoors without any shelter. Locking his mother in the house was the only way he could protect her and keep her safe when he wasn't there.

Elliott ran upstairs to his room and took the crystal from his pocket. Looking at it, he was reminded of the wonderful time that he'd had with Josie, and he smiled to himself. In his room stood a chest of drawers that housed his favourite minerals, and he was about to add this one to his collection, but he changed his mind. He wrapped it in the cotton handkerchief and put it back into his waistcoat pocket, where it rested next to his heart.

'Good morning!' said Elliott as his mother joined him in the kitchen the next morning. 'I've made some porridge.'

Mrs Dawson sat at the small kitchen table and watched her son as he picked up the pan and poured steaming hot porridge into two bowls, and then placed them on the table, whistling to himself while he worked.

'You're chirpy today,' she said.

'Aye, well, it's a nice morning out there.'

'It's good to see you happy, lad.'

Mrs Dawson sprinkled a teaspoonful of sugar over her breakfast and handed the sugar bowl to Elliott, who added four spoonfuls to his, stirring it into the gruel.

'Have you met a lass?' she asked.

'What makes you say that?'

'Mother's instinct.' She laughed. 'You were smiling to yourself. Well, have you?'

'Aye, I have.'

'Who is she?'

'You wouldn't know her, Mother. She's from Westgate.'

'Bring her here, lad. I'd like to meet her. If it's serious, that is?'

'Aye, I will.'

'That's good. Something for us to look forward to.'

'I'd better be off to work,' he said, as he put on his jacket. 'There's some dinner in the pantry for you'.

Elliott noticed his mother's puzzled expression, but she didn't say anything. Had she forgotten that he went out to work? His mother had been surprisingly lucid that morning, and he loved to see her like that, a brief glimpse of how she used to be. He grabbed his bait bag, which he'd already packed with his dinner, and left the house, locking the door behind him.

When he reached the mine, the men were loitering

around the entrance. He wandered over to one of his partners, who was leaning nonchalantly against a tub, puffing on his pipe.

'What's going on, Robbie?' Elliott asked.

'Looks like Geordie Henderson's been done in. They found him down there this morning.'

'Been done in. You mean murdered?' Elliott asked, shocked that something so horrid could happen in a small village like Rookhope.

'Aye, that's what they're saying. Apparently, his head's been smashed in, and there's blood everywhere. The bosses say we've got to stay out until they're finished — the police that is. They've been down there a while now.'

'The poor fella,' said Elliott. 'He seemed like a nice bloke.'

'Aye, he was,' said Robbie. 'One of the best. But they say only the good die young. He's got a wife and two young uns an' all — the poor bairns.'

Elliott sat down on the ground and leaned back against the tub, watching the adit for signs of the policemen returning to the surface, and while he waited, a thought struck him — if Henderson had been found dead that morning, there was a good chance that he'd been killed the day before. Was it Henderson who'd gone into the mine when he'd been down there with Josie? Or had the man they'd hidden from been the murderer?

It was over an hour later when the policemen emerged from the mine, two of them carrying a stretcher.

Geordie's body was covered with a woollen blanket, his muddy clogs sticking out at one end and his hat placed on his chest.

Once the miners were permitted to start work, they went through the adit, one by one. Elliott walked along the tunnel with them, but the usual camaraderie wasn't there — nobody laughed, and nobody spoke; the mood was sombre, and it stayed that way all day. Elliott usually enjoyed his work, but all he could think about that day was getting out of the mine and going home.

When the miners finished their shift, several policemen were stood outside the mine, waiting to question them. A burly constable approached Elliott, and he said, 'Good evening, lad. I'm Police Constable Emerson from Westgate. We're asking everyone who worked with Geordie Henderson a few questions. Alright?'

'Aye, I suppose you have to.'

The policeman took out his notebook and opened it at a blank page. Then, he removed his pencil from his pocket and licked the tip; when he was ready to take notes, he asked, 'What's your name?'

'Elliott Dawson.'

PC Emerson wrote the name at the top of the page, and then he asked, 'Can you tell me when you last saw Geordie Henderson?'

'On Friday, when we finished work. He was heading to the pub with the rest of the lads. They always do on a

Friday night.'

The policeman scribbled down Elliott's answer. 'You don't go to the pub with them, then?' he asked, raising his eyebrows.

'No,' said Elliott. 'I've got to get home and see to me mother. She's not well, and she's only got me to look after her.'

'I see. Sorry about that, lad. Where is it you live?'

'At 3 Railway Cottages,' said Elliott, and feeling obliged to fill the silence while the policeman wrote in his notebook, he added, 'It's just up the road from here.'

'Aye, I know where it's at. Empty your pockets, please.'

'I don't see why...'

'Just do it, lad. There's been a man killed.'

Elliott put his hands into his trouser pockets and took out a few coins and the house key. Then he reached into his jacket pockets and pulled out two tallow candles, a box of matches and a small hammer.

'What's the hammer for?' asked the policeman.

'It's for removing minerals.'

'A hammer that size!' He laughed loudly, and then looking directly into Elliott's eyes, he said, 'I'm not that daft, lad. Miners use mell hammers. So why are you carrying this little thing around with you?'

'We use mell hammers for breaking up minerals in the mine before we load them into the tubs. But this hammer is for breaking off small pieces — collector's pieces.'

The policeman raised an eyebrow.

'You know, bonny bits, like spar and quartz,' explained Elliott. From his waistcoat pocket, he took the fluorite crystal and unwrapped it. 'Like this,' he said.

'Understood. Well, that's all for now. We know where to find you if we need to speak to you again.'

Chapter 5

Rookhope
August 1895

The following Sunday, Josie rode Nutmeg over the hill to Grove Rake, at the head of the Rookhope Valley. Elliott wasn't at the mine when she arrived, so she sat by the river and waited for him. The sun shone down relentlessly, and Josie felt uncomfortable in the afternoon heat with no shelter from the intense rays. So, to cool down, she took off her boots and dangled her feet in the slow-flowing water, which offered some relief. She watched small fish dart back and forth beneath the surface, basking in the sun and seeking cover under the banks and the rocky river bed.

As she sat on the riverbank surveying the bleak landscape surrounding the lead mine, she recognised the evidence of ancient mining all around her, due to Elliott's tuition over the past few weeks. There were grooves on the hillside where miners had taken lead ore from the surface, shallow shafts like they'd seen at Middlehope, and mounds of waste material piled up by the river.

Absentmindedly picking a daisy, Josie twirled it in her fingers as she admired the wildflowers that could thrive in this harsh, lead-rich environment. Peeking out from the low-growing grasses and mosses, she spotted mountain pansies, purple and white clover, buttercups, and her favourite, bird's-foot trefoil. She'd always thought it looked more exotic than the others because of its tiny yellow fingers with red tips.

On the other side of the burn, she watched a brood of red grouse foraging amongst the heather, the young almost as large as their mother. The heather was beginning to flower, and Josie thought that in just another week or so the hills would look majestic, cloaked in purple.

As time passed, she became more and more restless. She removed her feet from the water and let them dry in the sun, and then she put on her boots. She stood up and looked down the valley, but there was no sign of Elliott, and she paced backwards and forwards along the river's edge. After waiting for what she thought was about two hours, she had to admit to herself that he wasn't coming. She was angry at him for letting her down and felt foolish for having wasted most of the afternoon waiting for him.

Wondering why he hadn't shown up as he'd promised, she thought that perhaps he hadn't enjoyed taking her into Boltsburn mine, or that maybe he'd decided it was too risky to take her underground again. After all, they had nearly been discovered the last time. But if that had been the case, wouldn't he have come anyway and told her that? She'd have been happy to go for a walk instead.

As she mounted Nutmeg and began the ride back to Westgate, Josie decided that there was only one logical reason for Elliott not being there that afternoon. He must have decided that he didn't want to see her again and he didn't have the decency to tell her. He'd let her waste a full afternoon hoping that he was running late and that he'd still come to see her. A tear ran down her cheek, and she hastily wiped it away with the back of her hand.

When she rode into the farmyard, her father and Uncle Joe were standing near the barn. She couldn't hear what they were talking about, but from their faces and the tone of their conversation, she knew they were discussing something serious.

Joe Milburn turned to greet her, saying, 'Hello, Josie. You look prettier every time I see you.'

'You always say that.' Josie laughed off his compliment as she dismounted, and then asked, 'Is there something going on?'

'We were just talking about that murder over at Rookhope,' said Joe. 'Did you hear about it?'

'Yes, Father told us about it.'

'Well,' said Joe, 'We can all sleep easier in our beds now. They know who killed him.'

'Who was it?' asked Josie.

'A young lad from Rookhope. Elliott Dawson. They

worked together.'

The colour drained from Josie's face. She felt faint and leaned against Nutmeg for support. Had Elliott killed a man? He couldn't have, could he?

Her father, mistaking her pallor for fear, said, 'There's no need to be worried, love. They'll soon catch him and put him behind bars.'

'They'll do more than that to him,' said Joe.

'Aye, no doubt he'll get what he deserves,' said Tom.

'Tell me what happened,' said Josie. 'Please.'

'Are you sure you want to know?' Joe asked, concerned that the story might upset her further.

'Aye, I want to know everything.'

'Well, it looks like Geordie Henderson, the man that was murdered, had been down the mine collectin' spar on Sunday afternoon. Boltsburn mine, that is, in the village. He didn't go home on Sunday night. His family were worried about him because he never stayed out all night, but they didn't dare say anything. They knew he shouldn't have been down there on a Sunday. Anyway, a miner found his body first thing on Monday on his way into work. Now, the police know this lad, Dawson, was in the mine on Sunday an' all. Someone saw him standin' outside the mine, and he admitted that he'd been collectin' spar.'

Josie realised that her uncle was talking about the afternoon that she'd been in Boltsburn mine with Elliott. Well, he hadn't killed anybody that day because she'd been with him the whole time. But she couldn't tell anyone that because he'd get into trouble for taking her underground.

'Just because he was there doesn't mean he killed him,' she said.

'Mebbe not,' said her father. 'But the police must think he had something to do with it because they've issued a warrant for his arrest.'

So, that's why Elliott hadn't come to Grove Rake that afternoon. It wasn't because he didn't want to see her again. She felt a brief moment of relief at that, but then her thoughts turned to where he could be. Was he hiding from the police? Had he run away? Or had they caught him already? With a sickening dread, she realised that if he were arrested for murder, he wouldn't just be locked up, his life would be in danger.

'Are you comin' in, Joe?' asked Tom.

'No, I'd better be gettin' back. The cows won't milk themselves.'

Joe mounted his horse and left the yard.

Josie unsaddled Nutmeg and led the horse back to its field. After she'd closed the gate, Josie watched the mare canter away and lie down and roll on the grass with her legs in the air, and then get up again and graze on the summer grass. Josie thought it must be nice not to have a care in the world.

In stark contrast, her mind was troubled as she walked back to the yard and put the saddle and bridle away.

Slowly, she walked back to the house and made her way upstairs to her bedroom. She needed time alone so she could think. Was there any way that she could help Elliott?

Chapter 6

Middlehope, Weardale
August 1895

The pitch blackness of the mine heightened Elliott's senses. He was near a shaft and at a junction where three tunnels diverged in different directions. If anyone entered the mine to search for him, he would hear them long before they could reach him, and he had the choice of tunnels through which to make his escape. They wouldn't catch him. Not while he was underground.

Elliott felt as though he'd been training for this moment all of his life. For years he'd explored the old mines of Weardale, and he knew them better than anyone. The majority of men, even experienced miners, wouldn't go into the Old Man's workings for fear of the unknown and possible unseen dangers. Elliott, although cautious, had loved to explore them and to look for connections between the workings.

There were tales of tunnels going all the way through the hill, connecting the valleys of Weardale and

Rookhope. His father had told him about a man from Wearhead who'd died in an accident at Grove Rake mine. His mates had wanted to take his body home for burial, but the roads had been impassable due to deep falls of snow, so they'd carried the dead body through old mine tunnels all the way from Rookhope to Blackdene. He'd heard rumours of Weardale men using the tunnels to walk to Rookhope to get to work when the weather was bad, rather than take their chances walking over the tops. He wouldn't have blamed them either. It was so easy to lose your way on the moors in the white-out conditions of a blizzard, or when thick fog descended, or get knocked to the ground by fierce gales, or soaked to the skin by torrential sleet and rain. At least underground, he thought, the conditions were predictable, and there were far fewer risks, so long as you knew what you were doing.

There were only two situations that would prevent Elliott from going underground: when the barometer fell, and low air pressure drew out foul gases from deep within the earth, which could suffocate men in minutes; and after heavy rainfall or melting snow, which could cause old mine workings to flood rapidly.

Whether these stories about tunnels connecting the valley were true or not, Elliott wasn't sure, but he knew for certain that centuries of mining had left the hills between the valleys riddled with tunnels, and luckily for him, he knew them better than most.

As he sat in silence, he mulled over the events that had

forced him to seek refuge in the old mine.

That morning he'd left the house to go to the chapel at Rookhope. He'd been alone. His mother hadn't accompanied him to the morning service for several months because the last time she had, she'd made a scene in front of everybody, saying that she didn't know him and that he was a stranger to her. The villagers knew that they were mother and son, so they hadn't interfered, they'd just thrown looks of sympathy in his direction as he ushered her from the building and out onto the front street, where he'd managed to calm her down and persuade her to walk home with him.

He hadn't got very far down the railway line that morning when he heard someone shout his name. He'd turned around and saw two policemen standing outside his house, banging on the back door and calling for him to come out. They hadn't seen him, so he'd crouched down behind a hawthorn bush, out of sight. One of them had shouted, 'Mr Elliott Dawson. We have a warrant for your arrest for the murder of Geordie Henderson. Come on out!'

He'd heard the words clearly enough. There was no mistake. Blood had pumped through his veins as he realised that he was wanted for murder. The police thought he'd killed Geordie Henderson. He couldn't be arrested. He couldn't leave his mother alone to fend for herself. And what about Josie?

Elliott had watched the scene unfold like a nightmare

in front of his eyes, knowing the whole time that he was wide awake.

The door of the middle house had opened, and his elderly neighbour appeared. The policemen spoke with him briefly, and then they left. Elliott reckoned they'd head for the chapel, as that's where Mr Westgarth would expect him to be on a Sunday morning.

Instinct had kicked in. Elliott had lain low until the constables were long gone, and then he left his hiding place and furtively returned home to check on his mother, who thankfully seemed oblivious to the visit from the police. Gathering together all the food he could find, he placed it on the kitchen table so that his mother could help herself when she was hungry, and he carried in as much water as possible until there were no more containers to store any more. Looking around the kitchen, he reckoned there were enough supplies to last his mother a week or maybe even longer. And then he'd gone to the place where he felt safe, to the place he knew better than anyone — the mines.

Now that he was secured away in his hiding place, his thoughts turned to Josie. Instead of sitting by himself down there in the dark all afternoon, he should have been at Grove Rake with her. It pained him to think of her waiting for him by the mine, wondering why he wasn't there, thinking that he'd abandoned her. He wished with all his heart that he could have gone to meet her, but he couldn't risk being seen in broad daylight, not when the police were looking for him. They could be anywhere. And word spread quickly in the dale. He guessed that there would be others searching for him too. He hoped that Josie would forgive him for his absence when she learnt the reason for it.

Elliott was sure that Josie would know that he hadn't killed Geordie because she'd been with him most of that afternoon. He prayed that she would tell everyone that he was innocent so he could come out of hiding and clear his name. But who would believe her? He'd never known a man to take his lass into a mine before. So, who would believe that he had? The whole situation was hopeless.

And there was a small part of him that feared Josie might think he'd gone back into the mine and killed Geordie after she'd left him and that he'd only wanted her there to act as an alibi. Would she want anything more to do with him?

He had to see her. He had to know.

Chapter 7

Westgate
August 1895

Josie wiped her brow with her apron. It was a warm day, made hotter by the fact that she and her mother had been baking all morning. She drank a glass of water and watched her mother take the last tray of cooked pies from the oven and place them on the table, where an array of scones and cakes were already cooling.

The kitchen door opened, and Tom Milburn came in, removing his boots at the door.

'Are the lads not back yet?' he asked. 'They should've finished fettling that dyke by now.'

'No, but I'm sure they'll show up as soon as there's food on the table,' said Mary, smiling at her husband. 'They usually do.'

'The police are out in force this morning!' he said, as he took a seat. 'They're up on the tops searching the fell for that lad. They've got dogs with them an' all, so if he's up there, they'll find him.'

Josie blanched as she sat down.

'Are you alright, lass? You look like you've seen a ghost,' said her father.

'I'm alright.' Josie hesitated a second before adding vehemently, 'Everyone's saying he's a murderer — but they don't know that. They can't be sure it was him.'

'What's got into you, young miss?' asked her mother. Do you know this lad?'

'Yes, as a matter of fact, I do.'

Her mother stared at Josie until she felt compelled to say more.

'I met him at the mineral exhibition, and he seemed canny.'

'You can never tell,' said Tom, shaking his head.

As Mary sat down next to her husband, she put her hand on his shoulder and said quietly, 'Tom Milburn, you've got a short memory.' She didn't need to say any more; her words had the desired effect.

'Aye, maybe I have,' said Tom. Looking at Josie, he said, 'You're right, love. He's innocent until proven guilty. But running away like that hasn't done him any favours — it makes him look guilty whether he did it or not.'

Josie lowered her head and didn't reply. She was very concerned about Elliott, not knowing where he was, or what he was doing. But if the police were still looking for him, at least they hadn't arrested him yet.

'Why do I get the feeling you know more about this lad than you're letting on?' asked Mary. 'Have you seen him since the exhibition?'

'Yes, a couple of times.'

'You've been cavorting with a lad that's wanted by the police!' exclaimed Tom.

Mary shot a look at her husband, and he shrugged his shoulders.

The sound of her brothers arguing outside the back door gave Josie an excuse to leave the kitchen, and she climbed the stairs to her bedroom. There was too much on her mind to worry about their silly disagreements. As she opened the door, she stopped suddenly and stared — a ray of sunlight shone through the window directly onto her half of the fractured crystal. Josie picked it up and held it to her heart.

'Oh Elliott, please be safe,' she whispered.

Later that day, after the family had finished their evening meal, Josie put the vegetable peelings and meagre scraps of food into a bucket and took them out for the pigs. It was a pleasant evening, warm and light, and she was in no hurry to go back indoors. The atmosphere inside had been tense, and she knew that her parents were concerned about her association with Elliott. If only they knew him as she did. But it was her fault that they didn't. She hadn't even mentioned Elliott to them, let alone introduced him.

She strolled to the pigpen, thinking about Elliott. He'd been on her mind all afternoon, and she hadn't been able to concentrate on anything else. She still hadn't decided on the best course of action, although she was seriously considering telling PC Emerson the whole story. He was a family friend, and she thought he'd listen to her.

Josie opened the gate of the pigpen, and called, 'Come on, girls. Come and get your supper.'

She emptied the food into a trough, and the pigs came over, grunting at her in greeting, and then they lowered their snouts and began to eat. As she watched them, Josie thought she heard something. She left the pen and closed the gate behind her, and then stood still, listening carefully.

'Josie.'

Someone whispered her name and a shiver ran down her spine. Instinctively, she wanted to run, to turn away, but there was something in that voice that begged her to stay.

'Josie, it's me.'

She recognised the voice. Looking around her, she asked, 'Where are you?'

'Behind the cart.'

With her back against the wall, Josie squeezed through the gap between the stone wall and the cart to get around to the back of the barn.

'Thank God, you've come out of the house at last,' said Elliott. 'I've been waiting for ages.'

'What are you doing here?'

'I don't know if you've heard, but the police think I

killed a man. There's a warrant out for me arrest.' Elliott ran his hands through his thick hair and looked directly at her. 'For God's sake, Josie, they think I'm a murderer!'

'But you're not,' she said. 'You can't be.'

'Of course, I'm not.' With tears in his eyes, he said, 'But I can't give myself up. Who'd look after me mother?'

Josie opened her arms and hugged Elliott, and he held her tightly. She could feel his body shaking, and she wasn't sure if it was from fear or if he was crying. When he'd settled, she pulled away slightly and asked, 'So, what are you going to do?'

'I've been hiding,' he said. 'Underground. And they haven't found me yet. So, I suppose that's what I'll keep on doing. I know most of the mines around here. The police don't. But Josie, I can't do that forever. I need to find a way to clear me name.' Looking her in the eye, he said, 'You believe me, don't you? That I didn't do it?'

'Aye, I know it wasn't you. I was with you the whole time.' She smiled reassuringly at him.

'Thank you.' He kissed her gently on the lips. 'This afternoon. I'm sorry. I wanted to go and see you so much, but I couldn't risk it.'

'I know. It's alright.'

When she saw a flicker of doubt on his face, she added, 'Really, it is. You had no choice.'

He rested his brow against hers.

'Do you remember when we went for that walk up at Middlehope? The small mine shaft with the wooden stemples?'

'Aye,' she said.

'That's where I'll be. I just wanted you to know.'

'I'll come over and see you tomorrow. I'll bring you some food.'

He smiled and said, 'I should be going. Your folks will be wondering where you are.

'Please, be careful, Elliott,' said Josie, tears forming in her eyes.

Elliott leaned back and looked at her, and said, 'I love you, Josie Milburn.'

He held her tightly in his arms and kissed her as though it might be the last time he ever did. Reluctantly, he pulled away and turned to leave.

'I love you, too,' she whispered as she watched him disappear from view.

That night, Josie couldn't sleep for thinking about the dire predicament Elliott was in, and the only solution she had come up with that might help him was to tell the truth. Yes, Elliott might get into trouble for taking her into the mine, and he might even lose his job over it, but that had to be better than being arrested on a murder charge.

As soon as the sun rose, Josie walked down to the village, reaching it before most of the villagers had stirred. Knocking loudly on the front door of the policeman's house, she stepped back and saw a curtain move in the upstairs' window, and then she heard movements from inside. The door opened, and PC Emerson stood in front of her in just his shirt and trousers. For some reason, she'd expected him to be in uniform.

'Good morning, Josie,' he said. 'You're up bright and early. Is everything alright up at home?'

'Aye, everything's fine. But I need to talk to you. It's important.'

'Well then, you'd better come in. It must be important if you're knocking on my door at this ungodly hour of the morning.'

He led the way into a small living room and invited her to sit in an armchair by the fire.

'By, I could do with a cup of tea. Would you like one?'

'Yes. Thank you.'

As she waited, she realised that her index finger was curling her hair, a nervous habit she'd had since childhood. She stood up and, looking into a wall mirror, she straightened her hair, and she was sitting back in the chair by the time PC Emerson returned to the room carrying two cups of steaming hot tea.

When he was sitting comfortably in a winged armchair on the opposite side of the fireplace, he said, 'Well now, you'd better tell me what brought you here so early this morning.'

'It's about Elliott Dawson. I need to tell you what happened last Sunday.'

The policeman raised his eyebrows and said, 'Go on.'

'I rode over to Rookhope that afternoon — to meet Elliott,' she said, her cheeks reddening.

'Did anyone see you together?'

'No, I don't think so. But I was there.'

'You'd better tell me exactly how you know Elliott Dawson, where you went with him and what you were doing. Now, listen, Josie. This is very important. You do realise that his life could be at stake, don't you?'

Josie gasped and covered her mouth with her hands. Slowly, she removed them and swallowed. Looking the constable in the eye, she said, 'I met Elliott at the mineral exhibition a few weeks ago. Since then, we've gone on a few walks together. Elliott knew how much I wanted to see inside a mine and he offered to take me into Boltsburn mine last Sunday, you see, he works there. We'd arranged to meet outside the mine, and we went in together. He showed me where he collects the best bits of spar. And then, on our way out, we saw a man walking into the mine. I don't know who he was, but he was on his own. We hid so he wouldn't see us and then we went out. I was with Elliott all the time that he was in the mine that day, so there's no way he could've killed anyone.'

'Oh, Josie!' said the policeman, leaning towards her. 'You remind me so much of your mother.'

'What do you mean?'

'Never mind,' he said dismissively, as though he'd spoken out of turn. 'I can see you think a lot about this lad, or you wouldn't be here, but I wasn't born yesterday.

Do you really expect me to believe that a miner would take his girl into a mine? I've lived in Weardale all of my life, and I know miners don't do that sort of thing.'

'But you don't know him,' said Josie, more frightened for Elliott's safety now that the policeman didn't believe a word she'd said. 'Elliott's different. He's not like other miners. You have to believe me. Please. I'm telling you the truth!'

'Now, now, there's no need for such a fuss. We just want to ask him a few questions. Do you know where he is?'

She looked away briefly before saying, 'No.'

PC Emerson's eyes narrowed ever so slightly, and she suspected that he knew she was lying. She quickly added, 'And I hope you never find him.'

'I'm sorry, Josie, but we will find him. It's just a matter of time.'

Josie stood up and ran for the door. As she opened it, she turned towards him, and through her tears, she said, 'He didn't do it. Please believe me. It's the truth.' She closed the door quietly behind her as she left. Her cup of tea remained untouched.

Josie couldn't settle all day. She had thought that PC Emerson would take her word for what had happened and call off the police search, and then everything would be back to how it should be. But he hadn't. She'd failed. And because of her failure, Elliott was still hiding in the old mine up at Middlehope. She thought of him sitting alone in the dark for hours on end and decided that she must go to see him.

After wrapping some bread, cheese and ham in a tea towel, she left the house without being seen. She walked up the road towards Middlehope, and when she reached the place where she'd met Elliott that day, she followed the narrow track that they'd taken. The mound that she'd thought resembled a volcano was a good landmark, and she headed for that and, remembering how he'd alerted her to the dangers on the fell, she paid attention to where she was walking.

A fox carrying a rabbit in its mouth ran across her path, startling her. Conscious of her quickened breathing and rapid heartbeat, Josie stopped for a moment to calm her nerves. She needed to think clearly to find Elliott's hiding place. The small shaft had been a short distance downslope of the track. She remembered roughly where it was, but the fact that it had been almost hidden from view made her concerned about finding it again. Eventually, she stumbled across the shaft and sighed with relief. Glancing nervously at the wild moorland around her, she was sure she was alone, so she knelt on the dry grass and whispered into the hole in the ground, 'Elliott, are you there?'

She waited for a reply, but there was none.

A little louder, she said, 'Elliott, I've brought you some food.'

Still, there was no response. Josie was tempted to

climb down into the mine, but the wooden rails didn't look very safe and, with there being water at the bottom of the shaft, she couldn't drop the food down for him. After wondering where she could leave it, she leaned into the shaft and tied the cloth around the top rail, hoping that he'd find it. She was disappointed not to see him. She'd wanted to tell him about her conversation with PC Emerson, and she'd wanted him to hold her and kiss her again as he had in the barn.

She wandered home with her head down, her mind on Elliott and the fact that he loved her, completely unaware of anything else going on around her.

Elliott heard a voice that, even though just a whisper, echoed through the mine. He was certain it was Josie. She'd kept her promise to bring him some food. His stomach rumbled loudly; he hadn't eaten since breakfast the previous day. He walked quickly through the water level and made his way towards the shaft, and when he got there, he looked up to the bright light and shielded his eyes with his hand. He couldn't see Josie. Longing to see her, he called her name, but she didn't appear. He noticed something suspended from one of the stemples, and he smiled — Josie had been there. He was disappointed to have missed her, but thankful that it had been her voice that he'd heard and not his imagination playing tricks on him.

Climbing up carefully to retrieve the package, Elliott

remembered which rungs were sound and secure, which were loose, and which were rotten and likely to break under stress. He'd tested them all thoroughly the day before when he'd decided to hide out there. He reached up, grabbed the package and began his descent back into the darkness. He heard the screech of a whistle and voices — men's voices, and they were close. The police!

Elliott jumped down the last few feet of the shaft and landed in the water with a splash. He fled through the tunnel as fast as he could, against the flow of water, moving deeper into the hillside. A shout rang out inside the mine, followed by a loud curse, and Elliott knew that one of the policemen had slipped and fallen in the shaft. They knew where he was hiding and were on his trail.

Sweat beaded on Elliott's brow and he wiped it off with his sleeve. He was back at his hiding place, and momentarily, he hesitated as he decided which way to go — east or west. Knowing there were more exits from the tunnel to the west, more escape routes, he went in that direction. Aware that the voices were getting closer, he ran faster, still carrying the bundle of food. Looking back over his shoulder, he saw two policemen with lamps turn into the tunnel after him. He continued to run, but somehow the policemen seemed to be closing the distance between them. There was a shaft in the floor of the level up ahead. He knew where it was because he'd cut a groove in the wall on either side, and he jumped over it easily, landing safely on the other side with a splash, and continued to run until he heard a scream that made him freeze on the spot.

'Help! Help me!' shouted one of the policemen. 'I can't swim!'

A large man stood in the tunnel and held out his hand to his colleague who'd fallen into the deep shaft. PC Emerson pulled the young policeman out from the deep pool and lifted him onto his feet. The man who'd almost drowned was shaking so badly that there was no way he could continue the pursuit.

'Blast it!' exclaimed PC Emerson. 'He's gettin' away.'

He held up his lamp and moved it in an arc in an attempt to see further into the mine, but he could see no more than about twenty yards in front of him. The constable looked almost directly at Elliott, before turning around and retracing his steps.

From further up the tunnel, Elliott watched them, knowing that they couldn't see him from that distance but, even so, he stood still against the wall with the white tea towel hidden behind his back.

Once the policemen were out of sight, Elliott's body slumped. He was safe. He remained where he was for a while because he couldn't take any chances.

Elliott was pleased that the young policeman was unharmed. If things had gone differently and the young man had been in difficulty, he would have gone back to help, even if it had meant giving himself up. There was no way he could have stood by and watched a man drown and do nothing to help.

Sweat ran down Elliott's face and dripped off his nose and chin. His heart was still beating rapidly. He was safe for now, but for how much longer? The police knew where he was hiding, and he was sure that they'd come back again in force. He would have to find somewhere else to hide.

Chapter 8

Josie was disappointed that she hadn't seen Elliott. She'd wanted to ask him what she could do to help. Her visit to the constable had failed miserably, and she didn't know what to do next. She hoped that her parents may be able to advise her. After all, they were older and should be wiser, she reasoned. She wished she'd told them about Elliott right from the outset. Now, since the only thing they knew about him was that he was wanted for murder, she faced a very difficult task.

When she returned home, she found her mother and father sitting at the kitchen table, sharing a pot of tea.

'Hello, Josie. Would you like a cup?' Mary asked.

Josie nodded.

Her mother took a cup from the dresser and filled it from the pot. Josie took the cup from her and took a long drink.

'What's the matter? Cat got your tongue?' her mother

asked.

'Sorry. Thank you.'

'Something's wrong, love,' said her father. 'Come on. Out with it.'

'There's something I need to talk to you about.' She paused as she thought of the best way to start what she had to say. She drained her cup and then said, 'Elliott Dawson didn't do what they think he did. He didn't kill that man in the mine.'

'And how do you know that?' asked Tom.

'I was with him,' said Josie. 'I was with him in Boltsburn mine that day.'

Tom and Mary looked at each other in surprise and then back at their daughter.

'Well, you have some explaining to do, young lady,' said Mary. 'First of all, what exactly is going on between you and this Elliott Dawson?'

Josie sat down at the table, and said, 'He was selling spar at the mineral exhibition, like I said, and we got talking. He asked me to go out with him. We've been for a few walks, down by the river and up on the fell. Anyway, he knew how much I wanted to go into a mine, and he said he'd take me into Boltsburn.'

Josie noticed that she was winding her hair into a tight curl and put her hands together on her lap.

'And you went with him?' asked her mother. 'You went into a mine with a man you hardly know, on your own, and you didn't tell anyone?'

'It wasn't like that, Mother. He didn't try anything. He's not like that.' Her cheeks coloured as she remembered the heated kiss that they'd shared in the barn the night before. 'We just went to look at the spar, that's all.'

'The day he took you into Boltsburn mine,' said Tom, 'that was the same day that fella was killed. Is that what you're telling us?'

'Aye, it was. But there was nobody in the mine when we went in. On the way out, we saw a man going in. He was by himself. It might have been the man who was killed. I don't know. We couldn't see him because we hid in another tunnel. Elliott didn't want anyone to see us underground because he knew he'd get into trouble for taking me in. The man was still alive when we left. Then, I came home, and Elliott walked up the railway. He lives up there with his mother.'

'Did you see him walk up the railway?' asked her father.

'No.'

'So, how do you know he didn't go back in after you left?'

'Aw, Father, I don't. But I know he didn't do it. He couldn't have!'

'You like him, don't you?' her mother asked quietly.

'Aye, I do. And he likes me. You believe me about the mine, don't you? That I went in with him.'

Her parents looked at each other and burst out laughing.

Her father said, 'I'm surprised it's taken this long, love.

You've wanted to go into the mines since you were a bairn.' And then with a straight face, he said, 'I only wish a fella hadn't been found dead down there at the same time.'

'I told PC Emerson but he didn't believe me,' said Josie. 'He thinks I was lying to protect Elliott. The police think he did it and they're still looking for him. Is there anything we can do to help him?'

'I don't know, love. Let me have a think about it,' said her father, going over to the fireplace and taking his pipe off the mantelshelf. Stuffing it with tobacco, he sat in the chair by the fire.

Josie knew that was the end of the conversation. Her father would sit and stare into the fire, puffing on his pipe, until he had an answer. She had watched him do the same thing time and time again. Her mother smiled at her kindly and then cleared the table.

It was over an hour later when Josie saw her father come out of the house in search of her.

'There you are,' he said, striding across the yard. 'Why don't we both go down to the village and have a word with Robert?'

'Really? Do you think that might help?'

'Well, I don't know. But it can't do any harm.'

Josie and her father walked down to the village of Westgate. When they reached the constable's house, Tom knocked at the door, and it was opened almost immediately by PC Emerson.

'Good afternoon, Tom. Josie. Didn't expect to you see you again so soon. What can I do for you?'

'Can we come in, Robert? There's something we need to have a chat about.'

'Aye. Just give us a minute. I've got a bit of a houseful at the moment, but they're just leaving.'

He disappeared back inside, and a few minutes later, two men in police uniform came out of the house. Josie noticed that one of them was limping and he held his arm against his chest as though it was injured, and the other man's clothes were soaking wet. Josie thought he looked like he'd been for a swim wearing his clothes. They nodded and mumbled a greeting as they passed.

'Come in,' said Robert, ushering Tom and Josie into his front room, where he rushed to a chair and removed a wet towel.

'What's been going on?' Tom Milburn asked his friend.

'Just police business. Sorry, I can't say any more. Now, what was it you wanted to talk about?'

'It's about the fella that was found dead at Boltsburn. I've been thinking about it, and there's something that just doesn't add up. I believe our Josie when she says she was in the mine with Elliott Dawson that day, and our Josie is a good judge of character. She's certain he wouldn't kill anyone. You know something, Robert, she reminds me so much of Mary at her age — it's uncanny.'

The policeman nodded in agreement, and said, 'You're

right there.'

'And thinking back,' continued Tom, 'I remember what it was like being accused of something like that. I can't say I blame this young man for doing a runner. The thought went through my head, I can tell you, but I couldn't have left Mary and Josie.'

Josie looked at her father with a puzzled expression; she had no idea what he was talking about.

'I hear what you're saying, Tom,' said Robert, 'but Elliott Dawson is the only suspect we have for this murder. We know that he was in the mine that Sunday, and when I questioned him, he had a hammer in his pocket that could have been a murder weapon.'

'That's a geology hammer,' said Josie. 'It's for collecting mineral specimens.'

'Aye, that's what he said an' all,' said Robert. 'But that's by the bye. We don't have anything else to go on, so we have to find Dawson and take him in for questioning.'

'Go easy on the lad, Robert. My gut feeling is that he's innocent.'

'We'll see soon enough once he's in custody.'

When Tom and Josie stood up to leave, there were tears in Josie's eyes. Tom put his arm around her shoulders and led her out of the house. As they walked home together, Josie said, 'They're going to catch him, aren't they?'

'Aye, love, they will. They won't give up until they do.'

'What'll happen then?'

'They'll take him to the police station and question him.'

'And then what?'

'It depends on if they think he did it or not. If they believe he's innocent, they'll let him go. If they think he did it, he'll be taken to Durham Prison and he'll stay there until his trial.'

'And if he's found guilty, he'll — he'll —'

Josie sobbed loudly. She had never felt so useless. Elliott's life was in danger, and she could do nothing to help him. Not wanting to talk anymore, she ran ahead and when she got home, she rushed to her room to be alone.

That evening, Josie went to the barn in the hope that Elliott might be there again, waiting for her, but he wasn't. She sat on the ground where he had been the previous night and thought about everything that had happened since they'd gone into the mine. If only she'd said 'no' that day, then none of it would have happened. She didn't know if Elliott had been captured, or if he was still tucked away underground. She hated not knowing where he was, and she needed to see for herself that he was safe.

A full moon lit up the sky as Josie walked up the hill to the old mine shaft. She sat down beside the hole in the ground and called softly, 'Elliott.'

There was no reply, and he didn't appear, so after a few

minutes, she called his name a little louder, and she heard her voice echo through the tunnels below. If he was down there, he must have heard her, she thought. She sat and waited, hoping that he was still there.

She guessed she'd been waiting almost quarter of an hour before she heard a splashing noise coming from inside the tunnel, and a few seconds later she heard his voice.

'Josie, are you there?'

'Yes,' she whispered.

'I'm coming up.'

Elliott expertly used the stemples to climb up the shaft and then he was by her side, his eyes filled with wonder.

'I can't believe you're here,' he said.

'I had to see you.'

'Oh, Josie.' Elliott's voice betrayed the depth of his emotion as he spoke her name. He took her into his arms and held her against his body. 'You wouldn't believe me if I told you how good it is to see you,' he whispered into her ear.

'Oh, I think I would.'

He kissed her neck and her throat, and she shivered with the sensations that ran through her body. She pressed up against him and turned her head so that their lips met, and he kissed her with a passion that she had never imagined possible. Before long, all she was aware of was her body and his body. His hands were caressing her back, pulling her to him, and she felt as though she was melting into him.

Suddenly he released her and stepped back.

'What's wrong?' Josie asked.

'What's wrong?' Elliott laughed as he sat down on the grass and took her hand so that she followed suit. He lay back on the grass and looked up at the starry sky.

'Why did you stop?' she asked.

'Because if I didn't stop then, I don't think I could have.'

'I didn't want you to.'

'Josie,' he said, his voice strained. 'You could torment the devil himself.' He propped himself up on one arm and looked at her lovingly. 'I want you so much right now — but this isn't the time.'

Josie couldn't meet his gaze.

Elliott took her hand and held it firmly. 'Listen to me. I'm wanted for murder. God only knows what's going to happen. Josie, I can't take you like this, and maybe give you a bairn, when I might not be around to look after you. I love you.'

Josie lifted her head and looked into his eyes. 'Oh Elliott, I love you too.' She leaned towards him, and he put his arm around her shoulder.

'The police were here today,' he said. 'They nearly caught me. I had to go further in to hide because they'll be back. There's no doubt about that.' Shaking his head, he said, 'I don't know how, but the sound of your voice carried all the way to where I was hiding. I came as quickly as I could, and you were still here — you waited for me.'

He lifted her hand to his lips and kissed it.

'Elliott, we could run away from here. Together.'

She noticed his eyes widen at her words.

'You'd do that for me?' he asked incredulously.

'Of course, I would. You can't risk getting caught. What if the police don't believe you're innocent? I dread to think what would happen. I want to be with you wherever you are.'

He lay down again and pulled Josie onto her side so that her head rested on his chest. She could hear his heart beating rapidly. She wondered how she could have fallen for this man so quickly and so completely that she would give up everything for him. His silence meant he was contemplating her suggestion, but was there anywhere they could go where they'd be safe?

'There they are!' A man's voice sounded from the moor.

Elliott leapt up and kissed Josie quickly before disappearing down the shaft.

Three policemen ran to where Josie stood. PC Emerson pointed at the shaft and asked, 'Did he go down there?'

'I don't know what you're talking about. Did who go down where?'

'You know who I mean, Josie.'

'I'm just out for a walk,' she said, with more bravado than she felt.

Another man, who she recognised as the sergeant from

Stanhope, said, 'Now don't come on with that, miss. We know he was here this morning. You came up here to see him, didn't you? You led us right to him.'

She looked down at the ground and didn't say a word.

The sergeant shouted down the shaft, 'Come out now and show yourself. We know you're down there.'

The sergeant looked at Josie, and he grinned wickedly. He shouted down the hole, 'This lass has been aiding and abetting a fugitive. Now, that's a serious offence that she could do time for. You wouldn't want to see your lass in Durham Prison, would you? With all those common criminals. I wonder what they'd do to a bonny lass like her? Come out now — and we'll let her go. Stay there — and she'll be taking a ride back to Stanhope with us!'

A voice boomed up from the depths. 'Leave her alone!'

Josie grimaced as she heard Elliott climbing up from the depths of the mine where he would have been safe. He was giving himself up to protect her. Her stomach churned at the thought of what might happen to him now. As he stepped out onto the surface, the sergeant immediately handcuffed him.

Elliott looked desperately into Josie's eyes, and she saw him mouth the words, 'I'm sorry. Love you.'

'I'll see that the lass gets home safely,' said PC Emerson. 'I'm sure you two can handle Dawson.' Without waiting for confirmation from his sergeant, he took Josie's arm and led her away across the fell and back to High House Farm. They walked in silence. Josie was mad at PC Emerson for following her and angry at herself for leading him to Elliott. She felt betrayed by her father's friend whom she'd turned to for help. And more than anything, she was upset because Elliott had given himself up to save her. By the time she got home, tears were flowing freely down her face.

The policeman knocked at the door, and it was opened quickly by her mother.

'There you are, Josie!' said Mary. Looking at PC Emerson, she asked, 'What's happened? Where did you find her?'

Josie stepped forward into her mother's arms and clung to her, her body shaking as she sobbed.

'Is Tom in?' asked the constable.

'Tom!' shouted Mary.

Tom rushed to the door and seeing the state Josie was in, said, 'Take her inside, Mary.'

After Mary and Josie went indoors, Tom stepped out and closed the door behind him. 'So, Robert, what's all this about, then?' he asked.

'We've got Dawson. The sergeant's taking him down to the station.'

'Well, that explains why our Josie's so upset.'

'Aye, I suppose. But that's not all. It was Josie who led us to him.'

Tom leaned against the house wall and looked at his friend, waiting for an explanation.

The policeman shifted uncomfortably and cleared his

throat before saying, 'When she came down to see me this morning, I could tell she knew where he was hiding, even though she denied it. So, we followed her up to Middlehope. To an old mine shaft. She had no idea we were watching her. After she'd gone, we went into the mine. We chased him, but we didn't catch him. We went back up tonight to surprise him. I'm sorry, Tom, I didn't think Josie would be there — not this late. I'm sorry she got caught up in it.'

'Caught up in what exactly?' asked Tom.

'The sergeant gave the lad an ultimatum. He said to the lad that if he didn't give himself up, he'd arrest Josie for aiding and abetting. By, I'll tell you something, Tom, I've never seen anyone give himself up so fast. He must think a hell of a lot about your lass. He just stood there and let us cuff him.'

Tom put his hand to his brow and let out a deep breath. After a short pause, he asked, 'Would you do me a favour, Robert?'

'That depends on what you're asking?'

'Would you show me where they found the body, and let me have a look around?'

'I don't see what good that would do.'

'Come on, Robert. I know you don't like going underground, but please, I can't stand by and see him charged with murder if he's innocent.'

Robert looked embarrassed. 'Aye,' he said. 'I suppose we could. How are you fixed for tomorrow?'

'Tomorrow's good for me,' said Tom. 'I'll pick you up at one o'clock.'

Chapter 9

The policemen who had captured Elliott led him to the road where the police carriage stood. Elliott walked with his head down, fleetingly wondering if he could make a run for it, but now that they had handcuffed him, it was too late. He wouldn't be able to take the cuffs off without the key. He could only hope that he could persuade them that he'd played no part in Henderson's death and that they would release him without charge.

The sergeant opened the carriage door. 'Get in, lad,' he said, giving Elliott a nudge. Elliott climbed in and moved to the far side. The sergeant followed him and sat by his side, whilst the constable climbed up to the driver's seat. The horse walked gingerly down the steep bank as they set off for the police station at Stanhope. When they reached the main road at Westgate, it was closing time, and drunken men were leaving the pubs and staggering along the street. They turned to stare at the police carriage.

When the miners realised that the murderer had been caught, they made such a racket, cheering and shouting loud enough to awaken many of the villagers who'd been sleeping soundly. Lamps lit upstairs' rooms, sash windows were opened, and men in nightgowns demanded to know what was going on.

A small group of men stood in the middle of the road, obstructing the carriage. The constable attempted to steer the horse around them, but the largest man in the group grabbed hold of its bridle and pulled the frightened animal to a halt.

A loud voice rang out clearly above the commotion, 'Mebbe we should take the law into our own hands. What do you think, gentlemen? We all know what murderers deserve, don't we? Anyone who murders a miner deserves to be brought to justice — by miners!'

The growing crowd roared in agreement.

The sergeant opened the side window of the carriage, and shouted, 'Clear the way!'

His request was met by a torrent of abuse and a man spat in his face.

The rioters began to rock the carriage from side to side, and Elliott braced himself for it tipping over onto its side.

'We have to get out of here,' the sergeant shouted to the constable, as he wiped his cheek with his sleeve. 'Hurry up!'

'Walk on!' screamed the constable. 'Move!'

Elliott heard the repeated crack of a whip, twice yielding a cry from the man restraining the animal.

Somebody opened the door on Elliott's side of the carriage, and a multitude of hands reached in to try to pull him out, excitement growing in their voices like hounds on the scent of a fox. Panic set in as Elliott realised that if these people managed to remove him from the carriage, they would kill him. There was nothing the policemen could do to stop them. He wedged his feet against the side of the carriage and tried his utmost to hold onto something, but with his hands tied, it wasn't easy, and he slowly felt his grip loosen.

'No!' shouted the sergeant as he grabbed Elliott's jacket with both hands, just as the horse lurched forward and the carriage moved away. The carriage shook wildly as the terrified horse galloped along the bumpy road, making its escape down the dale. Elliott found himself splayed across the seat. The sergeant reached over him and slammed the door shut. He heard the sergeant sigh loudly and, in the distance, the crowd jeering.

Elliott sat upright and took a deep breath. His face was dripping with sweat, but he was unable to wipe it as his hands were still fastened.

Every minute since the policemen had been at his house on Sunday morning, he'd feared being caught by them, but he reckoned his chances with them were much better than with the locals. Never in his life had he witnessed such hatred and anger, and he hoped never to see the likes again.

All night, Elliott had been locked in the cell at Stanhope police station, and he hadn't slept a wink. When a sliver of light appeared through the narrow window, high above his head, he sat up and ran his hands through his hair. It looked like it was going to be a lovely day again, but he doubted that he would get to see it.

Shortly after sunrise, a tall policeman unlocked the door and gave him a hunk of bread and a chipped mug filled with weak tea. The key turned in the lock, and he was alone again. The tea was too hot to drink, so he began to eat the bread hungrily.

He hoped that Josie was alright. She'd looked so frightened when he'd handed himself over to the police, but as far as he could see, he'd had no choice. He couldn't have let them arrest her when she'd done nothing wrong. She'd wanted to run away with him. He smiled to himself at the memory of her saying those words, spoken with love and naivety. For a moment, he'd been tempted. Aye, he had. He'd wanted to grab her hand and take her away from there, but it wasn't that simple. The police set up nationwide manhunts for killers. He and Josie wouldn't have been safe anywhere in England, or Scotland for that matter.

But more than his own safety, Elliott had his mother to think about. What would happen to her if they didn't release him? Could she manage on her own? He knew the answer to that — no, she wouldn't. She'd been dependant on him ever since his father had died. If they didn't let him go soon, his mother would end up in the workhouse.

A different constable came to the cell and unlocked the door. He held up a set of handcuffs, and asked, 'Are we going to need these? Or are you going to behave yourself?'

Elliott shook his head and looked down at his bruised wrists. He recalled the horrific journey the night before and thanked God that the crowd had failed to drag him from the carriage, for if they had, he doubted that he would have survived the night.

The constable led Elliott from the cell to a sparsely furnished room, with just a table and three chairs at its centre. 'Sit down. Wait here. And don't try anything.' He wagged his finger at Elliott in warning, as if speaking to an errant child, and then he asked contemptuously, 'By the way, do murderers drink tea?'

'I'm not a murderer,' said Elliott calmly, looking the man in the eye as he sat down at the table.

'I'll fetch you a cup — but just 'cos the sarge said I had to,' the policeman sneered.

The sergeant came in without saying a word and sat down at the opposite side of the table. He was followed by a smaller man who went to the far side and put down a notebook on the table before taking his seat. He then took a pencil from his inside jacket pocket, opened his book and sat poised, ready to transcribe the interview.

The constable returned with three steaming cups of tea

and placed them on the table next to each of the men, and then he left the room, chuckling to himself.

'Mr Dawson,' said the sergeant. 'You know why you're here. You've been arrested on suspicion of murdering Mr George Henderson of Rookhope, in Boltsburn mine, on the Sunday before last. Do you understand the charge?'

'I understand the charge — but I didn't kill him.'

'I need to ask you a few questions. Tell me about your relationship with Henderson. Did you get on with him?'

'I never had much to do with him. We worked for different partnerships at the mine. Some mornings I saw him going into work, and sometimes we finished about the same time. We passed the time of day. That's all.'

Elliott took a sip of his tea and spat it out across the table. 'There's salt in this!' he exclaimed, as he pushed the cup away.

Handing a handkerchief to Elliott so he could clean up the mess, the sergeant asked, 'Have you ever had a run-in with him? With Henderson.'

'No, I've never had a run-in with him. As I said, we passed the time of day, you know, we talked about the weather and stuff. Nothing else.'

The clerk recorded the conversation in his notebook, showing no expression whatsoever.

'What about his family? Do you know them?' asked the policeman.

'I know he had a family, but I've never met them.

They're incomers — they moved to Rookhope about a year back. And with me living outside the village, I don't get to see that many people. They must be church people 'cos I haven't seen them at chapel.'

Elliott thought the sergeant looked disappointed with the answers he'd given. They probably weren't what he was expecting to hear, but they were the truth. He had no reason to murder Geordie Henderson; he hardly knew the man.

'Henderson used to collect spar to sell to dealers, and we understand that you do a bit of collectin' an' all. You both went into the mine outside of work time to collect spar. Is that right?'

'Aye, I do. There's nobody minds us doin' it. The company's only interested in lead ore.'

'Was Henderson ever in the mine, outside of working hours, at the same time you were?'

'I don't think so. I don't remember seeing him.'

'That Sunday, when Henderson was killed, tell me what happened. From the time you left home in the morning,' said the sergeant.

'Well, I went to chapel in the morning, like I usually do. Then I went home to fix me mother some dinner. That afternoon, I'd arranged to meet Josie outside Boltsburn mine.'

'Josie being Josephine Milburn, the young woman who was with you last night?'

'Aye, that's right. I got there first, but I was only waiting for about ten minutes. Josie's very interested in minerals, and she hadn't been in a mine before, so I said I'd take her.'

The sergeant raised his eyebrows but didn't comment.

'I took her to one of the flats, and she spotted a nice bit of fluorite on the roof,' continued Elliott. 'It broke when I got it down for her. So, we shared it. I gave her one of the crystals, and I kept the other for myself. On the way out, we saw someone coming in. I couldn't see who it was. It might have been Geordie, I don't know, but whoever it was, he was on his own. We hid in West Level until he'd gone past, and then we went out of the mine. Josie got on her horse and rode home and I walked back up the railway line. I passed Jimmy Lonsdale and a few of the lads who'd been swimming up at Rispey. Then when I got home, I made tea for Mother and me.'

When Elliott finished, the sergeant nodded. The clerk put his pencil back into his pocket, stood up, picked up his notebook and left the room.

As the sergeant took him back to the cell, Elliott asked, 'What happens now?'

'We'll go through your statement. We'll have to check out your story. And then we'll let you know what we've decided to do. If there's a case against you, you'll be charged and sent to Durham to await trial. If not, you'll be free to go home.'

'How long will that take?' asked Elliott, thinking about his mother fending for herself.

'It'll take as long as it takes, lad.'

The sergeant opened the cell door and Elliott sat down on the wooden bench and put his head in his hands. He heard the key turn in the lock. All he could do now was wait. His fate was in their hands.

Chapter 10

Rookhope
August 1895

Tom pulled up the cart outside Boltsburn mine, climbed down and tethered Nutmeg beside the entrance. PC Emerson walked over to the mine entrance and looked into the dark depths of the earth.

'Come on,' said Tom. 'Let's get this done.'

Robert grunted, and said, 'You lead the way. I'll tell you when we get there.'

Tom hadn't been inside a mine since an accident at work over twenty years ago but, surprisingly, he didn't feel any fear when he walked down the horse level. If anything, he thought it felt like coming home. Walking underground was as natural to him as walking in the fields on his farm. He knew Robert didn't feel the same way about mines, he'd never liked them, and he could hear the unease in his friend's voice.

'The body was found around here somewhere,' said Robert, moving his arm in an arc around where he stood.

Tom looked around the large chamber. He could see bits of spar and quartz glistening on the walls and roof, but that wasn't what he'd come to look at. He began by walking around the edges of the cavity with his candle in his hand, looking for anything that might give him a clue as to what had happened there that day.

Something caught his eye, and he reached down to pick up a tin from the ground.

'What have you got there?' asked Robert.

He held up the tin so Robert could see it and said, 'It's Geordie's. His initials are on the lid.'

Tom passed it to Robert and watched the policeman open it. Inside were a couple of small spar crystals wrapped in a soft cloth.

'Looks like he collected these and put them in here before he was killed,' said Robert.

Tom continued his search, although he wasn't entirely sure what he was looking for. Several minutes later, he spotted something on the ground that looked out of place — a jagged piece of rock. He picked it up and inspected it closely in the candlelight. One end of the stone was encrusted with dried blood, and there were a few dark hairs stuck to it.

'Was Henderson wearing a hat when you found him?' asked Tom.

'He didn't have his hat on. It was on the ground next to him. We reckoned it must have come off in the struggle.'

'Did you find anything else near him?'

'A candle and a few matchsticks — that's about it. Just the usual stuff miners carry around.'

'Did you notice if the candle on his hat was burnt down?'

'Aye, it was.'

'And the candle on the floor was new?'

'That's right. It hadn't been lit,' said PC Emerson, looking puzzled.

Tom looked at the roof of the mine above where the dead man had been found and held a candle up close, moving it slowly so that he could see the top in detail.

'I think I know what happened here,' said Tom, holding up the rock he'd found. 'This is what killed him. Can you see the blood and hairs on it?'

Robert moved closer and nodded.

'That's how I knew he wasn't wearing a hat when he died,' said Tom.

'So, that's the murder weapon. I don't know how we missed that.'

'No, Robert. It's not the murder weapon. But it is what killed him.'

'I don't know what you're getting at.'

'Look at the roof here,' said Tom, pointing upwards. 'This rock fell from here recently. See that gap? It's exactly the same shape as this rock. I reckon Henderson must have been removing a piece of spar from the roof when his candle started to flicker or went out. Either way, he'd not be able to see what he was doing, and he wouldn't risk damaging the crystals he was after. So, he'd have stopped to replace the candle on his hat. Kneeling down here, he'd have taken off his hat and got a new candle and some matches out of his pocket. But before he had time to stick the new candle onto his hat, this fell from the roof and hit him on the back of the head.'

Robert looked at the rock in disbelief.

'It's not very big,' said Tom, 'but it's full of lead ore. Falling from that height, it's heavy enough to kill a man.'

Tom passed the rock to PC Emerson, and his hand dropped with the weight of the stone.

'Well, I never!' exclaimed the policeman. 'I see what you mean. It must be almost all lead.'

'By the weight, I'd say it is. You know, Robert, one of the first things I was told when I started mining was not to have me bait or change me candle where I was working because loose rocks might fall on me head. But for some reason, that's exactly what Henderson did — and it cost him his life. It was an accident, just an unfortunate accident.'

'I don't know what to say.' The constable took off his helmet and rubbed his hand through his thinning hair. Looking up at the roof, he hurriedly put his helmet back on. 'You should have been a policeman, Tom. I don't know how you worked all that out from just a few bits and bobs.'

'I know mining, and I know miners. That's all.'

'Well, I suppose that's good, then. We'd better get down to Stanhope and tell the sergeant. I guess your Josie's young man's in the clear. He cannot be charged with a crime that was never committed. So, she was right, eh?'

'Aye, she was,' said Tom proudly.

Shaking his head, Robert said, 'And I didn't believe her. I thought she was giving him an alibi to protect him.'

Tom looked at the constable. Although Robert could stand to his full height in this part of the mine, his shoulders were slumped forward, and he looked shorter than his six foot two inches. He was staring at the ground, but he wasn't looking at it. He appeared troubled.

'Mebbe it's time I quit. Retired, like,' said PC Emerson quietly.

Tom put his hand on his friend's shoulder and said, 'Because of this? No, Robert. Think about all the good you've done in the dale over the years. And anyway, you're not old enough to retire!'

Robert attempted a smile.

'Come on. Let's get you out of here. You've never been happy underground.'

Robert picked up the tin and the blood-covered rock. Holding them up, he said, 'We'd better take these with us — as evidence.'

Tom nodded, and the men made their way back through the tunnel to daylight.

After leaving the mine, Tom and Robert went straight

to Stanhope, and when they reached the police house, they jumped down from the cart. Tom tethered his horse before following Robert inside, where the sergeant, a constable and a clerk were deep in conversation.

'Elliott Dawson,' said PC Emerson. 'Where is he?'

'He's in the lock-up. Why?' asked the constable.

'He's innocent. He didn't murder anyone. Henderson's death was an accident.'

The sergeant said, 'Slow down, Robert. Now, who's this fellow that's with you?'

'I'm Tom Milburn, from High House Farm at Westgate.'

'Please wait here, Mr Milburn. Robert, you'd better come with me and tell me what this is about.'

Tom waited outside. He hoped that the sergeant would believe his version of events and accept that a murder had not taken place.

About ten minutes later, the sergeant and Robert reappeared. Robert nodded at Tom, and then Elliott Dawson was brought out by a constable, who removed his handcuffs. Elliott looked surprised to see Josie's father there. He recognised him from seeing him that night when he'd hidden in their barn waiting to see her.

The sergeant said, 'Mr Dawson, new evidence suggests that Henderson's death was most probably an accident. It appears a rock fell from the roof and hit him on the head and killed him. So, we don't need to question you any further. You're free to leave.'

'I'm sorry, lad,' said PC Emerson. 'We didn't know until this morning. You've Mr Milburn to thank. He's the one that worked out what happened.'

Elliott held out his hand to Tom, and said, 'It's good to meet you, Mr Milburn, and thank you very much.'

'No need for thanks, lad. I just wanted to set things right. Can I give you a lift? Either to your place, or ours?' Tom smiled.

'Does Josie know that it was an accident?' asked Elliott.

'Not yet.'

'Then I'd like to be the one to tell her, if that's alright?'

'Aye, she'll be glad to see you safe and well.'

Chapter 11

Josie had been moping around all morning. She couldn't settle to anything. Her mother had tried to keep her occupied, and Josie knew that she was trying to help, but no matter what Josie did, her mind kept returning to Elliott. He was in police custody, being questioned for a crime that she was sure he hadn't committed. Life was so unfair. He was by far the nicest lad that she'd ever met, and he didn't deserve any of this.

And it was all her fault. She should never have gone into the mine; she should have known better. All of her life, she'd been told that girls couldn't go underground because it was unlucky, and she'd gone and proved them right. It was unlucky; how else could she explain a man dying there the same day? Or Elliott being accused of murder? Two terrible things had happened already, and as bad things always come in threes, she dreaded what would happen next.

Josie stood by her bedroom window looking out at the barren hills on the opposite side of the valley. Her eyes travelled down over the green pastures and the emerald fields to the village in the valley bottom, where a movement caught her eye. Her father's cart was turning onto the farm track, but it looked like somebody was sitting next to him. Her brothers were both at home, so it wasn't one of them. She strained her eyes to see, and then stood back in surprise. It was Elliott, she was sure of it.

As she ran outside to meet them, so many questions swirled around in her mind. Had the police released him? Why was he with her father? And what on earth was he doing at High House Farm?

Elliott leapt from the cart and Josie ran into his arms. All she was aware of was his arms around her, his heartbeat, and tears on her face. She didn't know if they were hers or his, but all she cared about was that Elliott was back. He was safe. It was over.

They held each other for some time before she heard her mother shout, 'Tea's ready if you want some.'

Josie heard Elliott's stomach rumble, and she smiled up at him. 'You're hungry,' she said, and she took his hand and led him into the house.

When they went inside, Josie introduced Elliott to her mother and her brothers, and then they sat at the table and ate a hearty meal of mutton stew and dumplings. As they ate, Tom told the family about his discovery at the mine and explained how he'd proved Henderson's death had been an accident and that Elliott had been released because no crime had taken place.

When Tom finished his story, Josie was so proud of him. Her father had saved Elliott from being charged with murder and from the possibility of standing trial and being hanged. She would never forget what he'd done for them that day, and she could never thank him enough.

When everyone had finished the meal, Elliott said, 'Thank you again, Mr Milburn. I don't know how I can ever repay you. And thank you, Mrs Milburn, for the lovely tea. But I must go now. I need to check on me mother.'

'You're very welcome, lad,' said Tom. Winking at Josie, he said, 'It was worth it to see our lass smile again. Come on, I'll give you a ride over the hill.'

'I'll take him,' said Josie.

Looking at the tall clock, Tom said, 'It might be dark by the time you get back, love. I don't want you out on your own after dark. But you can come with us if you want?'

Josie nodded. She wanted to stay with Elliott for as long as possible.

Tommy and Matt harnessed Nutmeg and attached the flat cart. Tom climbed up first and took the reins. Elliott and Josie sat close together on the seat next to him, holding hands. They waved to her family as they set off for Rookhope.

As they descended the steep bank leading down into

the Rookhope valley, Josie asked, 'Is that smoke I can smell?'

'I can smell something,' said Tom, sniffing the air. 'Might be smoke.'

A little further down the bank, the acrid smell of smoke drifting on the breeze was unmistakable.

'Can we go any faster?' asked Elliott.

Josie noticed that his voice trembled as he spoke.

'Not on this steep bit,' replied her father, calmly. 'Nutmeg might slip and hurt herself.'

Looking towards the village, they saw smoke spiralling up into the sky, but couldn't see where it was coming from. As soon as the slope levelled out, Tom flicked the reins and Nutmeg began to canter, the cart rattling along behind her. Elliott held Josie's hand tightly and squeezed her fingers.

They turned a corner, and Railway Cottages came into view. The end house was ablaze. Smoke belched out of the windows and flames were eating away at the roof. Nutmeg whinnied and came to a sudden stop; refusing to go any nearer. Elliott jumped off the cart and sprinted to the houses. Tom and Josie ran after him.

Josie watched in horror as Elliott ran towards the fire, screaming at the top of his voice, 'Mother! Mother!'

The heat from the flames stopped him in his tracks. Tom ran up behind him and grabbed him in a wrestling hold to prevent him from going into the burning house, and manoeuvred him back to a safe distance. Elliott sank to the ground, his head in his hands, and wept. Josie knelt beside him and wrapped her arms around him and rocked him gently.

'What happened?' Josie heard her father ask an old man, who stood like a statue, his eyes fixed on the flames.

'I live in the middle one,' the man replied distantly. 'My house is on fire.'

'What about the end one?' asked Tom, pointing at Number One which was not alight as yet, but looked as though it soon would be.

'That one's been empty since the Watson's moved out.'

'How did the fire start?' asked Tom.

'How did the fire start?' The man repeated, still staring at the flames. After a pause, he said, 'Revenge for Geordie's murder, I reckon.'

'Did you see anyone?'

The man looked as though he was trying to remember, and then said, 'Lads from the village. Aye, it must have been lads from the village.'

Josie saw her father put his hand on the old man's shoulder.

'Who was it?' Tom asked. 'Did you see them?'

'I don't know,' said the old man warily.

'Don't you worry, the police will soon get to the bottom of this. Arson is one thing, but manslaughter, or maybe even murder, well, that's another thing altogether. The police won't rest until they find out who did it.'

'What do you mean? Manslaughter... or...or murder?'

'Elliott's mother was in the house. God rest her soul.'

'Mrs Dawson? She was in there? Oh, Lord!' Silent tears trickled down the old man's weathered face. 'I haven't seen her for months. I thought he was living there on his own — that the house was empty. Oh, Lord!'

Josie could feel Elliott sobbing as she held him, his whole body shaking. She couldn't begin to imagine the agony he must be feeling, knowing that his mother had died because the villagers had thought he was a murderer.

A crowd of onlookers had gathered to watch the fire and a policeman warned them all to stay back. Josie watched Tom walk over to him and she couldn't hear what he said but she guessed he was telling him about Elliott's mother. She heard the policeman say, 'Nobody's going in there tonight. Get the lad away from here.'

Somehow, Tom and Josie managed to get Elliott back to the cart. On the journey back to High House Farm, Elliott's head rested in Josie's lap, and she stroked his hair like he was an injured animal. His arms were wrapped tightly around her waist. She heard an occasional whimper or cry from him that sent shivers down her spine. He was hurting so much, and there was so little that she could do to relieve his pain.

When they returned to the farm, Tom helped Elliott up the stairs and led him into Josie's room, and left them there alone. Elliott's face was sooty, with streaks from tears running down his cheeks, and his clothes smelled strongly of smoke. He looked so lost. Josie removed his cap and his jacket, and put them on a chair and then took him into her arms and held him. He clung to her.

A few minutes later, there was a knock at the door, which was slightly ajar, and Josie went to open it fully. Her mother stood there, holding a large glass of whisky. Looking past her towards Elliott, and then back at Josie, she said quietly, 'Your father told me what happened. I'm ever so sorry. Give him this. God knows he'll need it to help him get through tonight.'

'Thank you.'

Josie took the glass and listened to the sound of her mother's footsteps retreating down the stairs. Closing the door, she turned to Elliott and handed him the glass. He didn't take it. So, she sat on the bed and patted the mattress next to her, encouraging him to sit down. When he didn't move, she got up and took his hand and pulled him towards her, and gently pushed him back onto the bed. When he was sitting on the edge of the mattress, she placed the glass in his hand and wrapped his fingers around it. At first, he took a small sip, and then knocked back the rest of the amber liquid in one gulp. His hand was gripping the glass so tightly that she thought it might break, so she took it from him and placed it on top of a chest of drawers. Then, she went back to him and held him. It was a long time before she heard his breathing become steadier and felt him relax in her arms. Still holding him, she moved so that he could lie down and within an hour or so he was sleeping. Josie kissed his grimy brow before leaving the room.

That night, Josie bunked down in her brothers' room which was next door to hers, but she couldn't sleep. Her mind was overactive; she couldn't stop thinking about the events of that day, from the relief at seeing Elliott after his release, to the horror of him losing his mother and his home. She knew that his mother was the only family he had. Josie hoped that Mrs Dawson had been asleep when the house was on fire and hadn't been aware of it. Anything else was just too dreadful to contemplate.

Her thoughts were brought to an abrupt halt when she heard Elliott sobbing in the next room. She slipped on a gown and went to him. Climbing onto the bed beside him, she took him into her arms and held him close for the rest of the night.

The next morning, Josie got up early and dressed. Elliott stayed in bed, not moving or speaking, but at least he was no longer crying. Josie went down to the kitchen where her parents were eating breakfast.

Her mother poured her a cup of tea, and asked, 'How is he this morning?'

'I don't know,' said Josie. 'He hasn't said a word since it happened. He cried a lot through the night, but he's stopped now. But it's like I'm not there. He seems to be in a world of his own.'

'That's shock, that is,' said Mary. 'Hardly surprising after what's he's been through. Maybe we should get the doctor up to have a look at him.'

'I think that's a good idea. Would Tommy go down for him?'

'Aye, I'll ask him. The police will want to talk to him. No doubt they'll call here today, an' all.'

'He's not up to talking to the police about the fire. He's not said a word to me yet.'

Josie sipped at her tea.

'Has Elliott got any family?' asked her mother.

'No!' said Josie defensively, thinking her mother wanted to send Elliott away.

'There'll be arrangements to make,' said Mary reassuringly, patting her daughter's hand.

'Oh. I hadn't thought about that. He told me his father died. I know he hasn't got any brothers or sisters. He's not mentioned anyone else.'

'I'll get started on it, then. The lad's not in any fit state to do anything.'

'Thanks, Mother.' After a few minutes of silence, Josie continued, 'I can't believe that anyone could be so evil. How could they set fire to a house with a woman inside it?'

'They didn't know she was there,' said Tom softly.

'But they shouldn't have set fire to his house in the first place!'

Putting an arm around Josie's shoulder and looking her in the eye, Mary said, 'No lass, they shouldn't have. But what's done is done. There's no going back. Now, what we have to do is pick up the pieces and get on.'

As tears welled up in Josie's eyes, she shook her head. She couldn't cry, not now; she had to stay strong for Elliott's sake. She sniffed loudly. Her mother handed her a handkerchief to blow her nose.

Mary poured another cup of tea and handed it to Josie. 'Take it up for him,' she said.

Josie smiled at her mother and said, 'Thank you.'

Elliott was still in bed. He sat up when he saw her walk into the room. She handed him the cup, which rattled in the saucer as he held it. He put the saucer down, on top of the quilt, and held the cup in both hands to drink the tea. When he'd finished it, she took the cup off him and placed it and the saucer on the chest of drawers. Then, she sat on the bed beside him, holding his hand, his head resting against her shoulder.

A short while later, there was a gentle knock at the door. Josie went to open it and greeted the doctor, showing him into the room.

'Elliott, this is Doctor Rutherford. He's come to see you. Would you like me to stay, or shall I wait downstairs?'

His eyes begged her to stay, and he held out his hand to her. She took it and stood by his side.

The doctor asked him to strip down to his underwear. Josie turned away, but Elliott pulled her back to his side.

'Stay with him, please,' said the doctor, observing Elliott's behaviour with interest.

Elliott didn't make any attempt to undress, so the doctor and Josie helped him to remove his dirty clothes, and then the doctor examined him thoroughly.

'You're in fine shape, Elliott. There's nothing to worry about. A few minor burns, but they'll heal in no time. I doubt they'll even leave a mark.'

There was no reaction from Elliott.

Dr Rutherford said, 'Now that you're stripped off, perhaps you'd like to have a bath and get cleaned up. Why don't you sit down for a few minutes? We'll get some warm water up here for you.'

The doctor indicated to Josie that he wanted her to follow him out of the room. Mary was waiting for them on the landing, and she closed the door behind them so that Elliott couldn't hear what was said.

'There's nothing wrong with him physically,' said the doctor. 'But he's had a terrible shock. What he needs now is time to come to terms with what's happened, and someone to keep an eye on him.' He smiled at Josie. 'It looks like he's chosen you for that job.'

'I'll look after him the best I can, but I don't know what to do to help him.'

'Let him cry when he needs to, let him talk when he needs to. Just be there for him. But I'll warn you, with something like this, it could take time.'

'I don't care how long it takes. I just want him to get better.'

Josie noticed a look pass between the doctor and her

mother.

'He will get better, won't he?' Josie asked anxiously.

'I have no reason to expect otherwise,' said the doctor matter-of-factly. 'I wouldn't let the police talk to him — not for a while yet. It could set him back.'

Looking at Mary, the doctor said, 'You've got a strong daughter. She's very much like you.'

'Aye, so everyone keeps telling me,' Mary laughed. 'We're happy for Elliott to stay here until he gets back on his feet, Doctor. I'll see you out.'

'Thank you,' he said, and inclined his head to Josie, before following Mary down the stairs.

As soon as Josie went back into her bedroom, Elliott grabbed her hand, and she led him back to the bed, where they sat down together. He held her hand tightly. The doctor was right, she thought. Elliott had chosen her to care for him. She owed him that much at least. Everything that had happened to him was because of her selfishness.

After his bath, Elliott spent the rest of the day either sleeping, or weeping, or looking out of the window as if in a trance, but he maintained his silence. That night Josie left him at bedtime and returned to her brothers' room, where once again, she was unable to sleep. She was worried for Elliott, and she desperately wanted to see him return to his usual self.

That night, she heard a petrifying scream coming from her room. She went out onto the landing where her mother and father already stood, looking anxiously at her bedroom door.

'You'd better go in, love,' said Tom. 'See how he is.'

'She cannot,' said Mary. 'It's not right — a young lass in his room in the middle of the night. I'll go.'

Tom put his arm around Josie's shoulder as Mary ventured into the bedroom. There was another scream, and Mary came straight back out.

'I think he's still dreaming,' she said. 'He looked terrified when I went in.'

'Maybe you should try, love,' said Tom. 'He seems to settle better with you around.'

Mary looked daggers at Tom.

'It's the only way anyone around here is going to get any sleep tonight,' he said.

Mary shrugged and went back to her room.

'Take no notice of her,' said Tom. 'She's just worried about your reputation. There's more than that at stake here. He's in a bad way, and he needs someone he trusts. And that's you. Don't worry, love; I'll sort things out with your mother.'

Josie kissed her father's cheek and went into the bedroom, where she found Elliott huddled up in bed, shaking and covered in sweat. He looked so frightened. His eyes turned to meet hers, and they pleaded for her to go to him. She wrapped him in her arms and held him.

And the pattern of that day was repeated over and over again.

Chapter 12

One morning, over a week after the fire, Josie climbed the stairs carrying Elliott's breakfast on a tray, and when she opened the door, he turned from the window and said, 'Good morning. That smells good.'

She was so surprised that she almost dropped the tray. Grinning, she said, 'Good morning! I've brought you bread that was baked this morning — it's still warm — and some eggs.'

Thrilled by the breakthrough, she sat and watched him eat, and savoured the sound of his voice when he commented on what a lovely day it was and that he'd need some braces or a belt to hold up his trousers.

Looking at him, she could see that he had lost weight since coming to stay at High House Farm, but that was hardly surprising when he'd hardly touched the food that she'd put in front of him. Apart from that, it felt as though nothing had happened. He was talking to her in his usual manner and appeared to be acting rationally, but she found it strange that he hadn't questioned her about why he was in her bedroom. He didn't mention his mother or the fire, and Josie decided not to broach the subject, thinking that he would bring it up when he was ready to talk.

After breakfast, Elliott stood in front of the chest of drawers that housed Josie's mineral collection, her fractured crystal taking pride of place in the centre of the display. He picked it up and looked at it closely.

'Your crystal!' exclaimed Josie in horror. 'Was it in the house when...?' She put her hand to her mouth when she realised what she'd said, and waited anxiously for Elliott's reaction.

'I keep it on me,' he said calmly. Patting his chest, he added, 'Right here.'

Reaching into his waistcoat pocket, he removed a handkerchief and opened it to reveal the other crystal. Holding one crystal in each hand, he moved them together, and they fitted perfectly. Elliott smiled, and Josie's heart melted. She watched him place hers back on the top, and then he carefully wrapped up his and put it back into his pocket.

After that, they spent a quiet and peaceful day together in her room. She followed his lead as the doctor had advised, listening to him when he talked and sitting in silence with him when he didn't.

As evening approached, Josie wondered if she should

stay in the room with Elliott overnight, now that his condition was improving. She'd acted like a nurse to him since the fire because he'd needed her to support and comfort him. That day, he'd been much better, almost back to normal at times, and she wondered how he would be during the night. The way he tossed and turned in his sleep, Josie knew he must suffer from awful nightmares. Sometimes he woke up shouting or crying, and sometimes he just sat there, looking incredibly sad. It broke her heart to see him like that.

Josie's mind drifted back to the night that she'd gone to Elliott on the fell when he'd been hiding from the police. She had loved being kissed and held by him. When he'd pulled away, she'd been disappointed and left wanting, but she knew he'd done the right thing. But what if he made advances towards her during the night? Would she be able to resist him?

Knowing that that was unlikely, she said, 'Elliott, I'm going to bed now. I'll just be next door if you need me.'

Elliott moved closer to her and took her hand, holding it tightly. He didn't say anything, but the look of fear in his eyes made Josie realise that, although he had shown improvement, he was still a long way from making a full recovery. If he could ever make a full recovery after his terrible ordeal, she thought sadly.

'Do you want me to stay?' she asked, already knowing the answer.

Fully clothed, Elliott climbed onto the bed. He watched

Josie wander over to the old armchair that she'd been sleeping in while he'd been using her bed.

'No,' said Elliott. 'You look tired. You need to sleep. Come here.'

He patted the bed.

As Josie climbed onto the bed next to him, Elliott kissed her gently on her cheek, and they cuddled up together, her back to his front. She didn't have time to worry about his intentions. She'd had so little sleep since the night of the fire, and she was so relieved that at last Elliott was improving, and she was so warm and comfortable in his arms that she soon drifted off to sleep.

The next morning, Josie woke early, still enfolded in Elliott's arms. She'd slept right through the night, which meant Elliott had slept well too. She hastily clambered off the bed and went into her brothers' room to change her clothes and tidy her hair. By the time Josie went back to her room, Elliott was up too.

'Good morning,' she said, a little shyly.

'Good morning,' he said, smiling at her.

'Do you feel up to having your breakfast downstairs today?'

'Aye, if that's alright, I think I will. I'm starving.'

Her parents didn't make a fuss when Elliott joined them at the kitchen table. They greeted him kindly, and Mary smiled at Josie in encouragement. Josie walked over to the stove and filled two bowls with porridge from a large pan.

As they ate, Mary asked her husband, 'What are you going to be on with today?'

'There's a dyke down in the top pasture,' he replied. 'Think I'll build that up. It needs fettling before we bring the lambs down for the sales. The lads can give me a hand. What about you?'

'It's washing day again. It doesn't seem like a week since the last one, but at least it's a good drying day. There's a nice warm breeze out there this morning.'

Her brothers had been watching Elliott with interest, and then suddenly Matt asked him, 'Will you be going to the funeral tomorrow?'

Josie was mortified that Matt had dared to mention it. She saw her mother fire a warning glance at her brother, and they all waited anxiously for Elliott's reaction.

Elliott looked up from his bowl and asked, 'Whose funeral?'

Josie put her hand on Elliott's knee under the table, and said quietly, 'Your mother's funeral.'

He swallowed, and then his face hardened.

'I couldn't miss me mother's funeral, could I? Of course, I'll be there.'

When everyone had resumed eating, Elliott turned to Josie, and he whispered in her ear, 'You'll come with me, won't you?'

'Yes, I'll come with you.' She smiled at him reassuringly.

'Right, that's settled then,' he said. 'I wouldn't mind a bit more porridge if there's any left in the pan, please.'

'Yes, there's a bit left,' said Mary, smiling at him. 'It's good to see you've got your appetite back.'

When Elliott had finished eating, he turned to Josie, and asked, 'Do you fancy a walk?'

'Yes, if you feel up to it.'

'Aye, it looks nice out there. I'll nip upstairs and get me jacket.'

While Elliott was upstairs, Josie said to her mother, 'He's changed all of a sudden. Do you think he's alright?'

'Changed for the better, I'd say,' said Mary. 'Just keep an eye on him. Has he said anything about what happened yet?'

'No, nothing. That's not normal, is it?'

'Who's to say? Everyone deals with things in their own way,' said Mary, shrugging.

When Josie and Elliott reached the summit of the fell, they turned around to admire the wonderful view of Weardale below them. The meandering river that shone like a silk ribbon, the patchwork of fields with dry-stone walls, and the limestone quarries that scarred the hillsides. The sun was high in the sky, lighting it all to perfection.

'It looks beautiful from up here, doesn't it?' said Josie.

'Aye, it does.'

'I can't imagine there are many places in the world that

can match it,' said Josie with pride. 'I love living here.'

'Really? Do you mean that?'

'Yes, of course.'

She looked at him questioningly as she sat down on a rocky outcrop. He came over and sat next to her, and said, 'Josie, I've been thinking. I cannot stay here. Not after everything that's happened. They'd have killed me the other night if they'd gotten hold of me.'

'What! Who would have killed you?'

'You don't know?' Elliott took a deep breath and shrugged. 'How could you? The night the police took me away, some blokes stopped us at Westgate and tried to drag me out of the carriage. If it wasn't for the sergeant grabbing me, the miners would have taken the law into their own hands that night. Luckily, we managed to get away.'

Josie couldn't believe what she was hearing. She'd lived near Westgate her whole life, and she couldn't imagine the men from the village would behave in that way, but she had no reason to doubt his word.

Bitterly, he said, 'But I suppose they did take the law into their own hands in the end, didn't they?' He shook his head. 'They didn't get to kill me, so they killed me mother. She didn't deserve that. She'd never hurt anybody in her life. How could they do that to her?'

How could Josie answer his question? She'd wondered the same thing herself many times since that night. They sat together in silence.

Elliott was looking down into the valley, when he said, 'You see a beautiful place, a place you call home. I don't see that anymore. I see a place where I don't belong, a place I'm no longer welcome.'

Josie turned to him, and said, 'But you didn't do anything wrong! That man's death was an accident.'

'We know that, but there'll always be doubt in some people's minds.' He sat back and sniggered. 'Where there's smoke, there's fire, and all that.'

'Elliott. Are you trying to tell me that you're going away?'

He looked down at the ground and mindlessly picked a reed and started to peel the outer coating away from the spongy centre. When he looked back at Josie, he said, 'Aye. I'm leaving. I'm going to America.'

Josie gasped. 'America? But...'

'I know it's a long way, but I know a lad that's been working over there for a few years. John Wilkinson. He wrote to me a while back asking if I'd be interested in going over to work. There's a desperate shortage of men to work in the lead mines there — you know, men that know what they're doing. I thought about it at the time. And if I hadn't had me mother to see to, I'd have gone.'

Josie's eyes glistened with tears as she said, 'But I thought...' She couldn't finish what she wanted to say. She had thought that they would be together, that they'd get married and have a place of their own — here in Weardale.

'I know, and I'm sorry.' He took her into his arms and held her. 'But you've got to understand that I can't stay here, not after everything that's happened. Oh, Josie, I'd love to take you with me, but I don't know what it'll be like over there. I'll have to find a job and somewhere to live.'

Loosening his hold on her so that he could see her face, he said, 'I'm not sure you'd want to come, anyway. Why would you leave your beloved Weardale to be with someone like me?'

'Oh, Elliott. Don't you remember? I offered to run away with you when you were hiding from the police, and I meant it. Surely you know how much I love you.' Josie started to cry, and through her tears, she said, 'I want to be with you, Elliott, wherever you are, and if that means going to America, then I'll go to America.'

'Josie, listen to me,' Elliott said, as he lifted his hands to cup her face gently. 'I can't take you with me. I have nothing. I've lost everything. As much as I want you to come with me, I can't support a wife. I can't even support myself. I need to find work so I can get enough money together for me passage, and when I'm settled out there, I'll send for you.'

Elliott had said wife. He did want to marry her. He wanted to be with her too.

'Do you promise?' she asked.

'I promise, on my life,' he whispered, kissing the top of her head. He held her gently until her tears stopped, and then he said, 'Come on. We'd better be getting back.'

They walked back to the farm in silence, each deep in their thoughts. When they reached the farmyard, Josie heard a man's voice that she didn't recognise coming from inside the kitchen. She led the way into the house and saw a man dressed in uniform sitting at the table, taking tea with her parents.

Tom turned to Josie and Elliott, and said, 'Ah, there you are! The sergeant has come to ask Elliott a few questions.'

Mary looked at her daughter sympathetically, and said, 'I told him that Elliott might not be ready to talk about it yet.'

Elliott reached for Josie's hand and gripped it firmly, saying to the man, 'What is it you want to know?'

'Why don't you sit down? The pair of you,' said Tom. 'We'll leave you in peace.'

'Please, stay,' said Elliott, as he and Josie sat at the opposite side of the table to the policeman.

'Alright, if that's what you want,' said Tom. He and Mary remained in their seats.

'I'd just like to say, first of all, that I'm very sorry about your mother,' said Sergeant Armstrong. 'It's a dreadful thing what's happened. We've talked to a few people, including Mr Milburn here, about the fire at your house. It appears it was started deliberately — while you were in custody. Do you have any idea who could have started the fire?'

'Aye,' said Elliott angrily. 'Take your pick. It could have been any one of those louts that tried to lynch me the other night because they thought I was a murderer! Or it could be anyone else from the dale for that matter! They all thought I was guilty.'

'I understand what you're saying, lad, and I know you're angry — with good right. I'm sorry about everything what's happened. It must have been very hard on you.'

Tom interrupted, 'The old man who lived next door to Elliott, I think he might have some idea about who started the fire. I don't know if he'll tell you, though. He looked frightened to me.'

'That would be Mr Westgarth. He's moved in with his daughter down in the village. We've already spoken to him, and like you say, he's not been very cooperative. He was pretty shaken up by it all.'

As he stood up to leave, the sergeant looked at Elliott, and said, 'We'll continue with our enquiries, and we'll keep you informed of any developments.'

Elliott nodded.

Sergeant Armstrong picked up his hat, and Mary showed him to the door. Josie heard him say to her mother, 'The poor lad, I wish there was more we could do.' And her mother's reply, 'Just find the person who did it.'

The next day, Josie and her parents took Elliott to

Rookhope for his mother's funeral. Although they sat side by side in the cart, it felt to Josie that there was a distance growing between them. He seemed to want her close to him, but their conversation had become stilted. She hadn't stayed in the same room with him since the night she'd slept in his arms, the night before he'd told her that he was going to America. Elliott was leaving, and she was staying behind. She wondered if he would stand by his promise and send for her when he was settled, or if he would forget all about her once he'd turned his back on Weardale.

But that day Elliott had to face his demons and Josie would be by his side to help him get through it. She took his hand as they walked into the chapel together. The building was full. It appeared that the whole village had turned out to show their respects to the poor lady who'd died in the tragic house fire.

After the service, the coffin was carried through the village, followed by a procession led by Elliott and Josie, with Tom and Mary walking behind, and then the villagers. Josie noticed that the curtains were closed in the windows of all of the houses on the road through the village as they made their way down to the peaceful churchyard beside the river.

Mrs Dawson's body was buried in a plot next to that of her late husband. Elliott stood at the graveside and held Josie's hand firmly. She knew why his head was down, avoiding eye contact with the other mourners. It wasn't because he was overcome with grief or emotion, as would be expected; it was because he knew that one or more of the people surrounding the grave could have been responsible for his mother's death. She could feel anger and tension radiating from his body, and at that moment, she knew that Elliott had made the right decision to leave the dale. It was clear to her that he had to get away.

Josie focused on the individuals there. Apart from Elliott, there was only one person visibly upset by the death of Mrs Dawson — the old man who had lived at Railway Cottages. He stood with his head down, but his shoulders betrayed the fact that he was crying. This was confirmed when he took a handkerchief from his pocket to wipe his eyes and blow his nose.

After the burial, there was no funeral tea. Josie stood with Elliott and watched the villagers disperse, walking in small groups back to their homes. Tom and Mary wandered towards the iron gates.

'Do you want a moment to yourself?' Josie asked Elliott.

'No, I'm done here,' he replied and led her to where her parents waited. They all walked back to the village together and then Tom drove them home.

When they arrived, Elliott went upstairs to Josie's room. Josie didn't follow, thinking he might appreciate some time alone. Instead, she went outside to find her father, who was in the stable grooming Nutmeg. Leaning over the stable door, she told him about Elliott's plan to emigrate.

'I can't say I blame him, love,' said Tom. 'I'm not sure I'd want to stay here after what he's been through.'

'I don't want him to leave, but it's what he needs to do. But he lost everything he had in the fire. He needs to make some money before he can go anywhere.'

'Ah! I see what you're asking, and the answer is yes. He can work here until he's earned enough to pay for his fare.'

'Thank you,' she said, giving her father a quick hug. Then she ran back to the house to tell Elliott the good news.

Chapter 13

Rookhope
August 1895

PC Emerson had questioned many people over the years, but he couldn't fathom out the man sitting in front of him. Instinct told him that something wasn't right about Mr Westgarth's account of the fire. He'd gone back to see him in the hope that he'd get more information out of him this time, something useful that might help him work out what had happened that night.

'Must I repeat how serious this matter is?' he asked Mr Westgarth. 'A woman was killed in that fire. You told Mr Milburn that it was lads from the village that started the fire. Did you see them? Who were they? What did they look like?'

Mr Westgarth looked out of the window and remained silent.

The back door opened and Mr Westgarth's middle-aged daughter came in carrying a handful of carrots, freshly pulled from the garden. Seeing the policeman sitting at the table with her father, she said, 'Hello! Can I get you a cup of tea or anything?'

'No, thank you,' replied the policeman.

Leaving the carrots in the scullery, she came into the front room, and said, 'If you're sure? I was going to go down to the shop. Is that alright? Or would you like me to stay here until you're done?'

Her father was still staring out of the window, ignoring her, so PC Emerson said, 'You go and get your shopping. We'll be fine.'

She grabbed a basket from the kitchen and went out of the front door, leaving them alone.

'Mr Westgarth,' the policeman said, 'if you're not going to give me their names, could you at least tell me what they looked like?'

Still, there was no response.

'If you don't cooperate, you could be charged — for withholding evidence, or perverting the course of justice, or aiding and abetting, or something of the sort.'

After a few minutes of silence, PC Emerson began to wonder if the man's mind had gone. It must have been a terrible shock for him to lose his home and his belongings, and to learn that his neighbour had died.

Getting to his feet, he said, 'Mr Westgarth, please stand up.'

The old man did as he was asked, but looked straight ahead, avoiding eye contact.

The policeman bent down to Mr Westgarth's height

and looked him straight in the eye. Losing his patience, he bellowed, 'I need to know who did this. What these men did was despicable! They killed an innocent woman, and they deserve to be strung up for it.'

A tear formed in Mr Westgarth's eye and it slowly rolled down his wrinkled cheek.

PC Emerson thought that he was finally making progress — at least he had managed to get a response, so he decided to carry on in the same vein.

'Men that could do such a horrid thing are evil, and they need to be stopped before they hurt somebody else. Tell me who it was, and I'll make sure they're locked up. They'll not be able to hurt you.'

Tears flowed freely down the old man's face now, and for the first time, he turned his eyes to meet the policeman's.

'I did it,' he confided. 'It was me.'

PC Emerson stepped back and rubbed his hands through his hair. My God, he thought, I never saw that one coming. When he'd recovered from the shock, he said, 'Sit down, and tell me exactly what it was that you did.'

They sat at the table. Mr Westgarth pulled out a large handkerchief from his pocket and dried his face, and then, without prompting, he began to speak.

'I was a miner up at Redburn. Mr Dawson, the lad's father, used to work there an' all. I never cared for the man, meself. He thought he was better than the rest of us. Anyway, when I heard that his lad had killed an honest, God-fearing, family man, I saw red, I did. I couldn't abide the thought of him coming back and living next door to me. So, I set my mind to firing his house. I never thought it would take hold like it did, and I didn't think that my house would go up an' all. And — and I didn't know Mrs Dawson was —'

His face crumpled, and he started to sob. After a minute or two, he sniffed loudly, and said, 'But the door was locked. Who locks the door when they're in the house?'

PC Emerson sat quietly, hoping he would say more now that he'd opened up.

'You're right,' said Mr Westgarth. 'What I did was evil. I killed Mrs Dawson, and I deserve to be punished for it. A life for a life. That's what the Bible tells us.'

Mr Westgarth got up quickly, for a man of his age, and darted into the scullery.

PC Emerson followed him and froze in the doorway when he saw Mr Westgarth pick up a carving knife and point it at his chest.

'No!' the constable screamed as he threw himself towards the old man, but he was too late. Mr Westgarth had already plunged the knife into his chest.

The old man lost consciousness as his blood spilled onto the floor, and PC Emerson looked on helplessly.

In the bottom pasture, Elliott grabbed a lamb by its fleece

and pushed it through the smoot hole in the dry-stone wall. That was the last one — all done. He blocked the gap with a large stone. When he turned around, Tom Milburn was walking towards him.

'Thank you,' shouted Tom, above the bleating of almost three hundred sheep and lambs. 'That's a good job done. Now, let's go and get something to eat. We can take the ewes back up to the fell later.'

'Aye, it's thirsty work in this heat,' said Elliott, wiping his brow.

As the two men made their way back to the farmhouse for dinner, they spotted PC Emerson walking towards them, and when their paths crossed, the policeman said soberly, 'Good afternoon, gentlemen.'

'How do, Robert? What brings you up here?' asked Tom.

'It's the lad that I've come to see. I've got some news for him — about the fire.'

Elliott shifted uncomfortably, and he felt Tom's steadying hand on his shoulder.

'Alright,' said Elliott, trying to stay calm. 'You'd better tell us what's happened.'

'I'll start at the beginning,' said PC Emerson. 'Mr Westgarth was the only witness to what happened that night — but he wouldn't talk. So, we went around every house in Rookhope and questioned everybody about where they'd been that night. We didn't get anything useful from the villagers so, as a last resort, I paid

Mr Westgarth another visit yesterday.'

Taking off his helmet and holding it in front of him, he said, 'I'm sorry to have to tell you this, but Mr Westgarth admitted setting fire to your house.'

Elliott stood with his mouth open and, finally, he asked in disbelief, 'Mr Westgarth?'

'Aye, lad. There's no doubt in my mind that it was him. He did it because he thought you'd killed Henderson. If it helps at all, lad, he didn't know your mother was in the house.'

Elliott acknowledged his words with a nod.

'And there's something else that might bring you some comfort,' said the constable. 'Your mother likely knew nothing about the fire. We found her body in an armchair.'

Elliott swallowed, and his voice was choked with emotion when he said, 'Thank you. That's a blessing, at least.'

There was a slight pause while Elliott regained his composure, and then he asked, 'What'll happen to him?'

'That's in God's hands now, lad,' replied PC Emerson. 'Mr Westgarth is dead.'

'Dead?' asked Tom.

'Aye. He took his own life.' Looking contrite, PC Emerson said, 'Mebbe I pushed him too far when I was questioning him. I don't know. He stabbed himself right in front of me.'

'I'm sorry, Robert,' said Tom. 'Most likely, his mind

was disturbed with the guilt of what he'd done. Don't blame yourself.'

Elliott had been standing quietly, looking at the ground, and then he raised his eyes to the men and said through gritted teeth, 'I hope the bastard rots in hell.' He turned quickly and stormed off, heading back uphill to the pasture.

Sitting with his back against a dry-stone wall, Elliott thought about his poor mother and everything she had endured. He thought it was unfair that she'd lost her husband, and then her mind, and that she'd died before her time at the hand of another.

All this time, he'd been blaming himself for his mother's death, because he was the one who had turned the key in the lock every time he'd left her at home alone, and he believed that it had been his fault that she'd been unable to escape from the house when the fire started. His decision to lock her in had been made with all good intentions. He'd never considered what would happen if there was a house fire, only the dangers of her wandering off. Thank God, his mother had not been aware of the fire. The policeman's words had offered him more comfort than he deserved.

As he sat there, he resolved to make the most of his life, for his mother's sake. The woman that his mother had been in her younger days would not have wanted him to feel sorry for himself. She'd have encouraged him to go out into the world and do something with his life and, more than anything, she'd have wanted him to be happy. From now on, he vowed that he would shed no more tears for her, and instead of dwelling on the past, he would look to the future, to his future. He looked up to the sky and smiled; he could feel her looking down on him.

Hearing a noise, he turned his head towards the gate and saw Josie walking towards him. She looked worried, and he knew Tom must have told her about the policeman's visit. Perhaps he'd even sent her up to make sure he was alright. Was he alright? Aye, he was now.

'There you are!' Josie exclaimed.

Elliott stood up and taking her hands in his, he said, 'I'm fine. I just needed a bit of time, that's all.'

'Good,' she said, smiling at him.

'Thanks for coming to check on me,' he said, as he kissed her lightly on the lips and hugged her. 'You've been so good to me.'

'Dinner's on the table,' said Josie. 'We should get back before the lads eat it all.'

Elliott laughed, and they walked back to the farmhouse, hand in hand.

Chapter 14

Elliott sat down for tea at the Milburn's table for the last time. In the morning, he would be leaving High House Farm to start a new life, where nobody knew who he was, or what he'd suffered. It was the right thing to do; he couldn't abide seeing pity in the eyes of everyone he met. His only regret was that he was leaving Josie, but he couldn't take her to a strange land and an uncertain future; it wouldn't be fair on her. She would be safe here with her parents. After all the time they'd spent together, his feelings for her had grown stronger and stronger, and parting from her would be tough. When he had a decent job, and a house that was worthy of her, he'd ask her to come to America, and he'd marry her. There was nothing he wanted more. But for now, he had to be patient.

Sitting next to him at the table, Josie kept glancing across at him, the pain in her eyes clear to see. Everyone was quiet, and even the lads had stopped their usual teasing and bickering.

After tea, Elliott asked Josie if she'd like to go for a walk, and he was relieved when she agreed. He couldn't begin to tell her what was on his mind, so they strolled together, hand in hand, and wandered across the fields.

'I've been thinking,' she said, breaking the silence. 'I'd like to see you off at the station in the morning.'

'Aye, if that's what you want.'

'It is. I want to be with you... for... for as long as possible.'

Stopping in his tracks, he turned to her, and said, 'I'll always be with you, Josie, and you'll always be with me.' Patting his waistcoat pocket, he said, 'I'll be thinking about you all the time that we're apart.'

She moved forward, and he took her into his arms, and they clung to each other.

The next morning, after breakfast, Tom, Mary and their sons gathered together in the kitchen to say farewell to Elliott.

Elliott shook Tommy's and Matt's hands, and said, 'You're like the brothers I never had. Thank you for making me so welcome. It's been great staying here and working with you on the farm. I'm going to miss you both.'

The young men wished him the very best of luck and then went outside to begin their chores.

'Thank you, Mr and Mrs Milburn,' said Elliott, 'for

everything that you've done for me. Without you, Mr Milburn, the police might still have me locked up in a prison cell.'

Tom reached into his pocket and took out a handful of coins, and he said, 'Take this, lad.'

'But Mr Milburn, I couldn't. That's far too much.'

'I've made me mind up. And this lot know I can be a stubborn bugger at times,' Tom said, laughing. 'Anyway, your need is greater than ours.'

'Thank you, Mr Milburn. That's very good of you. I'll take it on one condition.'

'What's that?'

'That you'll let me pay it back one day.'

'Aye, lad. That's fine by me. Treat it as a loan, eh? A long-term loan.'

The men shook hands.

'Mrs Milburn, you've been so kind, taking me in and treating me like one of your own. There aren't many who would have done that. Thank you so much.'

Mary opened her arms and hugged him, and whispered in his ear, 'Don't keep this lass waiting too long.'

'I won't, Mrs Milburn. Thank you again for letting me stay.'

Elliott picked up a small bag that contained everything he owned and then reached for Josie's hand. Her parents followed them to the door and watched the young couple walk down the track together.

Elliott and Josie stood on the platform at Westgate

Railway Station and waited. When the locomotive chugged into the station and pulled up beside them, Elliott took Josie into his arms and held her tightly.

'I love you, Josie,' he said earnestly.

'Oh, Elliott, I'll always love you.'

He kissed her passionately, and as they parted, she said, 'You will write, won't you?'

'Aye, I'll write.'

He stepped into the carriage and closed the door behind him. The guard blew his whistle, and the train slowly moved away. As Josie watched the engine disappearing into the distance, tears streamed down her cheeks. The man she loved had left her, and she didn't know when, or even if, she would see him again.

Chapter 15

Tom opened the back door of the farmhouse and went into the kitchen, where Mary was preparing dinner, and Josie was tending the fire. He closed the door quietly behind him, and without any preamble, he announced, 'Our Joe's taken to his bed.'

Josie stopped what she was doing and turned to look at her father, noticing that her mother's hands had stilled too. The news that her uncle was ill had shocked her too.

'He was fine yesterday,' said Tom, shaking his head. He took off his cap and sat on his armchair next to the fire, twisting and turning his hat in his hands.

'What's wrong with him?' asked Mary.

'It's his chest — he's having trouble getting his breath. I've asked the doctor to call in and see him.'

'Maybe I should go over?' suggested Mary.

'There's no need for that. Let's see what the doctor says first, eh?'

'Is it serious?' asked Josie, sensing her father's concern.

'I don't know, love. I've never known him to take to his bed before. Not ever — not even when he was a bairn. So, he must be feeling pretty bad.'

At one o'clock, Tommy and Matt came in for dinner, and the family sat down to eat. Tom told them about their uncle being unwell, and after that, there was barely any conversation. Josie wondered if they were all as worried about Uncle Joe as she was.

The silence was interrupted by a loud knock at the door, and Dr Rutherford, being an old friend of the family, let himself into the house.

'Good afternoon,' he said. 'I'm afraid it's not good news, Tom. It's no wonder your brother couldn't get out of bed this morning — he has pneumonia! He's burning up with fever. He really shouldn't be left on his own over there. Is there anyone who can stay with him until his condition improves?'

'I'll go,' said Mary decisively.

Tom looked at her with an expression that Josie couldn't fathom.

Mary perched herself on Tom's chair arm and took her husband's hand. 'Who else will see to him?' she asked. 'He hasn't got anybody.'

'You're right, I suppose. You should go over later after we've had our teas.'

Josie couldn't understand her father's reluctance to let her mother care for Joe. Surely he wanted his brother to get well? Josie turned to her mother, and said, 'I'll help, as well. He's going to need someone over there night and day until he's better. You can't do that all by yourself.'

'That's good,' said the doctor. 'That's sorted then. He'll be in good hands with you two ladies taking care of him.'

'Can I offer you a cup of tea or a bite to eat, Doctor?' asked Mary.

'No, thank you, but thanks for asking. Mrs Green has gone into labour, so I'd better go and check on her progress. This will be her tenth!' As he went to the door to see himself out, he said, 'I'll call up to see Joe again in the morning.'

'Thank you,' said Tom.

After the doctor had gone, Mary said, 'I'd better get a few things together to take over there. I don't suppose there'll be much in the house.'

'Probably not,' said Tom. 'He's not looked after himself very well since Connie died.'

As Josie helped her mother pack supplies, she said, 'Aunt Connie was so young when she died. No wonder Uncle Joe often looks sad.'

'Aye, it's no wonder.' Pulling a cover over the basket, Mary said, 'You can see to things here. I'm going over there now.'

'But Father said after tea.'

'Aye, I know what he said, but you never know with a fever. An hour or two can make all the difference.'

Josie went out into the yard with her mother, and said,

'I'll come over before it gets dark, then you can get home before bedtime.'

'Thank you,' said Mary, smiling at her.

Josie watched her mother walk away until she was out of sight, and then she went back inside to prepare tea.

When Mary arrived at Springbank Farm, Joe Milburn was sleeping peacefully. She wandered around the house for old times' sake, stirring memories long forgotten; long days working as a housemaid, Mr and Mrs Peart's friendly banter in the kitchen, and their daughter, Connie. Mary had never liked Connie, but even so, she would never have wished on her the hand that she'd been dealt in life. And now they were all gone.

Apart from the kitchen, the study and Joe's bedroom, it was apparent that nobody had used the other the rooms since Connie's death; they were filthy. In her mind, she could see Mrs Peart running her finger over the furniture, and hear her say, 'Good Lord, just look at all this muck.'

Mary shivered and pulled her shawl tighter around her body; it felt as though the house was full of ghosts.

Walking out into the yard, she saw the twins, Isaac and Jacob Rowell, who had just finished milking the cows. While Jacob took the cows from the byre back to their field, Isaac came over to her.

'How's he doing?' he asked.

'Not well from what I gather, but he's sleeping peacefully now.'

'With a good rest, he'll be as right as rain in no time.'

Mary smiled, wishing she had the same confidence in Joe's recovery. 'Would you do me a favour?' she asked.

'Aye, of course.'

'On your way home, could you call at the Green's cottage and ask if one of their lasses would come up and give us a hand cleaning this place up.'

'No problem.'

'Thank you. You'll need to speak to Mr Green or the eldest lass, Nelly. Mrs Green's having another bairn.'

Isaac tipped his cap at Mary, and she went back into the house.

Later that evening, Josie went to Springbank Farm. Her mother led the way to her uncle's bedroom, where Joe was lying in bed, propped up with pillows. Josie could hear his congested lungs trying to take in air, even from where she stood in the doorway, and she could see his chest heaving with the effort. Sweat beaded on his brow, and his face looked pale against his dark brown hair.

Her Uncle Joe was her father's only brother, younger by a couple of years, and he'd always seemed so robust. She'd seen him handle horses and cattle with ease, and work longer and harder than anyone else at hay-time and shearing. She would have described him as strong and determined, and a little sad, and she found it hard to comprehend that this was the same man lying in his bed, fighting to breathe.

Despite his obvious discomfort, he smiled at her when she walked over to him and stood beside his bed.

'Hello! How are you feeling?' she asked.

'Not good.'

'Mother's going home now. I've come to stay with you for a bit,' she said, as she saw her mother wave at her from the door before leaving.

'Thank you,' said Joe.

He looked like he wanted to say more, but the effort of speaking was too much for him, and he lifted a cotton handkerchief to his mouth and began to cough. When the bout of coughing ended, she sat by the bed with him, wiping his brow occasionally with a cold, damp cloth, and when eventually his breathing became a little more relaxed, she realised that he'd fallen asleep.

She walked over to a big, old rocking chair by the window and sat on it, hoping she could sleep for a while too. Leaning back, she let her mind wander, and she drifted into a light sleep.

'Mary!'

Josie was startled by her uncle, shouting for her mother. Without lighting a candle, she went quickly to his bedside to find him thrashing about in his sleep, and she imagined that he must be having a nightmare. She wiped his face with a damp cloth, which seemed to calm him.

'Mary? Is that you?' he asked quietly.

Coughing, Joe tried to sit up.

'It's Josie. Mother went home.'

'Josie? My Josie? You're here?'

He took hold of her hand, and she felt him relax back onto the pillows, so she sat with him until he went back to sleep. She thought it strange that he should have called her 'my Josie' and wondered if his fever might be worsening.

Joe slept for several hours before a fit of coughing woke him. When it subsided, he lay back against the pillows and shook his head, saying, 'So weak.'

'Would you like a drink or something to eat? Mother made some broth.'

'Broth — please.'

'Alright, I won't be long.'

Josie went to the kitchen and warmed some broth in a small pan, and then poured it into a bowl. She searched the kitchen drawers for a spoon and then carried them up to her uncle's room. Setting them on the dressing table, she propped more pillows behind his back so that he could sit upright, and then handed him the bowl and spoon.

'Can you manage?' she asked.

'Aye,' he said, as he took the bowl and started to eat. 'Good cook... your mother,' he said between mouthfuls. 'It's nice.'

He tired quickly, and when his eyelids started to close, Josie took the bowl from him. He'd eaten about half of what she'd given him. She removed the extra pillows so he could lie back and rest.

'Thanks,' he said, with a weak smile. 'You're an angel.'

Josie went back to her rocking chair and listened to his breathing until she heard him snoring softly, and then she closed her eyes and slept.

She was woken early the next morning by her mother coming into the room. Josie saw Mary go straight over to Joe's bedside and place her hand on his brow to check his temperature. And then Joe reached out and touched Mary's cheek tenderly.

'Mary,' he said softly. 'You came back.'

'I'm here, Joe,' she said, putting her hand on his. 'Are you feeling any better?'

'No. It hurts — when I breathe — feel weak.'

'We'll soon get you better. I hope our Josie's been looking after you?'

He nodded and smiled.

'And don't you worry about anything. Isaac and Jacob are here. They can manage the farm. Our Matt's going to come over to give them a hand. And me and Josie will take good care of you until you're back on your feet. Alright?'

'Aye,' he said, as his eyes closed again. 'Thanks.'

Josie wasn't sure what she'd just witnessed. She didn't know that her mother and Uncle Joe were close. But the way he'd touched her had appeared tender, like a lover's touch. Was her mother cheating on her father? Her parents had always seemed happy together; she was sure that they loved each other. She wondered if perhaps her uncle was confused again like he'd been the night before when he'd called her 'my Josie'. Maybe her mother was humouring him too.

Josie stood up, straightened her clothes, and tucked some loose hair behind her ear.

'Good morning,' she said.

'Good morning, Josie. I'm pleased you've managed to get a bit of sleep. How's he been?'

'He slept most of the night. I gave him some broth at about five o'clock this morning. He ate about half a bowl. He seemed a bit confused an' all, but that's probably just the fever. I think he's about the same as he was last night. No better. No worse.'

'Thanks, Josie,' said Mary. 'I'll take over now. You go home and catch up on your sleep. Will you come back again tonight?'

'Aye, of course, I will.'

She glanced towards the bed and noticed that her uncle was watching them with glassy eyes. 'See you later,' she said, smiling at him, 'I hope you feel a bit better by then.'

As she left the room, she heard him say softly, 'Bye, love.'

It wasn't like her uncle to use terms of endearment like her father did all the time. Perhaps his fever was taking a turn for the worse. She ran down the stairs and through the kitchen, and out into the yard, where she saw a thin, red-haired girl walking up the track. She waited for her.

'Hello, miss,' the girl said, shyly. 'I've come about the job. I'm Nelly Green.'

'Sorry, I don't know anything about a job.'

'Mrs Milburn sent for me to help with the cleaning.'

'Oh! You'd better come in.'

Nelly followed Josie into the house, and Josie called up the stairs, 'Mother, Nelly Green is here.'

'Right you are,' shouted Mary. 'Come on up, Nelly.'

Nelly smiled at Josie, and said, 'Thank you', before running up the stairs.

After a few hours' sleep in her own bed, Josie woke up and was surprised to see that it was early afternoon; she'd slept longer than she'd intended. Going downstairs, she heard voices outside, so she went to the kitchen window and looked out onto the yard. Her father was chatting to the postman, and he was holding something in his hand — a letter. They rarely received any post at High House Farm, and she'd been waiting for news from Elliott ever since he'd gone to America. She hoped it was from him. She paced around the room until Tom came back into the house. He held up the letter, and said, 'It's for you.'

Grinning, Josie took the envelope and ran to her room; she wanted to read Elliott's words in private. She opened it carefully, took out two sheets of paper and unfolded them, and then sat on the edge of her bed to read them.

30th October 1895
St Francois County, Missouri
My Dearest Friend

I hope this letter finds you there as well as I am here. The journey to this country was long and my thoughts turned to you often during my journey. How I wish you could have been there on the steamship with me to share this adventure. The ocean stayed calm and we made good progress. After eight days at sea though, it felt good to be back on dry land.

I travelled on the railroad from New York to the state of Missouri. The lead district is in a county called St Francois, in the foothills of the Ozark mountain range. The hills are covered in trees and there are some beautiful plants and flowers here. I think you would like it. In some ways it is similar to Weardale and in others it is very different. Houses here are built with timber rather than stone. It is much warmer too and even this late in the year it is like summer at home.

John Wilkinson came here two years ago from Rookhope and he works for the St Joseph Lead Company. He introduced me to the company manager and I was asked to start work that very same day. The land here is richer in lead than Weardale and it has not been worked for so long. Where the Weardale mines are coming to their end, these are only just beginning. New mines are being opened regularly and the first deep mines were only sunk a few years ago. There is a sense of opportunity here for everyone, no matter where they have come from. The pays are the best I've ever had, and I've already managed to save a decent sum.

I enjoy the work here but when I am finished for the day my thoughts return to you. I miss you dearly.

I am lodging with a family called Deschamps. The house is close to the mine where I work and it suits me well enough. The address is 2 New Row, Flat River, St Francois County, Missouri, America.

Please write back to me. I will look forward to receiving your letter.

Your loving friend

Elliott Dawson

Josie lifted the letter to her lips and kissed Elliott's signature. 'Oh Elliott, I miss you too,' she said, with a tear in her eye. After she had read it several times, she placed it in a drawer by her bed and went downstairs, where she found her father sitting in his armchair by the fire.

'What's your young man got to say for himself?' he asked.

'He had a good journey to America, and he's found work at a lead mine in Missouri.'

'Is that all? It took you a long time to read that,' Tom

teased. 'Well, whatever he had to say, it's nice to see that it's put a smile on your face.'

Josie blushed. 'Missouri sounds like an interesting place, and he likes the work. He said they're opening new mines there all the time.'

'Aye, I'm sure it is. I know a few men who've gone over to America for work, and I can see why. There's not much mining going on here anymore,' he said sadly. 'Anyway, how was our Joe last night?'

'He was in bed with a fever, but he was worse than I thought he'd be. His chest was making some awful noises when he breathed. He was a bit confused as well, but that would be because of the fever. Do you know if the doctor's been back to see him yet?'

'I haven't heard anything,' he said. 'No doubt, your mother will let us know when she gets back.'

Tom stared into the fire for a while in silence. Then he said, 'What's for tea, love? I've been shearing all day, and I'm starving.'

'I'll make some stew and dumplings.'

'That's good. I love stew and dumplings.'

Josie let herself into the farmhouse at Springbank Farm that evening and climbed the stairs to her uncle's room. Her mother was sitting on the edge of the bed, her head bowed.

'Mother,' she said. 'How is he?'

Josie took off her coat and hung it over the back of a

chair. When Mary turned to face her, Josie saw that her mother's eyes were red-rimmed.

'He's asleep now,' said Mary. 'The doctor came to see him earlier and left that bottle of medicine for him. You're to give it to him when he's coughing. There's some broth left in the kitchen if — if he'll take any.' Mary looked away.

'What's wrong?' asked Josie, going to her mother's side.

'The doctor said that Joe's worsened since yesterday — and that — and that he might not pull through.' A tear ran down Mary's cheek.

Josie hugged her, and said, 'You're tired. Go home and get some sleep. I'll take over.'

Mary stood up and took her shawl from the back of the rocking chair, and she pulled it tightly around her body. After glancing back at Joe, she left for home.

Josie noticed some writing paper, a pen and an inkwell on the dressing table, which she thought was odd because they hadn't been there the night before. As long as they were there, she would make use of them. Sitting down to write a reply to Elliott, she thought that the sooner she wrote to him, the sooner she would hear back from him. Picking up the pen and dipping it in ink, she began to write.

15th November 1895
Springbank Farm
My Dearest Friend

Thank you very much for your letter that I received today. I am very well, and I hope that you are too. It is good to hear that you are settled in lodgings and that you have found work so soon after your arrival. Missouri sounds like a nice place, but please be careful while you're there. I've read about men being killed by bears in the wilds of America, and I would be heart-broken if something like that were to happen to you.

The weather has been wet and miserable here, and the daylight hours are short. There is little time for me to do anything except to help my father and mother. In the dark evenings, Mother likes to read to the family, and she is reading 'Great Expectations' by Charles Dickens to us. Have you read it? I hope the story has a good ending. I think Pip deserves some happiness in his life.

Uncle Joe is unwell. The doctor says he has pneumonia. Mother and I are taking it in turns to care for him. I am in his room listening to his laboured breathing as I write this to you. My brother Matt is helping Isaac and Jacob Rowell on the farm until Uncle Joe is well again.

Please write back to me soon as receiving your letter was the best thing that has happened to me since you left this country. I miss you too.

As ever your friend
Josie Milburn

When she finished writing, she copied the address from Elliott's letter onto an envelope. Then she folded her letter, placed it carefully inside and sealed it.

She went to the rocking chair and sat down, thinking about Elliott and his promise that he would send for her when he was settled. As he'd already secured a job, she didn't imagine that it would be very long before he'd write and ask her to join him in America. Or perhaps he would come back for her and marry her here at Westgate, and then they could travel to America as man and wife. She knew in her heart that they belonged together and that somehow, someday, they'd be together. She missed him so much. When she closed her eyes, she could see his cheeky smile, and she could feel his arms around her, protecting her, keeping her safe and warm.

Josie woke with a start.

'Mary?' she heard Joe say quietly.

Josie walked over to the bed and looked down at her uncle's pale face. 'It's Josie. Can I get you something?'

'Sit.' Joe patted the edge of the bed gently.

Josie sat down where her mother had sat earlier, and Joe reached for her hand. 'Something — I want —,' he said, and his voice trailed off.

'What do you want?' she asked, watching his face for a clue. 'A glass of water? Some broth? Your medicine?'

'Tell you —'

Josie waited for him to catch his breath so that he could

finish what he wanted to say.

'Josie — you're my — my —'

A coughing fit stopped him from saying more. Josie let go of his hand and poured some medicine onto a spoon, and held his head as he took the dose. He looked exhausted.

'Sleep now,' she said quietly, taking his hand. 'You can tell me in the morning.'

She sat with him and watched his chest heave with every breath, and listened to the wheezing sound that accompanied the motion.

Thinking he was asleep, she kissed his brow and stood up, but she was certain that he smiled as she moved away. She went back to the rocking chair and made herself comfortable, and soon she was sleeping soundly.

When Josie woke, it was light outside, and the birds were singing. Surprised that Joe had slept through the night, she glanced across at his bed. She couldn't hear his raspy breathing anymore. Maybe he was better? She went over to the bed to check on him. He looked pale — too pale. She reached out for his hand — it was cold to the touch. She stepped back, her eyes wide. She'd been in the same room with her uncle all night, and she hadn't even noticed that he'd gone. She pulled up the sheet to cover his face.

Josie went downstairs to wait for her mother, and she paced up and down in the kitchen until, eventually, she heard the door open. When her mother walked into the kitchen, Josie's tears began to fall in earnest. Mary took her daughter into her arms and held her, and even in her state of distress, Josie knew that her mother was crying too.

Chapter 16

Joseph Milburn's funeral was held at St Andrew's Church in Westgate on a dismal autumn afternoon. Despite the rain, farmers and villagers turned out in force and, after the committal, most of them made their way to Springbank Farm.

A long table was set with a wonderful array of food that had been prepared by Mary and Josie; sandwiches filled with ham and pease pudding, cheese, and egg and tomato; meat pies, tatie cake, sausage rolls, fruit scones served with butter and jam, fruit cake with cheese, and sponge cake filled with fresh cream.

Josie and Mary were pouring cups of tea for the guests when Ned Routledge, a long-time friend of Joe's, approached them.

'Mary, thank you for everything you've done for Joe,' he said. 'I know he didn't deserve it, but you looked after him at the end. That's very good of you. I heard tell that you saw to all the arrangements as well, and you've put a good spread on for him today. He wouldn't have believed how much you've done for him.'

'Aye, well,' said Mary. 'Someone had to do it. And he didn't have anyone else, did he?'

'No, that's true enough.' After a moment's reflection, he asked, 'Any idea what'll happen to the farm now that he's gone?'

'I don't know. Tom was wondering that an' all. He doesn't think Joe had a will. Well, he's never been asked to witness one, anyway. I don't know what happens when there isn't a will. Do you?'

'Couldn't tell you. Mr Bainbridge will sort it out. He knows what he's doing.' Shaking his head, Ned said, 'Who'd have thought that Joe would have gone so soon, eh? Just a week ago, he was as fit as a fiddle. He'll be a big miss around here.'

'Yes, he'll be missed,' said Mary softly.

When most of the guests had left, Mr Bainbridge, the family solicitor, walked stiffly over to Tom.

'Mr Milburn,' he said. 'It's about time I read your brother's will. If you please, I would like to speak with you, your wife and Josephine Milburn — somewhere private.'

'Huh! I didn't think our Joe had a will,' said Tom. 'The parlour's empty. Why don't you go in there and make yourself comfortable? And I'll go and fetch Mary and Josie.'

A few minutes later, they were all gathered in the parlour, and Tom asked, 'Is this it? You don't need anyone else?'

'No, that's it. Just the three of you. Now, if you're ready, I'll make a start.'

Tom nodded to the solicitor and shrugged at his wife.

Despite Mr Bainbridge's frail body, his strong baritone voice rang out clearly as he read from a sheet of paper that shook slightly in his wrinkled hands.

This is the Last Will and Testament of me Joseph Milburn of Springbank Farm in the parish of Stanhope in the County of Durham, Farmer, I give to my eldest son, my real estate, the messuage house garden with all the appurtenances known as Springbank Farm situate near Westgate in the parish of Stanhope and it shall be enjoyed forever by his heirs. I give to my other children including Josephine Milburn my natural daughter a sum of £1,000 each. The remainder of my ready money, the household furniture, and my other personal estates I give also to my eldest son. And I do hereby nominate and appoint my solicitor Joseph Bainbridge Esquire sole Executor of this my will. In witness hereof I Joseph Milburn set and subscribe my hand and seal this thirtieth day of September in the year of our Lord One Thousand Eight Hundred and Seventy Four.
Signed by Joseph Milburn

Witnessed by Joseph Bainbridge, Solicitor, Stanhope and Edward James, Clerk, Stanhope.

The solicitor looked at Josie over the top of his spectacles, and said, 'Miss Milburn, according to this will you are to inherit £1,000 from Mr Joseph Milburn's estate.'

Josie sat in silence; her eyes fixed on her fidgeting hands.

'But while Mr Milburn was on his deathbed,' continued the solicitor, 'he wrote a codicil to amend this will. I have it here somewhere.'

Mary looked at Tom and said, 'I don't know how he managed that. Me and Josie were with him all the time.'

From his inside pocket, Mr Bainbridge produced a piece of writing paper and read it to them.

I Joseph Milburn of Springbank Farm, Westgate leave my property and all my worldly possessions to my natural daughter Josephine Milburn of High House Farm, Westgate.
Signed Joseph Milburn
Witnessed by Jacob Rowell and Eleanor Green
15th of November 1895

'You're a very wealthy woman, Miss Milburn,' said Mr Bainbridge. 'Joseph Milburn changed his will so that you would inherit everything. Now, I'll take my leave as I'm sure you have a lot to talk about, but I will need to see you again soon to discuss the finer details.'

The old man stood up slowly and left the room.

Josie looked at her parents in disbelief. Her mother was wringing her hands and looking down at the floor. Tom took a deep breath, readying himself for what was to come.

'What did he mean?' Josie asked them, her voice rising as she said, 'My natural daughter. What does that even mean?'

Tears formed in Mary's eyes, and Josie thought it was odd that Tom reached for Mary's hand to comfort her when he looked as much in need of support as her mother.

'I always meant to tell you, Josie,' said Mary. 'But the time just never seemed right. You loved Tom, and I didn't want anything to change that.'

'So, you're saying he isn't my father?' she asked, pointing at Tom, still grasping on to a sliver of hope that this unwelcome news might not be true.

Josie looked at her mother, who nodded her head in silence, a single tear running down her cheek.

'And Uncle Joe was my real father?'

'Yes.'

'Did you know about this?' she asked Tom.

'Aye, love. I've always known. Your mother had you before we got married. And I knew our Joe was your father. But I've loved you all these years as if you were mine, and I still do. That'll never change. And I hope that now you know, you'll still consider me to be your father because you'll always be my little girl.'

'I don't know what to say,' said Josie, standing up and folding her arms. 'Before he died, Uncle Joe tried to tell me something. I think he wanted me to know the truth. When he called me 'his Josie', I thought he was delirious.'

Josie was aware of her mother sobbing quietly in the background, but she was too distracted by her own thoughts to care. Her eyes were focused on the man that she'd called Father for as long as she could remember, who was not her father and never had been. Under her scrutiny, he sat stiffly, with a pained expression on his face.

'We should have said something sooner, love,' he said weakly. 'We just didn't know how you'd take it.'

'How I'd take it?' she laughed mirthlessly, shaking her head. 'What you mean to say is that you didn't know how I'd react to being told I'm a bastard!'

As the anger grew inside her, Josie looked at her so-called parents and thought they looked like two naughty school children who'd been caught misbehaving, and she fought the urge to laugh hysterically.

'When I was at school,' she said quietly, 'the bairns used to call me a bastard. I thought they were telling lies, and I used to hit them for it. But they weren't telling lies, were they? The children in the village knew more about me than I did. Huh! Is that why none of the lads wanted anything to do with me? They didn't want a bastard for a wife.' Putting her hands to her head, she said, her voice breaking, 'I don't believe this. Why didn't you tell me?'

'I'm so sorry,' said Mary sincerely. 'Please forgive us. We only wanted to protect you. I should have known that you'd find out somehow, sooner or later. If I'd thought about it, I should have said something before the funeral. But even when Joe was bad, I didn't think he'd die. And when he did, well, we didn't know he had a will.'

'So, you had no intention of telling me, ever?'

She looked at each of them in turn and then stormed towards the door, from where she turned and shouted, 'I need to get out of here!'

As Josie left the room, she noticed her mother get up to follow her, but Tom held Mary back and took her into his arms. They looked upset, but so was she, and she had every right to be. For her whole life, her parents had deceived her. There was no way that she was going to feel sorry for them! It was her that had been wrongly done by.

She walked briskly up the path towards the fell. How could they hide from her something as significant as who her real father was? She loved them both dearly, but she was so angry at them for keeping quiet all this time and letting her find out from Mr Bainbridge.

Throughout her childhood, Uncle Joe had always been around. Living on the neighbouring farm, he'd often called in, and she'd visited his farm regularly too. She'd thought he favoured her over her brothers, but she would never have guessed the reason for it. But now she felt as though she hadn't known him at all. Not properly. She wished more than anything that she could speak with him again, and hear what he had to say. It had only been a week since she'd watched over him, and she wished that she could turn back time and encourage him to finish what he'd wanted to tell her. He'd wanted her to know the truth about her birth, but she'd stopped him by saying he could tell her tomorrow. Well, for Uncle Joe, there had been no tomorrow.

The wind picked up, and she pushed the hair that had come loose away from her face, and as she did so, she noticed that her face was wet with tears.

Josie wondered what had happened all those years ago. Her stepfather had said that she'd been born before he'd married her mother. So, her mother and Joe must have been lovers. But for some reason, they hadn't married when her mother fell pregnant. Why hadn't Joe married her? Was he already married to Aunt Connie at the time? There were so many questions that she wanted to ask.

Although whatever had happened, it didn't change the fact that she was baseborn. Despite having been brought up by loving parents, she'd been born out of wedlock, and she was illegitimate — a bastard.

Elliott! How would he react to the news? Would he still want to marry her? Would he still love her as he had before? Perhaps he would say that it wasn't important who her real father was, that she was still the same person and that it didn't matter in the slightest. Maybe she was worrying unnecessarily. But there was a chance that when he found out, he'd not want anything more to do with her, and turn his back on her as all the local boys had. Perhaps it might be better if he didn't know. He was in America, so it wasn't likely that he'd find out unless she told him. So, she decided there and then that she would not tell him about her illegitimacy because she didn't want to risk losing him.

Tom Milburn, the man she'd always looked up to and respected, was not her father by blood — but he was a good man, and she loved him. He'd cared for her and loved her as much as any real father could have. She'd never questioned that he was her father; there had never been any doubt in her mind, even when the children at school had taunted her.

Looking back over her childhood, she'd been happy. She'd been blissfully unaware of the dark secret that her parents had been hiding from her. But the secret was out now, and before long, everybody would know that she was Joe Milburn's bastard daughter because he'd left everything to her.

Without noticing, Josie had walked down the fields and onto the road in the valley bottom, and she was making her way back up the hill towards Springbank Farm. Her farm.

She'd been so preoccupied with finding out about her parentage that she hadn't given any thought to her inheritance. She looked at the familiar buildings with new eyes. The house was a two-storey, double-fronted Georgian building, far grander than High House where she'd grown up. There was a garden to the front, with overgrown shrubs around the edges, and weeds growing through the flagstone paths. She could remember when it had been a beautiful garden, with colourful flowers and neat lawns. But now it looked thoroughly neglected. Joe hadn't bothered with it since his wife had died.

As she neared the farmyard, a horse came out from the yard and galloped towards her, passing within a few feet. She didn't recognise the rider. He was an elderly man with a white beard and piercing blue eyes, and the look he gave her sent chills through her body. She made a mental note to ask her mother who he was.

When she entered the house, the villagers had left, and she found Tom and Mary clearing up in the kitchen.

'Do you need a hand?' she asked calmly.

'Yes, please,' replied Mary. 'Could you bring the dirty dishes through from the dining room?'

As Josie left the room, she noticed the smile of relief that passed between them.

Chapter 17

Although Josie had met Mr Bainbridge on several occasions, she had never been to his office at Stanhope. From the other side of the street, she looked at the front of the building and wished that she'd accepted her mother's offer to accompany her to the meeting, but pride had stopped her, and now she stood outside, alone. She knew she was too stubborn for her own good sometimes, and this was one of them. Well, she couldn't put it off any longer. She crossed over the road and knocked loudly at the door.

A young woman opened it; she greeted Josie formally and invited her inside. The woman knocked at an oak door before opening it, and she spoke quietly to the occupant. A few moments later, Mr Bainbridge emerged from the doorway.

'Miss Milburn, it's so nice of you to come. I see you've met my granddaughter, Phoebe.' Turning to Phoebe, he said, 'Would you be kind enough to make us a pot of tea, my dear.'

Ushering Josie into his office, Mr Bainbridge pointed to a red leather chair, and she sat stiffly on it. He hobbled around to the other side of the desk and sat down. His desk was covered with papers and ledgers, which he moved to one side so that he could see her clearly.

'We have rather a lot to discuss,' he said. 'Mr Joseph Milburn was a very wealthy man. He wrote his original will shortly after he inherited Springbank Farm from his father-in-law, and at a time when he expected that he and his wife would be blessed with children. That was not to be. So, as his only child, you are to inherit his entire estate.'

'What do you mean by 'entire estate'?'

'Put simply — everything he owned. Now let me see—'

He opened a file and peered through his spectacles at the notes. 'Springbank Farm — that's nearly four-hundred acres of meadow and pasture land, with stints on the fell, the barn and other outbuildings and, of course, the farmhouse. Then, there's the stock on the farm — horses, cows, sheep, pigs, poultry and his dogs. Also, there's the carriage and the flat cart, the fodder, hay and straw in storage, and all the tools and implements. Everything inside the house too — that includes the furniture, pictures, plate, crocks, glassware, linen, clothes and jewellery. And finally, there's the money in the bank — which amounts to £12,562 plus any interest owing.'

Josie's jaw dropped as the solicitor worked his way through the list, but when he mentioned the sum of money in the bank, she gasped.

Mr Bainbridge lifted his spectacles and looked at her from across the desk.

'Are you alright, Miss Milburn?'

'Yes, that's so much more than I expected.'

They were interrupted by a tap at the door, and Phoebe brought in a tray and poured tea into two china teacups before leaving the room. Mr Bainbridge picked up a cup and saucer and placed it in front of Josie, and took the other for himself.

'I realise this must have come as a shock to you,' said Mr Bainbridge. 'Mr Milburn lived his life modestly, and the two of you weren't close, so you weren't to know that he was a man of means. Now, may I ask if you've considered what you would like to do with the farm?'

'I — I have no idea. I need to talk to my father — to Tom Milburn.'

'That would be wise. Mr Milburn is a sensible man, and I'm sure he'll advise you well. The way I see it, there are three options. You could sell the farm and have a very considerable sum of money to live off. You could employ a farm manager to run the farm and receive an annual income from the profits. Or you could find a husband. That shouldn't be too difficult now that you have money of your own. In the event of a marriage, everything would pass to your husband, and he would take control of it.'

'There is another option,' said Josie quietly. 'I could manage the farm myself.'

'Now, now, Miss Milburn! Manage the farm yourself?' He chuckled. 'Whatever made you think of that?'

Josie bristled at the insult but bit her tongue. Being a young woman did not mean that she couldn't be a farmer. She'd lived on a farm most of her life, and she had helped her stepfather with all aspects of farming. She knew enough to manage a farm, and she could learn about the business side of things as she went along.

Mr Bainbridge continued, 'If you require anything further from me, please do come and see me again.'

He held out his hand to her, and she shook it firmly.

'Thank you, Mr Bainbridge.'

'Good day, Miss Milburn.'

Josie stepped out into the fresh air and looked up the street. People were going about their daily lives as usual, and as she watched them, she thought that most of them had enough money to put food on their tables, but that was about it. They wouldn't be able to comprehend the sum of money that Joe Milburn had left her; Josie could barely believe it herself. She was a wealthy landowner now, which meant she had options for her future. Then, the smile slowly slid from her face as she remembered that she was still a bastard, and there was nothing that could change that, and most of these humble villagers would look down their noses at her because of it — whether she was wealthy or not.

As she walked over to her pony, Josie noticed that she was being watched by a stranger standing outside the bakery — a gentleman judging by the way he was dressed. He looked to be about forty years of age, and he was a little on the plump side. When he realised that he'd been seen, he tipped his hat and smiled, before walking across the road.

'Good morning, Miss Milburn.'

Josie was at a loss; she had no idea who he was.

'Good morning,' she replied.

'Charles Chapman, at your service. May I be of any assistance?'

'I beg your pardon.'

'Perhaps I can help you mount?'

'Thank you, but I'm quite capable of getting onto my pony myself.'

'In that case, the very least I can do for such a beautiful lady is to hold the animal still.'

The man's compliment and his attention made Josie feel uncomfortable, and she was eager to be on her way.

'Thank you,' she said, as she put her foot into the stirrup and lifted herself effortlessly into the saddle.

'Good day, Miss Milburn. I hope to see you again soon.'

She inclined her head in a non-committal fashion and urged her Dales pony forward. On the way home, she wondered why Charles Chapman had made himself known to her. Men didn't usually pay her any attention, except for Elliott. The thought of Elliott pushed the recent encounter from her mind, and she spent the rest of the ride daydreaming about him.

When Josie returned to High House Farm, she found her mother in the kitchen, rolling out pastry. Josie had realised long ago that her mother baked whenever she was worried, and she wished again that she'd accepted her mother's offer to accompany her to the solicitor's office. While she could have done with her support at Stanhope, her mother had been fretting at home.

Mary looked up and wiped her face with the back of her hand, leaving a white smear of flour on her cheek. Josie walked over to her and wiped it off.

'Well, what did he have to say?' asked Mary.

Josie sat down at the table, and said, 'Uncle Joe left me the house and everything in it, the farm and the stock. He had a fair bit of money in the bank as well.'

'Did he? How much is a fair bit?'

'Over twelve thousand pounds.'

'Oh, my word!' After a brief pause, Mary said, 'Well, I suppose he must have inherited quite a bit from Mr Peart, and he was never one for spending money where it wasn't needed.'

'Mother, now that I know that Joe was my father, I can't stop wondering why you didn't marry him, and why you married Tom instead. I just don't understand it. Maybe it would help if I knew what had happened back then.'

Mary slowly sat down at the table next to Josie and

sighed. 'I'm sorry, I always intended to tell you about Joe when you were old enough to understand. But you were so happy and content when you were growing up. I didn't want to take that away from you.'

'I know that, Mother, but please tell me what happened — with you and Joe.'

Mary smiled sadly. She took hold of Josie's hand and said quietly, 'You were called Josephine, after Joe. I never told you that either.'

'Oh! But how...'

'Shush! It's not easy for me to think about that time, never mind talk about it, but you deserve to know the truth. I only wish I'd told you sooner.' Mary swallowed before she continued. 'As you know, I used to work for Mr and Mrs Peart at Springbank Farm. I was seventeen when I went there, and I'd never been far from home before that. I met Joe Milburn. He was handsome and funny back then, and I fell for him. Anyway, when I told him I was expecting you, he walked away and left me. I didn't know what to think. He abandoned us. And not long after, he married Connie Peart.'

'But why did he marry her when you were having his child?'

'Hmm. I know I shouldn't speak ill of the dead, but it was because Connie was the heiress to Springbank Farm and Joe was a selfish, greedy man. He wanted that farm more than anything else. You know, if it hadn't been for Aunt Lizzie taking me in, you'd have been born in the workhouse.'

'I'm so sorry,' said Josie, detecting the anger and hurt from all those years ago in her mother's voice.

'I still can't believe how lucky I was when Tom asked me to marry him,' said Mary nostalgically. 'I couldn't have hoped for a better husband or a better father for you.' Looking into Josie's eyes, she said sincerely, 'I hope you find someone like him.'

'Aw, Mother. I don't need a man.'

'You say that now, but you'll see.'

'Thank you for telling me.' Josie stood up and hugged her mother. Remembering that there was something else that she wanted to ask her mother, she stepped back, and said, 'On Joe's funeral day, an old man left Springbank Farm in quite a hurry. Do you know who he was?'

'Aye, I do. That was John Peart — Mr Peart's brother. He lives over at White Wells Farm near St John's Chapel.'

'Why did he rush away like that?'

'I don't know, lass. Tom wondered if it might have something to do with Joe's will. He thought John overheard him telling Ned that you'd been left the farm. I saw the way he galloped down that track. Reckless he was. He was lucky he didn't fall off and break his neck.'

'He nearly ran me down.'

'Oh! Something's burning!' Mary exclaimed, as she jumped up from her seat and rushed to the oven. She took out a tray of oatmeal biscuits and placed them on the table. The biscuits looked darker than usual, well-done but not burnt. With a laugh, she said, 'Well, they'll be nice and crunchy.'

Tom came into the house and sniffed the air. 'Something smells good,' he said.

Looking down at the over-cooked biscuits on the kitchen table, he said, 'Well, there's a first time for everything! I've never known you bake anything that wasn't perfect, Mary.'

Mary gave him a warning look, and he laughed loudly. He picked up a biscuit and took a large bite.

'Mmm. They taste good an' all!'

Josie laughed. Her parents had always been happy together. She thought back to what her mother had said about finding someone like Tom, and she smiled ruefully. The only man she'd ever been interested in was Elliott, and he was thousands of miles away.

Chapter 18

Mary opened the study door and found Josie looking through the contents of a desk drawer.

'So that's where you are!' she said. 'We've brought your things over on the cart.'

'Thank you,' said Josie. 'Have you all come over?'

'Yes, I think Tom and the lads wanted to have a look around the place if you don't mind.'

'I don't mind, but it would have been better if they'd waited until I got everything cleaned up. It's such a mess. Nelly made a start when Joe was bad, but she didn't get very far.'

'You can't manage to do all this yourself,' said Mary. 'It was hard enough to keep on top of it when it was in good order, and I should know! I did all of the cleaning, the washing and the cooking here at one time.'

'I know, Mother. It must upset you to see the state it's in, but I'll soon have it back to its former glory.'

'What you need is a maid.'

'I don't need a maid,' said Josie, laughing at the idea. 'I'll manage.'

'If you intend to run the farm, you'll have to have someone to help in the house. You can't do everything yourself.'

Josie paused for a while before she said, 'Aye, I know I'm taking on a lot.'

'Maybe you should invite Nelly back to work for you,' said Mary. 'She's a nice lass, and she'd be good company. It would help Mr and Mrs Green out too, with one less mouth to feed and a bit of extra money coming in. Her poor bairns always look so tatty. How many times can clothes be handed down, eh?'

'Alright, I will.'

'Shall I tell our Matt to go down and ask her?'

'Yes, thank you,' said Josie, putting the papers back in the drawer. 'I hoped to clear out some of these drawers, but most of these papers look too important to throw out.'

'Aye,' said Mary. 'I suppose that's what happens when so many generations of a family live in the same place. Nothing gets cleared out properly.'

When Josie's family went home, she was left alone at Springbank Farm. It was too strange for her to think of it as her house. She couldn't believe that it was really hers and that she owned it outright, and that from now on it would be her home — Miss Josephine Milburn of Springbank Farm.

She wandered along the corridors, looking at each room in turn, and she saw that the whole house was well-furnished, but it was all desperately in need of a good clean. It was evident that many of the rooms hadn't been used for years because everything in them was covered with a thick layer of dust. She hadn't realised just how large the house was — there were so many rooms. Her mother had been right about her needing help. It would take a lot of elbow grease to make the house beautiful again.

She chose a large room at the front of the house for her bedroom and went to the window which looked out across the fields, the view obscured by years of grime on the glass panes. It wasn't until she opened the sash window and a blast of fresh air rushed into the house that she realised how stuffy it had been. She decided to open all the windows in the rooms that she intended to use, to freshen them up, and then she began to clean her bedroom in earnest, starting at the top.

As she worked, she thought about the farm and the responsibility that came with it. The cows were in the byres for the winter, the horses were in the stables, and the sheep were on the fell. The animals all needed food and water every day, and the cows needed milking twice a day. She'd been relieved when the Rowell twins had agreed to stay on and work for her; she'd been a little concerned that they mightn't want to work for a woman. Tommy was always busy at High House Farm, but Matt had offered to lend a hand if needed, and Tom was more than willing to help her with the business side of farming.

When Josie had left High House Farm that morning, Mary had insisted that she took a set of clean bed linen with her and, seeing the dust motes floating around the room when she removed the old bedding, she was pleased that she had. The weather had been unseasonably dry lately and, if it stayed that way, Josie thought she'd get the dirty linens washed and dried outside the next day. She closed the window and lit the fire so that the room would be warm when she went to bed. Looking around her bedroom, at the polished furniture, the clean bed, and the clear view from the window, Josie was delighted with her first day's work.

Her stomach rumbled, reminding her that she hadn't stopped to eat all day. In the kitchen, she lifted the cover off a basket that her mother had left for her, and took out a ham and egg pie and, as she removed the plate, a letter caught her eye. She sat at the table and ate a large slice of cold pie, with her mind on the letter that had arrived before Christmas — but remained unopened.

Usually, Josie couldn't wait to hear Elliott's news, and she wasn't sure why she hadn't read this letter yet. But deep down, she did know. When she read his letter, she would feel obliged to write back, and there were things that she didn't want to tell him.

When she'd finished eating, she went to the basket and removed the letter. Turning it over in her hands, she sat back down at the table, lit the oil lamp and opened the envelope.

5th December 1895

St Francois County, Missouri

My Dear Josie

I am well, thank you, and I hope you are too. Since my last letter to you, I have come into some good fortune. I was promoted to foreman at the mine very shortly after starting there and I had a substantial increase in pay. On Saturday afternoons and Sundays, I have been prospecting for new areas to mine lead ore. The land here is even better than I had at first thought. I am very pleased to tell you that only last week I set up the Dawson Mining Company and opened my first mine.

John Wilkinson is working with me. Just the two of us for now. It is a very exciting prospect but it is also a little frightening because I have had to invest nearly all of my money. I hope we reach a good vein soon and find that our efforts and the expense have been worthwhile. John is a good miner but unfortunately he is not a suitable business partner, for although he has been here for several years, he does not have any money to invest in the venture. He frequents the public houses in the evenings — and he blames them for taking all his money!

It would be good to have a partner to share the

risks and returns. The quicker we get to the galena, the sooner we can mine it, sell it and make a profit. I have made enquiries in the area but, as yet, no investment has been forthcoming. The people here do not know me and I have no history in business. As I see it, it's a good opportunity for an investor because the profits are almost guaranteed. I cannot see how the mine can fail to produce good quality ore.

There are frosts here now which hardly lift during the day. It is bitterly cold. It does not affect our work.

I hope your Uncle Joe made a swift and full recovery from his illness.

My best wishes to you and your family for Christmas and the coming year.

Your good friend always

Elliott Dawson

The thought of Elliott owning a mine brought a smile to Josie's lips. She was pleased that things were working out for him. After everything that he'd been through, he deserved some good fortune. She wished she'd been there to see his face when he'd started to dig his mine. Remembering the day that they'd walked by the river to look at mineral veins in the riverbank, she recalled what he'd said and chuckled to herself.

Josie went to the desk for some writing paper and ink, and then returned to the kitchen table to write back to him.

3rd January 1896
High House Farm
My Dearest Elliott
Thank you for your letter dated 5th December. It arrived here just a few days before Christmas and I was very pleased to receive it and to hear your good news. Congratulations! It is hard to believe that you actually own a mine.

I remember when we walked by the River Wear and you said, 'That will the day when a Dawson owns a mine' or some similar words. Well, that day has come and I am delighted for you.

I am well as is the rest of my family, all except for Uncle Joe who died shortly after I wrote my last letter to you. That was a shock to us all as he had been fit and well just a few days earlier.

We had a quiet Christmas with just the family. At the New Year, Tommy was our first-foot for the first time. It had always been Uncle Joe before. Father made Tommy stand outside until after midnight, and then he came in with a piece of coal and Father gave him a tot of whisky which he almost choked on! I hope Tommy brings the household good luck for 1896.

There has been no snow here yet but no doubt it will come soon.
Your dear friend

Josie Milburn

When she put down the pen, Josie felt like a fraud. She had always hated telling lies and, although she hadn't lied outright in the letter, she hadn't exactly told Elliott the truth about what had been going on in her life. She'd omitted the most important things that had happened. She'd even used her old address because she couldn't tell him where she was living without revealing the full facts. So much for being his friend, she thought.

That night, something in Elliott's letter kept coming back to her. He wanted a business partner to invest in his company. Could she be that investor? She had plenty of money. Nevertheless, there were several problems that she could see. She doubted that his pride would let him take money from her, and she didn't want him to know that she'd inherited a small fortune. But a plan was starting to form in her mind.

As Josie rode down to Stanhope to visit Mr Bainbridge the following morning, the pony's hoof beats were silenced by the snow-covered roads. She admired the shimmering frost on skeleton trees and the glistening fields. She loved winter. Everything looked so clean and bright, and the air was crisp and fresh.

By the time she arrived at the solicitor's office, she had difficulty tethering her pony because her fingers were numb. She blew on them to warm them up and then knocked at the door.

'Miss Milburn,' said Phoebe, looking a little flustered. 'Come in. You look frozen — it's nice and warm in here. Do you have an appointment?'

'No, I haven't. But I would like to speak with your grandfather about a business matter if he's available.'

'Please, go into his office and take a seat.'

'Thank you.'

She sat in the leather chair and glanced out of the window, wondering how to begin her proposal.

'Good morning, Miss Milburn. May I ask what brings you here today, my dear?' asked Mr Bainbridge, as he hobbled around the desk and sat in his chair.

Josie cleared her throat and said, 'I'd like to invest in a mining company. It's in America. And I want to remain anonymous. Is this possible?'

Looking at her over the top of his spectacles, the old man said, 'Well, that's certainly unexpected. Let me think for a moment.' He tapped his fingers on his desk for a few seconds, and then said, 'Yes, it would be possible. How much do you intend to invest in the company?'

'Two thousand pounds.'

'Really! Two thousand pounds. That's a large sum of money. How much do you know about this company?' he asked, peering at her over the top of his spectacles.

'Enough to know that if anyone can make a profit from mining lead, it's the man who owns this company.'

'And you've made this decision yourself? Nobody has forced you into it?'

'No, sir. It's my decision, and I've discussed it with nobody but you. The owner knows nothing about my involvement, and I don't want him to either.'

'Alright, so be it. Please let me have the details. I'll set everything up, and once that has been done, I'll arrange with the bank manager to transfer the money. Please come back at the end of the week, and I'll have the paperwork ready for you to sign.'

Josie handed a sheet of notepaper containing the relevant details to the solicitor, and said, 'Thank you very much for your assistance, Mr Bainbridge.'

'You're welcome, Miss Milburn. Anytime.'

Josie walked out from the solicitor's office with her head held high. It felt wonderful knowing that her decision to invest in Elliott's company would help him enormously. Her only regret was that she wouldn't see his reaction when he received the news.

While she was at Stanhope, there was something else that Josie wanted to attend to. She walked further down the street and looked at a window display of jewellery, watches and clocks. Opening the shop door, she went inside and was greeted by a middle-aged man with a friendly smile.

'Good morning, miss. What can I do for you?'

'Good morning.'

Reaching into her pocket, she pulled out her half of the fractured crystal and held it up to show him.

'I'd like you to make this crystal into a pendant, with a

gold setting and chain.'

He took the crystal from her, and said, 'But it's spar, miss. Spar's not a gemstone. It doesn't polish up well.'

'No!' she exclaimed. 'I don't want it to be polished. It must look exactly the way it does now. Is that something you could do?'

He held the crystal up to the light and rotated it between his fingers.

'Nobody's ever asked me to set spar in gold before, but if that's what you want, aye, I can do it.'

'Thank you.'

'Alright, leave it with me, and I'll have it ready for you to collect on Friday.'

'Please be careful with it. It means a lot to me.'

He filled out a receipt stating that she'd handed over the fluorite crystal to him and also quoting a price for his work.

'Will that be satisfactory, miss?'

'Yes, that's fine.' She smiled at him. 'I'll see you on Friday.'

She left the shop and walked back to her pony, and was startled when a man stepped out from behind it. It was Charles Chapman.

'Miss Milburn, fancy seeing you here! I did wonder if this was your pony.'

'I was just leaving, Mr Chapman.'

'Really, there's no need to hurry. It's such a cold day. I'd be honoured if you would accompany me to The

Phoenix for a cup of tea. It would warm you through before your ride home.'

Josie was still cold from the journey to Stanhope, and the short time that she'd spent in the solicitor's office and the jewellery shop had done little to warm her. The thought of drinking hot tea in front of a roaring fire at the public house was very appealing.

'I would appreciate a cup of tea, but I insist that I pay for it myself.'

'That is perfectly fine by me.' He bowed slightly before holding out his arm. Josie tentatively took hold of it, and a few moments later, when she slipped on ice, she was pleased that she had. If it hadn't been for Mr Chapman's grip on her arm, she would have ended up on her backside in front of everyone. How humiliating that would have been! She laughed nervously as she thanked him, and he simply smiled down at her, kindly, and held her more firmly.

They went into the inn, where Josie was delighted to see a log fire burning in the dining room. A waitress came over immediately and showed them to a table by the window, which offered a view of the marketplace, and once they were seated, the woman took their order and rushed back to the kitchen.

'Well, here we are, Miss Milburn.'

'May I ask,' asked Josie, 'how do you know who I am?'

'Everybody in the dale knows who you are, my dear.'

'Oh! It seems you know all about me, and I know

nothing about you.'

'What is there to say? I live at Overton Hall on the outskirts of Stanhope. I'm a widower — my wife died last year during the cholera outbreak.'

'I'm sorry to hear that, Mr Chapman. Do you have children?'

'Yes, I have children.'

She was pleased to hear that he hadn't been left alone after his wife had passed away.

'What do you do for a living?' she asked.

'I don't have a profession, as such. My father left me the house and a good sum of money when he died, so I had no need for employment.'

'I'm sorry. I'm being very rude, asking so many questions.'

Charles smiled warmly. 'Don't be silly. I don't mind in the least.'

Josie felt sorry for the man sitting beside her. It must have been hard for him to lose his wife and to bring up their children alone. She hadn't taken much interest in him, but now, as she looked at him more closely, she thought that he might be considered handsome, in a fashion. He was smartly dressed. His dark brown eyes were set into a pleasant face, and his brown hair was greying at the temples. His smooth hands had long slender fingers, and she noticed that his nails were clean and neatly trimmed. She should have realised that he didn't work for a living. All the men she knew were farmers or miners, and their hands were large and rough.

'I didn't expect to see you again so soon,' said Charles. 'Do you visit Mr Bainbridge, often?'

'No, not really.'

'Well, the next time you come to Stanhope, I would be delighted if you would call on us. Overton Hall is less than a mile down the road. It's the large house between here and Frosterley. You can't miss it.'

Josie wasn't sure about accepting his offer but thought that it might be considered rude to refuse his invitation outright, so she nodded, noncommittally.

The next morning, Nelly Green knocked at the door at seven o'clock, just as Josie was about to sit down for breakfast, and she came into the kitchen carrying a small bundle.

'Hello, thanks for coming,' said Josie. 'Have you had anything to eat?'

'No, miss, I came straight here.'

'There's porridge in that pan.' Josie pointed to the stove. 'And you'll find a bowl on the dresser and cutlery in the drawer.'

Nelly helped herself to some breakfast and sat down at the table next to Josie. While they ate, Josie explained to Nelly that she was the new owner of Springbank Farm and that she'd like Nelly to help out in the house with cooking and cleaning.

When they'd finished eating, Josie said, 'I'll show you

where you'll be staying.'

They walked up the wide staircase together, Nelly following Josie like a shadow. Upstairs, the long, dark corridor had doors on both sides. Josie opened one of them, and said, 'This will be your room.'

Nelly's eyes widened, and she asked, 'You mean I'll have a room to myself? I won't have to share it with anyone?'

'No. It's just for you.'

'I've never even had a bed to meself, never mind a whole room!' Nelly laughed.

Josie smiled to herself; she'd often wondered how the Greens managed to squeeze all their children into their tiny cottage.

'Leave your things here, and I'll show you around. I know you made a start downstairs when you were here before, but most of the house hasn't been bothered with for a long time. If we work together, I'm sure we'll soon get on top of it.'

They explored the upstairs rooms first. When Josie opened the door to her bedroom, revealing her growing collection of crystals, Nelly looked surprised to see them.

'I don't want you to touch any of these, Nelly. Don't try to clean them, and don't move them to clean the furniture underneath. I'll see to them. Do you understand?'

Nelly nodded her head.

After they'd completed a tour of the house, Josie said, 'I think we should start with your room today. What do you think?'

Nelly grinned. 'Yes, please.'

As they worked, Josie learnt that Nelly was seventeen years old, and the eldest of ten children, most of them girls. It didn't take long for Josie to realise that her mother had been right — Nelly was good company, and she was also sensible and a quick learner. She was so glad that her mother had talked her into taking her on. The saying about many hands making light work was true.

Chapter 19

It was a dull morning with a slight drizzle, but that did not deter Josie. Since she'd moved into Springbank Farm at the New Year, she'd familiarised herself with the house, but still wanted to get to know the farm better, so she'd arranged for Isaac and Jacob Rowell to show her around. After wrapping up well, she went outside to meet the twins in the farmyard.

'Morning, Miss Milburn,' they said at the same time. They had a habit of doing that, and it brought a smile to Josie's lips. She'd known these men since she was a child.

'Good morning, gentlemen. Why did you call me Miss Milburn just then? You've never done that before.'

Isaac looked at his brother, and when Jacob didn't reply, he said, 'Well, you're the boss now.'

'I might be the owner of the farm, and I might be the one who'll be paying your wages, but I'm the same person that I've always been. Please call me Josie.'

The twins nodded in agreement, and then she set off with them through the gateway. They climbed up each of the muddy fields in turn until they reached the fell wall. Beyond it was open moorland, common land, where she had grazing rights for her hill sheep. They turned back to look down upon Springbank Farm — a patchwork of green, separated by grey, dry-stone walls, with a cluster of buildings almost at the bottom of the hill. Trees grew in patches that appeared randomly spaced across the landscape, but Josie knew that they marked areas that were not suitable for ploughing because they were too stony or too steep; or where potential danger lurked from old mine workings, small quarries or shake holes.

In the valley below the farm, she could see three lines running along the valley floor. The river Wear that flowed from Wearhead to Wearmouth on route to the North Sea, the road that ran through the Pennines connecting the counties of Durham and Cumberland and the passenger railway line to Bishop Auckland.

Isaac pointed out each plot of land in turn and told her their names. She'd already studied the map that Mr Bainbridge had given her. It had been with the property deeds, and it was old, but very little on the property had changed. There were a few more buildings around the farmyard, and that was the only difference that she could see from their bird's eye view.

Josie couldn't believe that she owned the land down to the riverbank in the distance, and as far as she could see both to the west and east. The task of running a farm this size was daunting, but she knew she could rely on Isaac and Jacob; they had worked there for so long that they knew all there was to know. With support from them and her family, Josie was confident that she could make a success of the farm.

On the way back to the farmhouse, she asked the twins, 'Is there anything that needs doing urgently?'

Jacob said, 'Aye, there's a dyke down in the Little Field. That needs building back up.'

'Is that all?'

Isaac replied, 'The bull's getting on in years, and he's a bit lame. We should be looking to get a younger one. There's a sale at St John's Chapel in April. We should go and see if there's anything decent.'

'Alright, we'll do that. Is there anything else?'

'No, just the regular jobs, so long as the snow stays away.'

The thought of snow sent a shiver down Josie's spine. She dreaded bad winters and the dangers that came with them. Ever since she'd been a child, her parents had drummed into her how important it was to prepare for the winter months, with plenty of fuel for the fires and provisions in store, and to stay indoors whenever possible.

'Please could you check that there's plenty of coal and wood in the sheds?' she asked them.

'They're well-stocked,' said Isaac. 'We spent most of

November chopping wood.'

'That's good. Thank you.'

She left the men to get on with their work and went back indoors, where she checked the pantry. There was meat hanging from hooks in the ceiling, sacks full of potatoes, turnips and carrots edged the room, onions hung on strings, and she smiled when she found a basket of apples — she loved apple pie. There was only one sack of flour, and it was crawling with mites. Carrying it outside to dispose of it, she thought it must have been there a long time. She couldn't image Joe using flour for baking or thickening soups and gravy. She wondered how he'd managed to live there so long without a wife or housekeeper.

When she went indoors, she sat at the kitchen table and made a list of the provisions that she needed from the village shop. She'd go that afternoon and make sure the pantry was ready for winter.

It was still wet and miserable a few days later when Josie returned to the jewellery shop. The jeweller recognised her instantly.

'Good morning! I have your pendant ready for you, and it looks stunning, even if I do say so myself.'

He pulled open a drawer behind the shop counter and took out the necklace, which he held up to the light. The gold chain and mount shone brightly, setting the purple crystal off beautifully.

'A beautiful necklace — for a beautiful lady,' he said as he handed it to her.

The man was right — it did look stunning, and she was relieved to see that he hadn't altered the crystal's cubic form at all. As she gave him the payment and a little extra, she said, 'Thank you, you've done an excellent job.'

'Thank you,' he said, smiling at her as she left his shop.

Dodging the puddles, Josie crossed the road to the solicitor's office. Phoebe showed her straight into Mr Bainbridge's room, where he was waiting for her, paperwork spread out all over his desk.

'Ah, there you are, Miss Milburn. Please take a seat.'

He appeared to shuffle the papers and then place them into a neat pile in front of him. Peering over his spectacles, he said, 'I have prepared all of the legal documents for your investment in the Dawson Mining Company of Missouri. Once these are signed, a notice will be sent to Mr Dawson informing him that an anonymous investor would like to invest two thousand pounds in his company for a share of the profits. I would suggest for this amount of money that we ask for fifty percent. He will have to agree to these terms before your bank will send the payment. Do you understand?'

'Yes, I understand, but I don't want fifty percent of his company. That would make me an equal partner. I want Mr Dawson to keep control of his company.'

'But it would be in your best interests —'

'I know, but I'd be happier with a forty percent share.'

Mr Bainbridge cleared his throat. 'I must advise you that —'

'Please, Mr Bainbridge, I've made up my mind.'

'And you want to go ahead at forty percent?'

'Yes, I'm certain.'

Passing a pen to her, he said, 'I need to complete the details of the offer, and then you can sign the papers.'

When Mr Bainbridge had completed the paperwork, he took off his reading glasses and sat back in his chair, and said, 'That's it done. This is your last chance to change your mind. Once these documents leave my office, there's no going back. I must advise you that mining is an expensive and risky business.'

'I won't change my mind.'

'In that case, I sincerely hope, for your sake, that this gamble pays off.'

'Thank you, Mr Bainbridge. I'm sure it will.'

Chapter 20

Springbank Farm
February 1896

When Josie heard a light knock at the door, she put the hot iron down on the hearth. She looked up to see the back door open.

'It's only me,' Mary said. 'I thought you had a maid to do your ironing now.'

'Nelly has plenty to do. She's upstairs lighting the fires and then she'll be making our teas.' Folding a newly ironed shift, Josie said, 'Anyway, there are some clothes I like to iron myself.'

Mary smiled and raised her hand. In it was a letter.

Josie's heart skipped a beat.

'It's for you,' said Mary. 'It came yesterday. I've not had a chance to bring it over 'til now.'

'Thank you,' said Josie, her heart beating wildly, as she took the letter from her mother. She'd been waiting anxiously for Elliott to write to her about the new investor in his company. But her face fell when she saw the writing on the envelope.

'What's wrong?' asked Mary.

'Nothing — it's just that I thought it would be from Elliott.'

'Oh, well, never mind. Open it, then, and see who it's from.'

Josie opened the envelope and took out a sheet of folded paper. The neat copperplate writing looked very formal, and she read it out loud.

> *Dickinson & Black Solicitors,*
> *Silver Street,*
> *Durham.*
> *6th February 1896.*
> *Dear Miss Milburn,*
> *I understand that you are the sole beneficiary of the estate of Mr Joseph Milburn of Springbank Farm, Westgate.*
> *However, Mr John Peart of White Wells Farm, St John's Chapel, has contested the validity of the codicil attached to the late Mr Milburn's will and therefore your right to inherit his estate.*
> *The codicil will be examined in court and its validity decided by the judge. Your presence is requested at the Probate Court, Durham on Tuesday, 17th March 1896.*
> *Yours sincerely*
> *William Black Esq.*

Josie's hands were trembling. She put the letter down

on the table and looked across at her mother.

'I don't believe it,' said Mary, shaking her head.

'Why is he doing this?' implored Josie.

'I don't know.' Her mother shrugged.

'Is it because I was born out of wedlock? Does he think I'm not fit to inherit because of that?'

'Maybe, who knows what goes on in other people's minds? But Joe wanted you to have this farm, so you should fight for it if that's what it takes. Mr Bainbridge must have thought you were the rightful heir or else he wouldn't have given it to you in the first place, and he's been a solicitor for a very long time. You know, there'll always be some who'll be jealous of others' good fortunes. I reckon that's what's behind this. Jealousy. He never got to have the farm.'

Josie shook her head and slumped into a chair.

'The probate court in Durham,' she said with trepidation. 'Can't Mr Bainbridge see to this? I don't have to go, do I?'

'Yes, you have to go. It says here that your presence is requested.'

'Do you think Father would come with me?'

'Of course, he would. You know, Tom will always think of you as his daughter and he'd be proud to stand up for you. I don't envy you, though. It'll be a tough day for you both, but you'll get through it.'

'I'd like him to come. Would you ask him for me?'

'You can ask him yourself. He said he was coming over

this morning. He's missed you since you moved out.'

Josie laughed. 'I'd better get the kettle on then.'

After her parents' visit, Josie sat down at the kitchen table and stared into space. Since the arrival of the solicitor's letter, there had been something weighing heavily on her mind — the inheritance money that she'd invested in Elliott's company. What would happen if the court decided that she wasn't the rightful heir to Joe's estate? She guessed that everything would be taken from her and it wouldn't go unnoticed that a large sum of money was missing. There was no way that she could repay two thousand pounds unless she recouped the money from Elliott, but if the investment were to be pulled out of his company before he'd reached the mineral vein, it would probably bankrupt him.

She made a cup of cocoa and sat by the fire, hypnotised by the yellow and orange flames. At one time she thought that having money would solve a lot of problems, but now she was learning that it could cause them too.

'Miss Milburn, are you there?'

A man's voice brought Josie out of her trance. She turned to see a large man standing in the doorway. She didn't know who he was, but she remembered seeing him at Mrs Dawson's funeral.

'Sorry, miss. I hope I'm not disturbin' you. I knocked, but you mustn't have heard me.'

'Good afternoon,' she said, getting to her feet. 'What can I do for you?'

'I'm Jimmy Lonsdale. I work at Boltsburn mine over at Rookhope. I've taken to collectin' a bit of spar and doing a bit of sellin'. There's a shortage since that bother last year with Geordie and Ell, and the dealers have been desperate for it.'

At the mention of Elliott, Josie felt a sudden pang of sadness. She said, a little brusquely, 'So, what's that got to do with me?'

'I heard that you're interested in minerals, and wondered if you might be interested in buyin' some off me. I've got some nice bits.'

'Have you brought them with you?'

'Aye, I have.'

Josie had plenty of room to extend her collection now that she was at Springbank Farm, and she thought it might cheer her up to get a few more pieces. Anyway, there was no harm in having a look.

'Would you like to come in, Mr Lonsdale?'

Jimmy took off his cap and followed Josie to the kitchen table, where they sat opposite each other. He opened his bag and took out each piece in turn, and laid them out on the table for Josie to inspect. There were eight pieces altogether, two of which caught her eye. She picked them up to take a better look.

'How much do you want for these two?'

'A pound each.'

'One pound each? You must be joking,' she said. 'I'll give you one pound for the pair. Take it or leave it.'

'Thank you, miss. You drive a hard bargain.' He held out his large hand to shake on the deal.

She shook it firmly, and said, 'Thank you.'

'Can I come back again, when I've got more to sell?'

'Yes, of course, you can. I only want the very best pieces, though.'

'I can see you've got a good eye, miss.'

Josie watched him wrap the discarded pieces and put them back in his bag. He took the coins that she'd placed on the table and left with a big smile on his face. She heard him whistling as he walked out of the yard, and she smiled to herself as she took her new specimens to her bedroom.

Chapter 21

Springbank Farm
March 1896

Matt knocked at the door of Springbank Farm and went into the kitchen, where Josie and Nelly were cleaning the silver and brasses. He smiled at Josie and held up an envelope, waving it in the air.

'I've brought a letter from your boyfriend,' he said smugly.

'Thanks, Matt,' said Josie, jumping up from her chair, but as she reached for it, he pulled his hand away.

'You little pest!' She exclaimed although he was several inches taller than her, and she laughed as she tried to grab the letter from him.

He walked around the kitchen table, keeping his distance from her.

'How much do you want it?' he laughed. 'Enough to give the bearer a shilling?'

'A shilling. What do you want a shilling for?'

Matt stopped still, and his face fell. 'It doesn't matter,'

he said. 'Here, you can have your letter.' He dropped it onto the table.

'What's the matter, Matt?'

He sat down, and his cheeks reddened.

Nelly looked embarrassed, and said quietly, 'I'll make a start on the butter. I'll be in the dairy if you need me.' And then she hurried outside.

Josie waited for her brother to speak.

Looking at the floor, he said, 'There's a lass I like, and I want to take her out, but I don't know if she likes me or not.'

'Who is she?'

'That's none of your business!'

'Huh! Do you want my help or not?' asked Josie, raising her eyebrows.

'Aye, I suppose. What d'you think I should I do?'

'Ask her. You'll never know if you don't ask.'

'Thanks, Josie,' he grinned. 'It's not the same at home without you.'

'I'm not far away, and you're welcome to come over here whenever you want.'

'Thank you.'

Matt walked to the door and paused to wave to her. She threw him a shilling, and he grinned back at her.

'Thanks, Josie.'

As soon as the door closed behind him, Josie rushed to the table and tore open the letter.

24th February 1896

St Francois County, Missouri

My dearest Friend

Thank you for writing back to me. I look forward to receiving your letters so much. I am glad that you are well, as am I, but I was sorry to learn of the death of your uncle.

I have some very good news from Missouri. I have an investor in my company and the extra capital has allowed me to employ three more men at the mine. We have just reached the vein. I called it Josie's Vein — after you. It looks very promising and I hope it proves to be as good as I expect. With more hands, we can get the lead out faster. Lead is fetching a good price in America at the present time and I hope that it will not take too long before my investor and I recoup our initial investments. I plan to blast a cross-cut through to the next vein which is about 40 yards further into the hillside. It has been hard work getting to this stage but I cannot think of anything that I would rather be doing.

A few inches of snow fell last week and it aroused a lot of interest. Some of the miners here had not seen snow before. Can you believe that? They didn't believe me when I told them that snowdrifts in Weardale are often taller than men.

I still think of you often and have fond memories of

the time we spent together in Weardale.
Your friend always
Elliott Dawson

Josie was delighted with Elliott's progress at the mine and could feel his enthusiasm through his words. Making a profit from her investment was not important to her; she just wanted Elliott to achieve his dream. She wished that she could be there with him, but that could never happen, not now that circumstances had changed their destinies.

Anyway, it seemed as though Elliott was happy enough there without her. He had 'fond memories' of the time that they'd spent together. Was that it? After all that they'd gone through together. There was no mention of sending for her, or about coming home to see her, or of marriage.

Elliott Dawson had been on her mind most of the time since he'd left England. Every little thing reminded her of him. Knowing he was happy brought her some comfort. But what she wanted, more than anything, was to be with him. If only things had been different. With a heavy heart, she began to write.

16th March 1896
High House Farm
Dear Elliott
I am so pleased to hear that your mining venture is doing well and that you have found a business partner. It must be a very exciting time for you.

We are all well here and continue to farm as usual. Seasons come and seasons go but very little changes. Weardale is Weardale. We do the same things year in and year out, I suppose as our ancestors did for generations before us.

The winter has been a mild one so far with little snow to speak of. A few nights ago, I woke up thinking that it was daylight. The aurora was so bright and colourful. It was a wonderful sight to see.

There is nothing more to tell from here so I shall wish you well and look forward to hearing your news in due course.

Your friend

Josie Milburn

Josie hated holding back information from Elliott. Recently, she'd questioned her decision not to tell him who her real father was and about the inheritance that he'd left her. She wished she could confide in him about the upcoming court case that was troubling her too. Through her dishonesty, she was losing him as a friend. Her deceit, she concluded, was the reason for his coolness towards her. He must think that she was losing interest in him. Holding the letter to her chest, she felt that nothing could be further from the truth. Her love for him was as strong as ever.

Yet, the need to tell someone about Joe's will being contested was overwhelming; it was too much to keep to herself. She wondered if perhaps Charles Chapman would be able to advise her. He was a man of means, and he might have some knowledge of wills and probate.

The next morning was damp and grey, but the weather was better than it had been for several weeks. After greeting Isaac and Jacob, and discussing what they would be doing that day, Josie set off for Stanhope. As she rode down the road, she enjoyed the sights and the sounds of the dale. The hilltops were covered by cloud, and the lower slopes spotted with pretty yellow primroses. Water in the River Wear rushed over the stony bed as it made its way down the valley. The sound of birdsong surrounded her; thrushes, tits, finches, robins and blackbirds and a few she didn't recognise.

She rode through the town of Stanhope without stopping, continuing towards Frosterley, until she saw a large detached house not far from the road. She took the track down to it. The building looked old, with its low roof and mullioned windows. She noticed children playing in the yard, but by the time she got there, they had disappeared.

Josie dismounted and tethered her pony next to a water trough by the stable block, and then she made her way to the house. As she raised her hand to knock at the door, she heard a voice calling her.

'Miss Milburn. What a delightful surprise!'

Charles Chapman walked through a gateway into the

yard, with a dog at his heels.

'Good morning,' she replied.

'Do come in!'

Charles held open the heavy oak door, and Josie ducked to avoid hitting her head on the wooden door frame as she stepped over the threshold. The hall was dark and gloomy, with a sweeping staircase and dark oak furniture, in stark contrast to its owner who was dressed impeccably in a light tweed suit and a colourful cravat.

Smiling brightly, he asked, 'Would you care for tea?'

'Yes, please.'

'Come and take a seat in the morning room. It was my mother's favourite room.'

He led the way and gestured for her to sit at a table by the window.

'I'll be back shortly,' he said, leaving her alone.

As she waited for him to return, Josie noticed that the fire was unlit. The room felt cold and damp, and there was an unpleasant smell of mould. Wallpaper was peeling away from the wall around the window. The furniture, crammed into the room, was coated with a fine layer of dust, which took the shine and the colour from the wood, making it dull and grey. The faded red carpet was well-worn and had certainly seen better days. Josie thought the house was missing a woman's touch and wondered why Charles hadn't hired a housekeeper or, at the very least, a maid after his wife's death.

She spotted a wedding photograph on the sideboard

and went over to take a closer look. The bride and groom stood in the centre of the picture, with their parents on either side. Charles hadn't changed much — he'd gained a few pounds over the years, and his hair was tinged with grey. His blonde bride was pretty, very slim with delicate features and large doe-like eyes. The tall man standing beside her looked familiar, but she couldn't place him.

Charles carried in a tray and put it down on the table and said, 'There we are.' He sat at the opposite side of the table. 'Would you like to pour, or shall I?' he asked.

'I don't mind,' replied Josie. She picked up the Delft teapot and poured the contents into two blue and white cups. 'What a lovely tea set!' she remarked.

'I think it was my grandparents, or perhaps it was their grandparents.' He laughed. 'It's been in the family for years. Now then, to what do I owe the pleasure of your visit?'

'I hope you may be able to help me or at least offer me some advice.'

'Oh, I do hope so. What advice are you in need of, my dear?'

'As you know, I recently inherited Springbank Farm from my uncle.'

Charles nodded and smiled.

'Somebody has contested the changes that he made to his will. I've been summoned to the probate court in Durham later this month, and a judge will decide what will happen to the estate. I could lose everything.'

'I see,' said Charles, fidgeting with his cup. 'Do you think the complaint might be upheld?'

'I don't know. I hoped you might advise me. Do you know anything about probate and wills?'

'I'm afraid I don't have much experience in such matters. When I inherited my father's estate, there were no issues. But as the eldest son, who could have contested my rights?'

'I see, thank you, anyway,' said Josie, trying to hide her disappointment. Changing the subject, she asked, 'Were those your children playing in the yard?'

'Yes. They've gone upstairs to the nursery. They're a little shy of strangers, but I hope you won't be a stranger to them for long.'

'How many children do you have?'

'Six,' he said, with a strained laugh.

'They must be a handful. Do you have someone to help?'

'Good heavens, no. There's really no need. They're at school much of the time.'

Josie replaced her empty cup onto its saucer and stood up. 'Thank you very much for the tea, but I should be on my way.'

Charles reached out and took her hand and said, 'So soon? But you've only just arrived. Perhaps I could show you around the house, or the grounds?'

'I really should be going.'

'Alright, if you must. May I call on you sometime?'

Josie thought it would be rude to refuse when she had imposed on his hospitality, so she replied, 'Yes, of course. That would be nice.'

His eyes bore into hers as he lifted her hand to his mouth and kissed it. She wanted to get away, and without waiting for him to lead the way, she walked quickly to the front door and opened it herself. It felt good to be outdoors again — in daylight and fresh air.

'Good day, Miss Milburn. I hope to see you soon.'

She climbed onto her pony, inclined her head, and rode away at a canter.

Chapter 22

Springbank Farm
March 1896

The day that Josie had been dreading arrived quicker than she would have liked. She didn't feel ready for it. It was still dark outside when she got out of bed and dressed. The sun began to rise as she stood outside the farmhouse, waiting for a ride to the station. A horse and cart came up the track, with her brother Tommy holding the reins. Her stepfather, dressed in a suit, sat by his side, and as the horse came to a standstill, he moved across the seat to make room.

'Good morning,' he said brightly, as Josie climbed up beside him.

'Good morning,' she replied as a matter of course, although she couldn't think what was good about it.

'You look nice, love. Is that a new dress?'

'Aye, it is. Mother thought I should have one to wear today. To look my best.'

'It'll be fine, lass. Don't worry yourself.'

Tommy dropped them off outside Westgate station, and they travelled by train to Durham. Josie sat and looked out of the window for most of the journey, trying to get her thoughts into some sort of order. She was worried. Very worried. Although she hadn't owned the farm for long, she was concerned about losing it; she already loved it, and she'd grown accustomed to the freedom that it offered. But by far, her greatest fear was for the future of Elliott's company if she had to withdraw the money that she'd invested in it.

It had crossed her mind that details of the trial and the facts surrounding her birth would appear in the press. She thought it was unlikely, but she asked herself what would happen if one of those newspapers were to find its way across the Atlantic and into Elliott's hands. It would certainly be a shock for him to find out in that way. It wouldn't take him long to realise that she'd deceived him, and he'd wonder why she hadn't told him. Had she done the right thing in keeping quiet?

Her thoughts returned to the day she'd found out that Joe was her real father. She'd been so angry at her mother and Tom because she would have preferred to hear about that from someone she loved. With hindsight, she could see that they'd held back the truth of her birth to spare her the pain that the knowledge of her illegitimacy would undoubtedly have caused.

And then Josie realised that she was just as guilty as her parents had been. She'd tried to protect Elliott by evading the subject but, in so doing, she'd made things even worse. If he found out that she'd withheld vital information from him, he'd be angry, and he'd feel betrayed, as she had. But there was no point in telling him now. When he knew what she was, he'd not be interested in her anymore.

Durham was bustling when Josie and Tom walked from the station to the courthouse. Josie had rarely been to the city, and under normal circumstances, she would have been excited to see the castle and cathedral and to browse in the market and the shops, but today they all passed by in a blur.

As they climbed the steps to the courthouse, Tom took Josie's hand. She was grateful for his support. They were shown into a small courtroom where John Peart and his solicitor were already seated.

Everyone stood up when the judge entered the room and, after waiting for them all to take their seats, he began the proceedings. Looking at John Peart, he said, 'I understand that you wish to contest the will of Mr Joseph Milburn of Springbank Farm, Westgate. Please state your case.'

The solicitor stood up and introduced himself. 'Your Honour, I am William Black, of Dickinson and Black of Durham City, and I represent my client, Mr John Peart of White Wells Farm at St John's Chapel in Weardale.'

Josie wished that she'd consulted with Mr Bainbridge and brought him along to speak on her behalf.

Mr Black continued, 'Miss Milburn is named in the original will of Mr Joseph Milburn. As his illegitimate daughter, Mr Milburn left her a very generous sum of one thousand pounds. My client does not contest that she is entitled to that sum of money. He does, however, contest her entitlement to Springbank Farm and claims that it should not have been given to her. Please let me explain why. A codicil that amended Mr Milburn's will was signed and witnessed the day before he died. There were two witnesses present when he signed it: Mr Jacob Rowell, a farmworker in Mr Milburn's employ, and Miss Eleanor Green, a newly hired servant girl.'

'Of that, we are aware. What exactly is your point?' asked the judge.

'At the time Miss Eleanor Green witnessed the signature of Joseph Milburn, she was seventeen years of age — too young to act as a witness to a legal document.'

The judge cleared his throat, and then said, 'Do you have evidence to support this claim?'

'Your Honour, I have a copy of her birth certificate here.'

A clerk took the paper from the solicitor's hand and passed it to the judge, who studied it carefully.

'After reviewing the document,' he said, 'I can confirm that the codicil is, indeed, invalid for the reason stated. In this case, the original will signed by Mr Joseph Milburn on 30th September 1874 must be reinstated. Miss Josephine Milburn is entitled to the sum of one thousand pounds. And as there is no surviving spouse or legal issue, the remainder of the estate is subject to the laws of intestacy. What this Court now needs to determine is who is the closest living relative of Mr Joseph Milburn, and thereby the rightful heir to his estate.'

Tom stood up and said, 'Your Honour, I'm Thomas Milburn, the elder brother of the late Joseph Milburn. I believe Josephine Milburn, his daughter, is my brother's closest living relative.'

'Ah yes,' said the judge, 'but as an illegitimate child, Miss Josephine Milburn, cannot be considered as an heir. The laws of intestacy are clear in this respect.'

Josie saw John Peart sneering at her from across the room, and she looked down at her hands. She wished that she could be anywhere other than here in this courtroom at this time. She hated being the centre of attention, and hearing her illegitimacy discussed so openly was beyond humiliating. She wished she could sink into the floor and disappear, which made her think about the time she'd spent underground with Elliott, and how he'd held her. She knew that she would feel safe anywhere in his arms, and wished that he was with her.

Tom reached down and held her hand. She turned to him, and he smiled reassuringly. 'Don't worry, love,' he whispered. 'You can't miss what you never had.'

'Mr Milburn, do you have any surviving older brothers?' asked the judge.

'No, there was just Joe and me.'

'And you are his full brother by blood, not a step-brother, or brother-in-law?'

'Yes, I am. We shared the same father and mother.'

'And you were born to them within the confines of matrimony?'

'Yes, they were married well over a year before I was born.'

The judge shuffled some papers noisily, and then he addressed the room.

'In that case, I can say with absolute surety that Mr Thomas Milburn is the closest living relative of Mr Joseph Milburn and that he is the rightful heir to his brother's estate.'

'But Joe wanted Josie to have it!' Tom exclaimed, looking flustered for the first time that day. 'That was clear from the note he wrote. It doesn't matter to me that one of the witnesses was underage. They both saw him write it. Look, our Joe loved Josie, and there's no doubt in my mind that he wanted her to have it.'

'Thank you, Mr Milburn, but the court has reached its decision. We will inform Mr Bainbridge and, as executor of the original will, he will ensure that the estate is transferred to you.'

Then turning to Josie, he said, 'Miss Milburn, the circumstances surrounding this complaint are unusual, and it's unfortunate for you that the complaint has been upheld, but it is the right decision according to English law, by which we must abide.' Looking at her sadly, he asked, 'You do understand that the estate will be taken from you and passed to Mr Thomas Milburn, don't you? You will keep one thousand pounds, and that is all.'

'Yes, sir. I understand,' said Josie quietly.

John Peart glared across the room and smiled cruelly, showing his yellowed teeth.

'And Mr Peart,' said the judge, 'you have witnessed that the complaint you made has been upheld. Do you have anything further to say?'

John Peart stood up and said, 'Springbank Farm belonged to my family for centuries. My father and my brother were both honest, upstanding men and they would turn in their graves if they knew that their land had been given to a girl, and a bastard one at that. Now I've said my piece and I've done what's right.'

He folded his arms, and he sat down with a smug look on his face.

Tom moved forward in his seat and glowered at John Peart.

Tears came to Josie's eyes. Tom turned to her and put an arm around her shoulder and said, 'Don't worry love.'

Rather than going straight home from Durham, Josie went to High House Farm with Tom. When they arrived, Mary was standing by a table full of pies and cakes. The room smelled wonderful, and the loud rumble from her stomach reminded Josie that she hadn't eaten all day.

'Sit down, lass. There's tea in the pot. Get yourself something to eat, and then you can tell me all about it.'

'Do you not want to know what the judge said?' asked Josie in surprise.

'It can wait.' Mary smiled at them both. 'But you do need to eat, so reach up.'

After they had eaten their fill, Josie told her mother all about the trial and explained how the judge had reached a decision.

'Well, I never!' said Mary. 'John Peart did all that out of spite. It must have cost him a pretty penny for solicitors and everything.'

'Aye, it's hard to believe,' said Tom.

'It's like something Connie would have done,' said Mary. 'But traits run in families — he was her uncle. I remember when I worked at Springbank Farm, Mr Peart and John weren't on speaking terms for years. Mrs Peart told me it was because John had been jealous of Mr Peart when he'd been left the farm after their father died, and John didn't get anything. But that's the way it works. The eldest son has always inherited from the father. John should have expected that.'

'Aye, it's the way it's always been,' said Tom. He took out his pipe and pulled his chair up to the fireplace, as he did when he wanted to think.

'I'll head back now,' said Josie. 'Thanks for the tea.'

As she walked back to Springbank Farm, she wondered how much longer Tom would allow her to stay at the farm now that it belonged to him.

Josie was black-leading the kitchen fireplace when she heard a knock at the back door and then a man shouting, 'Miss Milburn! It's only me.'

Recognising the loud voice as Jimmy Lonsdale's, she went to the door and opened it.

'Come on in, Jimmy. Sit down.'

'I've got some belters for you this time, miss.'

He sat at the table and opened his bag. He carefully removed three pieces and set them on the table in front of Josie. She looked at them and couldn't help but smile.

Picking each one up and examining them closely, she said, 'Yes, these are exactly what I want. They're beautiful.'

Jimmy looked relieved. 'They're not cheap mind. I need a good price for them,' he said.

'I'll give you a fair price for them. Just give me a minute.'

She left the kitchen and returned with some coins, which she put in front of him.

'That's more than I was going to ask for,' he said, his eyes wide.

'It's what they're worth.'

'Thank you, miss. Thank you very much.' And then sadly, he added, 'I'm afraid that's going to be the last lot though.'

Josie raised her eyebrows, silently waiting for a reason.

She'd just given him an excellent price for the minerals she'd bought in the hope that he'd continue to supply her.

'I'm off to the Klondike next week — to find gold!' He grinned. 'You never know, I might come back after I've made me fortune.'

'Oh, I see,' Josie said, relieved that she hadn't offended him. 'I read about the gold rush in the paper. Alaska is a long way to go, but I wish you luck!' She showed him out.

The thought of such a long journey brought Elliott back to mind and, feeling unsettled, she decided to go outside to check on the animals.

The twins had brought the ewes down off the fell and put them in the lower fields for lambing, and she walked among them, pleased to see that they were looking well. Most of them stood nibbling at small piles of hay dotted around the fields. Isaac had informed her that the first lambs would be born in early April and, despite the long hours and hard work involved with lambing, she was looking forward to seeing playful lambs in her fields. She corrected herself — in Tom's fields. And she wondered if she would even be at Springbank Farm when the lambs were born.

Chapter 23

High House Farm
April 1896

Josie approached High House Farm, anxious about the meeting to which she'd been invited. Her mother had asked her to be there for nine o'clock sharp because there was something important that Tom wanted to discuss. She suspected that he might ask her to leave Springbank Farm and move back home so that he could sell the farm, but she didn't know for sure. The other possibility was that he wanted to move the whole family into Springbank Farm and give up the lease on High House. She wouldn't blame him if that's what he decided to do. With no rent to pay, farming Springbank Farm would be much more profitable for him.

As she turned the corner, she recognised Mr Bainbridge's horse and trap in the yard, and she sighed. What was he doing there? She'd had enough of solicitors and legal matters.

Putting her hand to her mouth, she came to a sudden

halt. A wave of nausea swept through her as she thought that Tom must have discovered that some of the money was missing. Had Mr Bainbridge told him about her investment in Elliott's company?

She walked to the back door with trepidation and took a deep breath. Whatever it was Tom wanted to talk about, she would have to face it and the sooner, the better. She needed to put an end to all the speculation that was driving her crazy.

Opening the door, she saw that the kitchen was empty. Voices drifted from the parlour, and she headed towards them.

'Come in,' said Tom. 'Sit yourself down.'

'Good morning, Miss Milburn,' said Mr Bainbridge, peering over his glasses at her.

'Now that everyone's here,' said Mary, 'I'll make a pot of tea.'

'Sit down, love,' said Tom, smiling at Josie reassuringly.

He can't know about the money, she thought. As she sat on the sofa, she registered that her stepfather remained standing by the fireplace. Why had she been invited?

'Josie,' said Tom more seriously.

Josie's heart began to pound.

'I thought it was very unfair that the court took the farm off you when it was clear that Joe wanted you to have it. So, I asked Mr Bainbridge to see to it that you get what's rightfully yours. The deeds for Springbank Farm have been changed back into your name, and the money has been returned to your bank account. It's like the complaint in court never happened. It's all yours, love.'

Not believing what she was hearing, she asked sceptically, 'Can you do that after what the judge said?'

Mr Bainbridge sat up straight in his armchair, and said, 'Mr Milburn here is within his rights to do whatever he wants with his property and money. If he wants to gift it all to you, then that is his prerogative. It will be yours, and nobody can take it from you.'

'I don't know what to say,' said Josie, mixed emotions flooding her mind. She had lost the farm that she'd grown to love and the chance of an independent future, it had all been taken away from her, and now Tom was offering it back. His generous gesture had taken her completely by surprise. She knew he was doing it with the best of intentions, but he was depriving himself and his sons of a secure future. After everything he had done for her, how could she let him do that?

'You don't need to say anything, love,' said Tom. 'It's all done. It's all legal and above board. And the most important thing is that it's what our Joe wanted. That farm was his life.'

Josie rushed into Tom's arms and hugged him tightly. She said, 'Thank you. Thank you so much.'

She noticed Mr Bainbridge give her a wink, which she guessed meant that her secret investment had remained a secret. Turning to him, she said, 'Thank you, too.'

He stood up unsteadily and held out his hand to her, but she surprised him by kissing him on the cheek.

Mary came in carrying a tray with a teapot, cups and saucers, and a delicious-looking Victoria sponge cake.

'That looks lovely, Mary,' said Tom, 'but I think I'd like something stronger than tea. This is a celebration, after all. What about you, Mr Bainbridge?'

'I wouldn't say no,' said Mr Bainbridge, his eyes twinkling as he smiled.

Tom walked over to a wooden cabinet, opened the door and took out a bottle of scotch. He poured two glasses of whisky for Mr Bainbridge and himself, and two glasses of sherry for the ladies, and passed them around.

Holding up his glass, he said, 'To our Josie and Springbank Farm.'

That night, Josie slept soundly in her bed despite the high winds whistling outside her bedroom window. After all the uncertainty about the ownership of the farm, she now knew for sure that it belonged to her and nobody could take it away from her again.

The next morning, Josie woke early and went down to the kitchen for breakfast. She'd just filled the kettle when Nelly rushed into the kitchen shouting, 'Miss! Miss! The hens are dead.'

Josie got quickly to her feet, and asked, 'What! All of them?'

'Yes, the whole lot.'

Walking towards the door, she asked, 'Where are they?'

'In the hen house.'

Josie followed Nelly to the hen house. The door was wide open and lying on the floor were more than twenty decapitated chickens. There were feathers and blood splatters everywhere, but there was no sign of the missing heads.

'What's happened to them?' asked Nelly.

'A fox must have got in, but I don't know how. I closed the pop hole last night, and I checked that this door was bolted as well.'

'It was wide open this morning when I came out,' said Nelly.

Josie picked up the dead chickens and cleaned the coop and, while she did, she thought about the previous night. The wind had picked up around the time she'd gone to bed, but no amount of wind could have undone the bolt, and a fox certainly couldn't have. After she'd shut in the hens at dusk, somebody must have opened the door. But who would do such a thing?

Chapter 24

Horses and carts lined the road into St John's Chapel. Isaac found a space and tethered the pony, and then he helped Josie down from the cart. They walked towards the mart together, Isaac nodding to the farmers as they made their way to the livestock pens that contained sheep and cattle, and a few pigs and geese.

'The bulls will be over this side,' said Isaac, leading the way.

When they got there, they saw that there were only two shorthorn bulls entered in the sale.

'There aren't many to choose from,' said Josie.

'You only need one.'

Isaac checked both of the bulls thoroughly, looking at their overall shape, conformation, markings, legs and feet, and then running his hands over their bodies. When he'd finished his examination, Josie asked, 'Which one do you think we should get?'

'Either of them would do, but the darker one is better marked.'

'We'll get him then. Do you know who's selling him?'

'I am.'

Josie was startled by a familiar voice right behind her. She turned quickly to see Charles Chapman standing there.

'Good morning, Mr Chapman. I didn't know you were here.'

He smiled at her. 'Perhaps we could find somewhere to have a pot of tea. There's an inn just up the road from here that serves a very decent brew.'

Isaac moved forward protectively, and said, 'We're here on business Mr Chapman, please excuse us.' He took Josie's arm and led her away.

'Why did you do that?' asked Josie, embarrassed by his behaviour. 'It was rude to walk away. He was just being polite.'

'He's being over-friendly, inviting you to tea like that in front of our neighbours.'

'Now you're behaving like my father!' said Josie huffily, but she knew Isaac had a point.

The sale was about to commence, and Isaac led her to a place where the auctioneer could easily see them. The first lot to be auctioned was a shorthorn heifer. The auctioneer asked for bids in his sing-song voice and sold the cow in seconds.

Josie said, 'I didn't understand a word of what he said,

and I've no idea what she sold for. I think you'd better do the bidding.'

'Aye, lass, I will.'

All of the cows were sold, one by one, and then it was time for the bulls to go under the hammer. The darker one was led to the ring first, and a skinny man walked him around so everyone could see him. Josie sat on the edge of her seat, eagerly waiting for the auctioneer to begin.

Isaac looked very relaxed as he raised his hand to accept the auctioneer's starting bid. Another two farmers joined in the bidding. Isaac inclined his head slightly to show his continued interest.

A drunken voice shouted, 'Are you buying this animal for that bastard?'

Josie shrank back in her seat and saw John Peart at the entrance to the mart, glaring at her. Then he raised his hand into the air and kept it raised. The price of the bull went up and up.

Josie touched Isaac's arm and whispered, 'Stop bidding. Let him have it. We'll get the other one.'

When the auctioneer turned to Isaac, Isaac shook his head, and then the auctioneer announced, 'Sold, to John Peart, for forty guineas.'

'How much?' John exclaimed, his face reddening. He looked daggers at Josie and Isaac, his eyes blazing, and he swore under his breath.

The auctioneer repeated the selling price, and John

cursed loudly before turning away, pushing people aside as he marched outside.

Isaac bought the second bull for twenty-four guineas. He turned to Josie and said, 'You got a good deal there. Peart paid way more than t'other was worth.' He shook his head and added. 'He should know better than come to a sale full of drink.'

At the end of the sale, Isaac went to collect the bull from its pen and Josie went to the office to pay. On her way back, she almost collided with a man just inside the office doorway. About to apologise, she looked up and saw John Peart glaring down at her, his face hard and his beady eyes cold with hatred. He barged past her, knocking her against the wall. Her head hit the stonework. She lifted her hand to her head; it felt wet and sticky. There was blood on her hand, and she felt dizzy.

Looking for help, she recognised a few faces, Charles's included, but nobody came to her aid. She slithered to the floor and sat with her back against the wall until she could see more clearly. John Peart was complaining loudly about the cost of the bull while the cashier counted out his money on the desk. Then, the sound of his footsteps got closer, and as he passed her, he kicked her outstretched leg with his hobnailed boot and laughed when she screamed with pain.

Ned Routledge's large frame appeared in the doorway, and he grabbed John Peart's arm and dragged him out of the office.

'Get that damned animal, and get out of here!' roared Ned. 'And if I ever see you near that lass again, you'll have me to answer to!'

Isaac was oblivious to what had taken place as he walked towards the office leading the bull, and he was shocked to see Ned so riled up. He'd known Ned for years, with him farming at Westgate. He'd been a pretty good wrestler in his day, but he wasn't a troublemaker. John Peart must have done something pretty serious to upset him, and Isaac guessed it had something to do with Josie. He should never have left her alone. He rushed back to the office and found her sitting on the floor holding her leg.

'What did he do?' he asked.

'He pushed me against the wall and I bumped my head. And he kicked my leg,' said Josie weakly.

Isaac handed the bull's lead rope to Ned and ran out of the office in the direction that John had taken. John hadn't gone very far. He was staggering along the road with the bull he had bought following calmly behind him. Isaac soon caught up with him and grabbed the lapels of his jacket. Looking into the older man's face, he said, 'You coward! Why don't you pick on someone your own size?'

John's face twitched and, as soon as he raised his hand, Isaac punched him soundly on the jaw. John fell to the ground and wiped a little blood from the corner of his mouth with the back of his hand.

Ned had followed Isaac, knowing what he'd been likely

to do, and witnessed the whole thing. 'Come away, Isaac,' he said. 'You've made your point.'

Isaac was still staring at John, waiting for him to make a move so that he could punch him again.

John stayed down on the ground, cursing under his breath. He didn't look at either of the men towering over him.

Ned took hold of Isaac's arm and pulled him away. They left John sprawled on the road and headed back to the mart. Josie was standing outside the office, waiting for Isaac. 'Where did you go?' she asked when he returned.

'There was something I needed to take care of,' he said gruffly.

'My leg hurts. Would you mind helping me back to the cart?'

To her surprise, Isaac picked her up and carried her to the cart and lifted her onto the seat. Ned brought out the bull and tied him to the back of the cart. Isaac thanked him, and they said their farewells.

When Isaac picked up the reins, Josie noticed that the knuckles on his right hand were grazed, but she didn't say anything. She could guess what he'd done and was pleased that he had.

As they turned into the farmyard, Isaac asked, 'Do you want me to fetch your mother over, to check you're alright?'

'There's no need. I'll be fine.'

'Alright, if you're sure. I'll go and get the bull settled in the garth.'

Josie limped to the house. She was met by Nelly, who fussed over her, cleaning her wounds and washing the dried blood from her hair. While the girl went to fetch a clean towel, there was a knock at the door. Rather than get up to open it, Josie shouted, 'Come in!'

PC Emerson entered the kitchen and took in her injuries.

'Do you mind if I ask you what happened today?' he said kindly.

'Come in and sit down.'

The policeman pulled out a chair and sat at the table.

'I heard there was a commotion at the mart earlier,' he said, 'and I can see you've been knocked about a bit. Was it John Peart that did this to you?'

'Aye, it was.'

'Do you know why he attacked you?'

'I can guess. Probably because I'm back here — on the farm.'

'Tom told me about him taking you to court and all that. You want to be careful of him. He's taken a dislike to you, and he's out to hurt you in any way that he can. There are enough witnesses to what happened today to put him behind bars, if that's what you want, or I could go and have a word with him?'

'If he went to prison because of me,' said Josie, 'it would only make matters worse. I'd be more worried about what he'd do when he got out again.'

'Aye, I see your point. But if you change your mind, come and have a word with me. A man like that shouldn't get away with beating up young lasses. I shouldn't condone what Isaac did, taking the law into his own hands, but if I'd seen John Peart hitting you, I'd have done the same.'

PC Emerson got up from the table and walked to the door. Before he left, he turned and said, 'If you have any more bother with him, you let me know.'

'I will. Thank you.'

Chapter 25

High House Farm
June 1896

Josie opened the door to High House Farm and went into the kitchen, where Tom sat at the table, carving a piece of wood that was slowly taking the shape of a tup. He looked up and said, 'Morning, love.'

'Happy birthday!' said Josie.

She sat down next to her stepfather and held out a gift, which he took, saying, 'You shouldn't have bothered. There's nothing I need.'

'I wanted to get you something. Now, open it.'

He unwrapped the present, and inside was a photographic portrait of Mary and Josie in a silver frame. He studied the image and then looked up at her.

'When did you —'

'When we went to Bishop Auckland to get the dress material.' She smiled, pleased at his reaction. 'It was Mother who gave me the idea. We passed a photographer's studio, and she pointed out that we didn't have any photos of our family, so I took her inside, and we had this taken. What do you think?'

'It's lovely, lass. Thank you.'

'I'm pleased you like it. You should have heard Mother complaining about having to sit still for so long to have her picture taken.' Josie laughed.

'Aye, I can imagine,' said Tom with a chuckle.

'I thought she'd be here. Where is she?'

'She's just popped down to the village. She needed a few things from the shop. She shouldn't be much longer.' Tom cleared his throat, 'Josie, can I ask you something?'

Josie inclined her head.

'Where is it that Elliott lives, exactly?'

'Missouri. He's staying in a little place called Flat River. Why do you ask?'

'It's just that there was something in the paper yesterday.'

'Oh! What about?'

'There was a tornado. A bad one. In Missouri.' He paused and waited for Josie to say something, but she didn't, so he continued, 'St Louis seems to have got the worst of it. A bridge collapsed, and a lot of houses were damaged. They reckon over two hundred people have been killed, maybe more.'

The colour faded from Josie's cheeks. Was Elliott one of the dead? She pictured him running around, trying to save other people with no concern for his own safety. Her mind flooded with images of him lying crushed under fallen timbers, being swept down a swollen river and caught up in a fire. The thought that Elliott could have been killed was just too terrible — it couldn't be true. Without saying a word, she stood up and rushed for the door, where she bumped into her mother.

'Josie! What's got into you?'

Josie was trembling. Mary took her into her arms and held her.

'Sorry,' said Tom sheepishly. 'I was just telling her about the tornado.'

Safe in her mother's arms, Josie began to cry.

'He'll be alright,' said Mary.

After a minute or two, Josie pulled away, and said, 'I wish I'd gone to America with him. I've done nothing but worry about him ever since he went!'

She flew out of the door and ran back to Springbank Farm.

Josie added the column of figures in the account book for the third time. She couldn't concentrate on what she was doing. It was almost two weeks since her father had told her about the tornado and she'd been worried about Elliott ever since.

When she heard a knock at the door, she ran to it in case there was news of him. She flung open the door and saw Charles Chapman standing in the yard. He smiled and said, 'Good afternoon.'

'Oh, it's you.'

He laughed. 'May I ask who were you expecting?'

'I'm sorry. It's just that I'm waiting for some news. You'd better come in.'

As he followed her into the house, he asked, 'News about what, may I ask? The court case?'

'No. The court case has been and gone. I'm surprised you haven't read about it in the paper or heard the gossip.'

'I don't listen to gossip. As you are still here, I presume it's safe to say that the hearing went in your favour?'

'You could say that,' replied Josie, not wanting to explain the circumstances that allowed her to stay at the farm.

'Thank goodness for that.'

'Would you like some tea?' asked Josie out of politeness.

'No, thank you. However, I would like it very much if you would accompany me for a ride. It's such a beautiful day! Much too nice to spend it indoors...'

'Yes, you're right,' she said and followed him out into the yard where his horse, a tall chestnut thoroughbred, stood.

She went into the stable to saddle up the trusty Dales pony that she'd ridden since she'd moved to the farm. Joe's black stallion neighed loudly and pawed at the bedding in his stall, and she thought that he looked a much better match for Charles's horse. She'd never ridden Jet before, but he belonged to her now, and she decided that this was as good a time as any to get to know him. Gathering up his tack, she saddled him quickly and, because he was much taller than the pony, she led him to the mounting block in the yard.

'What a stunner!' said Charles, looking her in the eye. 'I should say, I was referring to your horse, but the same does apply to you.'

Josie blushed slightly but ignored his comment. She led the way out of the yard towards a track which led up to the hills, and it wasn't long before they were riding side by side up the pasture and towards the fell. Once they were on open ground, Josie struggled to hold back the stallion. The horse hadn't been exercised much since her uncle had died, and he was full of energy and raring to go. Josie began to wish that she'd chosen the pony to ride instead; she was much steadier.

'He's a bit of a handful, isn't he?' said Charles, whose gelding, Chester, was behaving perfectly.

Jet pulled at the bit and shook his head, trying to loosen Josie's grip on the reins, but she sat firmly in the saddle and held him back. An adder appeared from the rushes and slithered across the path in front of them. Jet reared up in fear. Josie managed to keep her seat, but she lost her grip on the reins, and the thin leather straps slipped through her fingers. Jet took off at speed, following a path across the fell. Josie leaned forward and grabbed hold of his mane, but she had no control over him. Her legs were useless; they were shaking too much.

She'd never travelled so fast on horseback. Jet's hooves pounded the ground, his mane flew up into her face and the scenery rushed by in a blur as he tore across the moor. She could do nothing but cling on to him.

They had travelled at least two miles before Jet slowed down and eventually came to a stop, snorting loudly, and then he lowered his head to graze on the coarse grass.

A few moments later, Charles pulled up next to them and dismounted.

'Are you alright?' he asked, looking up at Josie's ashen face.

'I will be. I just need to rest for a while, and I'll be fine.'

She slid down Jet's side, but when her feet touched the ground, her legs refused to support her weight. She felt Charles's arms around her, holding her up. He turned her to face him and held her close against him. After such a frightening experience, it felt good to be to wrapped in his arms, and she nestled into him. For a moment, she imagined that it was Elliott who was holding her and she felt safe and well.

Charles lowered his head and kissed the top of her head, and his hands moved down to below her waist and rested on her behind.

She pushed him away sharply and stepped back.

'I feel fine now,' she said, 'but I'd like to go home.'

'Are you sure that animal is safe to ride? I'll tell you what. I'll ride your horse, and you can take mine.'

'Thank you.' She was grateful for his offer. She didn't

want to admit it, but she was a little afraid to get back on Jet after he'd taken off with her.

Charles swapped the saddles and helped Josie mount Chester.

On the way home, Jet walked leisurely alongside Chester. Either Jet had worn himself out, or Charles was an accomplished rider. The silence was awkward, but since it was her who had rebuffed his advances, she thought it was her place to start a conversation. They talked about horses for a while, and the farm, and she was surprised by how quickly the time passed as they rode back to Springbank Farm.

Isaac came out of the stable to greet them and, although he looked surprised to see Charles on the stallion, he didn't say anything. He held Jet still while Charles dismounted, and then Charles held Chester while Josie jumped down. Isaac swapped the saddles back and took Jet into the stable.

'Miss Milburn,' said Charles. 'May I call you Josephine? Surely, we know each other well enough by now to drop the formalities, don't we?'

'Yes, I suppose we do. But everyone calls me Josie.'

'Josie,' he said with a smile. 'I would very much like to call on you again.'

He leaned forward and surprised her by kissing her on the edge of her mouth, before hastily mounting his horse and riding away down the track.

Matt ran into the farmhouse at Springbank Farm. He

was breathing heavily and waved a letter in his hand. 'Mother said I had to bring this over for you as quick as I could. I ran all the way.'

'Thank you,' said Josie, tentatively taking the envelope from her younger brother. She hesitated to turn it over to see the writing on the front. When she did, she slumped down onto a chair and wiped away a tear.

'Are you alright?' asked Matt.

'Aye, I'm fine.'

Taking his sister at her word, he said, 'I don't know why he's still sending letters to our house. You should tell him you've moved in here.'

Josie stared at Matt. He didn't understand that if she told Elliott she was living at Springbank Farm, she'd have to explain everything.

'Anyway, I hope it's good news!' he said, as he backed towards the door. He turned quickly and almost knocked Nelly off her feet.

'Sorry!' he said, looking startled.

'Don't worry, Matt,' replied Nelly, looking down at the floor.

'As long as you're alright?' he said to her.

'I'm fine,' replied Nelly, looking up at him.

Josie watched them, wondering why they were so uncomfortable around each other. Matt appeared hesitant to leave, and she was anxious to read her letter in private.

'There's no harm done,' said Josie. 'So long, Matt.'

When he'd left, Nelly said, 'I've finished in the dairy. I'll go and collect the eggs now unless...'

'Yes, please go and collect the eggs.'

Josie stared at the envelope again. It was Elliott's handwriting, and the postmark was dated after the storm. The relief she felt was immense. She tore open the envelope and began to read the letter.

10th June 1896

St Francois County, Missouri

My dearest Friend

I hope that you are in good health and everything is well with you and your family. I received your letter early in April. Please accept my apologies for not writing to you sooner.

There was a terrible storm a few weeks ago. Wind like I've never seen before tore down everything in its path. Houses and bridges were wrecked and many people were killed. The house where I was staying was made from timber and it was badly damaged. The whole roof blew off. Luckily none of us inside were hurt, other than a few cuts and bruises.

Everybody in town had to help the injured, clean up the town and repair the houses. Me and John fixed roofs from daybreak to nightfall — even on Sundays.

Work at the mine stopped for two weeks because of it, but now the mine here is producing good ore and plenty of it. I am considering taking out a lease on another site that has become vacant. The new site is about two miles west of here. It will cut into the same veins as the first and will hopefully prove as fruitful. Many miners have left here to go to the Klondike. I suppose you will have read about the gold rush in the newspapers. There is plenty of opportunity here without travelling over 3,000 miles to Canada. In the time that it will take them to get there, I will have made a good profit from my lead ore.

There is little wind here and the sky is cloudless. The sun shines down relentlessly and it is very hot and muggy, almost unbearably so. There is no relief from it except to cool off in the river. The temperature at night makes it hard to sleep.

I am renting a small house at the edge of town now. Please note the new address on the back of the envelope and remember it when you write your reply to me.

Your last letter gave me cause for concern that something is troubling you. I hope whatever it is, that it is not of my doing. You know you can always confide in me. Isn't that what friends are for?

Your very dear friend
Elliott Dawson

Josie's eyes welled up with tears as she read his words.

Thank God, Elliott was alive and unharmed. And he'd noticed that she'd been more distant in her last letter and he wanted her to confide in him. But she couldn't. The truth was too terrible.

As she put the letter down on the table, she looked out of the window and wished more than ever before that things had been different and that she could be with him. She missed him more than she thought possible.

After dinner that evening, she sat in the kitchen and wrote a reply.

29th June 1896

High House Farm

My Dearest Elliott

I was so pleased to receive your letter today and to hear that you are safe and well. News of the tornado arrived weeks ago and I was worried that you had been hurt, or even killed, and when I hadn't heard from you for so long, I feared the worst. You have no idea how much receiving this letter means to me.

News of the gold rush caused a great deal of excitement here and several men have left the dale to go there. There are some that you might know. Jimmy Lonsdale is one of them. He used to fetch me Boltsburn spar for my collection, so I will miss him. I will have to find a new supplier. My collection has grown considerably since you last saw it in my room at High House Farm. It seems such a long time since you left here and I miss you so very much.

Please take care over there. I couldn't bear it if anything bad happened to you.

My family send their very best wishes.

Your loving friend

Josie Milburn

Chapter 26

Springbank Farm
July 1896

On hearing a commotion in the yard, Josie went to investigate and was met by a horse's muzzle when she opened the door. Charles Chapman was attempting to turn a trap around in the small yard and was finding it difficult.

'Ah, there you are,' he said. 'It's a glorious day again. Would you like to come out for a drive with me?'

Josie didn't have any plans for the day that couldn't wait, so she said, 'Yes, why not?'

'Excellent. If there's anything that you'd like to take with you, go and get it now while I turn this contraption around.'

By the time Josie had put on her hat, and found a shawl in case it dropped colder, Charles had managed to manoeuvre the horse and trap so that they were facing out of the yard. He took her hand and helped her up onto the green leather seat.

'This is nice,' she said. 'Very comfortable.'

'Yes, it is, isn't it? My father had it made years ago. I wonder, have you ever been to High Force?'

'No! I've heard about the waterfall, but I've never seen it.'

'Then, that's where we shall go.'

They headed up to Westgate and turned onto a road which climbed steeply up the southern slope of the dale and over the hill into the neighbouring valley of Teesdale. Chester struggled to pull the trap up the steeper parts of the bank, and Josie wanted to get down and walk alongside him to lighten his load, but Charles wouldn't hear of it. Other than that, their conversation was enjoyable on the journey over the fell.

Josie loved being high up in the hills. The wide-open space gave her a feeling of freedom, and the cool breeze was refreshing. An old mine that they passed reminded her of the walk at Middlehope with Elliott — that had been a wonderful day.

They descended the steep slope into the valley and travelled along a narrow road until they reached the High Force Hotel. Charles helped Josie down, and then he went into the inn. The boy who followed Charles out unharnessed Chester and led the horse to a paddock to rest for a while.

Meanwhile, Charles offered Josie his arm, and they walked along a wooded path by the River Tees. Josie could hear a roaring noise that got louder and louder as they approached the waterfall, and when it came into view, she stopped and stared, stunned by the height of the falls and the power of the water. White water cascaded down from a cliff into a dark, turbulent pool below. Although she was some distance from it, she could feel the fine spray on her skin. Charles led her to a seat on the edge of the path — a perfect viewing point.

'It's magnificent, isn't it?' he asked.

'It's incredible,' she said, still staring at the waterfall in wonder.

'It's a very special place,' he shouted over the noise, and added more quietly, 'and you're a very special lady.'

They sat in silence for a few minutes, admiring the view, and then Charles said, 'While we're here, Josie, there is something that I would like to ask you. Would you do me the honour of being my wife?'

Josie turned to him. 'I'm sorry. Did you say something?'

Charles looked disgruntled and raised his voice above the sound of the water. 'I said, would you do me the honour of being my wife?'

Josie turned to look at him, her eyes wide, and said, 'You want to marry me?'

'Yes, I do.'

He reached into his pocket and took out a small leather box, and opened it to reveal a gold ring set with a large ruby in the centre, surrounded by smaller diamonds. It was beautiful.

'It was my grandmother's,' he said, tugging at his collar as though it had suddenly become too tight. 'It's a family heirloom.'

He took the ring out of the box and held out his hand to take hers.

'I'm sorry, Charles,' she said sincerely. 'I had no idea you felt that way. We hardly know each other. But I don't want to be married, to you or anybody else for that matter.'

'Surely it would make your life easier for you if you had a husband to protect you and to manage your affairs. I would be honoured to do that for you.'

'I'm quite capable of looking after myself, thank you. I don't need a husband.'

'But don't you get lonely?' he asked, leaning forward. 'Especially at night?' He lifted his hand to her neck and stroked it gently.

She found his question and his touch irritating, and she pushed his hand away. Yes, she got lonely at night, but it wasn't Charles that she wanted in her bed.

'I'm sorry, Charles. The answer is no, and I'm not going to change my mind.'

'You'll live to regret that, I promise you. You'll not get a better offer.'

Like a petulant child, Charles stormed off back up the path towards the inn, leaving Josie to walk back alone. She wondered why he'd had to spoil such a good day out with a proposal of marriage. And now she dreaded the long journey home with him.

The innkeeper came out to greet them. 'Would you like some refreshments, sir? Drinks? Or something to eat? My wife's a great cook.'

Josie realised she was hungry and looked at Charles.

'No, we'd better get back on the road,' Charles replied. 'Get the horse ready, would you?'

'Johnny, harness the horse for this gentleman.'

The boy brought Chester back from the paddock and harnessed him to the trap. Charles climbed up without helping Josie first and threw the boy a coin. The innkeeper stepped forward and, as he helped Josie up, said, 'You take care, miss.'

Charles flicked the reins over Chester's back. Startled, the horse whinnied as he set off at a trot. When they reached the steep bank out of the dale, Charles didn't let Chester slow to a walk, and it wasn't long before the horse was breathing heavily. Josie was worried for him.

'Slow down, Charles. He can't keep up this pace on these hills.'

'How dare you tell me what to do?'

He shouted at Chester to go faster and brought the whip down on the horse's flank with a loud crack.

Josie held her tongue after that as she figured Charles would make the gelding suffer even more if she said anything. The journey was a silent one, and it seemed to last an eternity. She tried to distract herself by looking for wildlife on the fell, but all she saw was a single hare running away from them. By the time they got back to Springfield Farm, Chester was covered in white foam, and he was gasping noisily.

As soon as he stopped, Josie jumped down and stroked his sweat-soaked muzzle.

Isaac came out of the barn, and when he saw the distressed animal, he ran over to him.

'What on earth have you done to him?' he asked accusingly.

'What business is that of yours? He's my horse.'

Isaac looked Charles in the eye, and said, 'He won't be anyone's horse for much longer if you don't let him rest.'

Charles looked at Chester, and it slowly seemed to dawn on him what he'd done to his horse.

Josie said to Isaac, 'Lend him one of the ponies so he can get home, and do what you can for this poor fellow.' She went into the house without even a glance in Charles's direction.

A week later, Josie went to the stables to check on Chester's progress. Isaac was in the stall with the horse that he'd been caring for since the day Charles had pushed him to exhaustion.

'How's he doing?' she asked.

'He's getting better by the day. Aren't you owd fella?' said Isaac, reaching up to stroke Chester's neck.

She was surprised at the change in the horse. His coat was shiny, his eyes were bright, and he almost looked as if he was smiling.

'He looks well. You wouldn't think he was the same animal.'

'Good food, gentle exercise and a lot of love.' Isaac smiled to himself. 'I've taken quite a shine to him.'

'So, I see.'

'He's not as old as I thought, either. By his teeth, I reckon he's no more than about twelve. There's plenty of life left in him yet.'

'There is now, thanks to you. Charles would have killed him if you hadn't stepped in.'

'Aye, he surprised me that day. I didn't think he was that sort.'

'What do you mean, that sort?'

'You know, cruel. Some men are bad through and through and think nothing of hurting animals, or people for that matter. Chapman never struck me as that sort. But the look on his face that day. I've never been good with words, lass, I can't explain it, but it looked to me as if he was losing his mind.'

Josie knew that Charles had been upset when she'd turned down his proposal — he'd not even tried to hide his anger. But could Isaac be right about him losing his mind? She hoped not for his children's sake. They'd already lost their mother, and it would be dreadful if they lost their father too. What would happen to the poor little mites?

'Are you alright?' Isaac's eyes showed concern.

'Yes, I'm fine. I hope you're wrong about Charles though.'

'Time will tell.'

A few days later, Charles Chapman appeared at Springbank Farm, riding the Dales pony that Josie had loaned him. As Josie opened the back door of the house and went into the yard to meet him, Isaac and Jacob came out of the barn.

'Good morning, Miss Milburn,' said Charles. 'I've come to collect Chester. I'm sorry it's taken me so long to get back, I've been away on business.'

'Isaac, could you bring Chester out please?' asked Josie.

Isaac went into the stables.

Although Charles was chatting cordially, she was pleased that Jacob had stayed outside with them, so that the conversation couldn't turn to personal matters. She knew Charles wouldn't say anything about what had happened at High Force when there were others present.

Isaac reappeared and led Chester into the yard.

Charles let out a low whistle when he saw his horse. 'What have you done to him?' he asked. 'He looks very well. Very well, indeed!'

'Isaac's been working with horses since before I was born,' said Josie. 'What he doesn't know about them isn't worth knowing.'

Charles reached into his pocket and said, 'I should repay you for what you've done for him.'

'There's no need,' said Isaac. 'I get paid well enough for what I do here. Just take good care of him. He's a good horse.'

'Well, that's very kind of you. Thank you.'

Jacob harnessed Chester and attached the trap, and then Charles climbed up and tipped his hat at Josie.

'Oh, I almost forgot,' said Charles. 'I met the postman on the way here. He gave me a letter for you.' He reached into his pocket, took out the letter and handed it to her.

'Thank you.'

'It's been nice to see you again,' he said as he pulled away and waved.

'Unbelievable!' said Isaac as he came to stand by Josie's side. 'He's a completely different fella today.'

They watched him ride down the track towards the main road.

'Aye,' she said. 'As nice as pie.'

Isaac shrugged and went back to work.

Walking back to the house, Josie looked at the envelope and was pleased to see that the handwriting was Elliott's. She went into the study and closed the door behind her. Sitting at the desk, she opened the letter and began to read.

31st July 1896
St Francois County, Missouri
My dearest Josie
Thank you for your letter. I am sorry to have caused you so much upset at the time of the storm.

I would have written sooner if I had known how distressed you were. I can assure you that I am completely well, and I hope you are too.

I wish I had good news to share about my company but truth be told there has been a major setback. The vein came to an abrupt stop. One of the miners in town reckons there's a throw in the vein of about 20 feet, so it's back to dead work for a while until we track it down again. Thank God for the new investor because without his money I'd not have been able to buy dynamite to blast this hard rock.

The heat here is unimaginable now. Even in the night it is like a summer's day in England. We've had some heavy rain showers recently, a bit like summer thunderstorms in Weardale, with a quick burst of sheeting rain for just a few minutes and then nothing.

Apart from work at the mine, I have very little else to tell you except that I still miss you every single day.

Sending all my love.

Your friend

Elliott Dawson

When she had finished reading it, she decided to walk to High House Farm and pass on Elliott's news to her family. When she arrived, Tom was leaning over a wooden gate and pointing out various sheep to Tommy and Matt.

'Hello!' she said. 'What are you doing?'

'Hello, love,' said Tom. 'We're choosing the sheep we'll take to Chapel Show this year.'

Josie scoffed. 'I don't know why you bother. All that washing and preening just to win a rosette!'

'You think that's why we do it?' exclaimed Tom. 'Well, lass, you're wrong there. The reason we put them in the show is so that everyone can see how good our stock is on this farm.'

'So, it's to show off then.'

'No, lass,' said Tom, rolling his eyes. 'You've still got a lot to learn. The shows come just before the lamb sales. If people see you've got a good stock on your farm, there'll be more interest in your lambs when they go to market, and they'll fetch a better price.'

Josie kissed him on the cheek and said, 'Thank you. I'd better pick out some of mine and start washing them, then. Is Mother in?'

'Aye, she is.'

Josie left the men to their job and went in search of her mother.

The show field at St John's Chapel was already bustling by the time Josie arrived with Nelly, Isaac and Jacob. They'd walked up from Westgate together, with a tup and two ewes that Josie had hand-picked herself. She'd spent hours the day before getting them to look their best, with a little help from Jacob who had trimmed their wool with a pair of shears.

As soon as they'd gone through the gates of the show field, Nelly had run off to find her family. When her sheep were safely penned beside the show ring, Josie and the twins weighed up the competition.

'I reckon you stand a good chance,' said Jacob, as they came to the last sheep pen.

Josie smiled as his optimism. Feeling as though she was being watched, she turned full circle, but couldn't see anyone looking at her. When her attention was back with Isaac and Jacob, she realised that they'd been whispering to each other.

'Would you mind if we had a bit of time off today?' asked Isaac. 'We'll be back when it's time for the sheep to go in the ring. It's just our folks are here. It'd be nice to have a wander around with them.'

'Of course, go and see them,' replied Josie.

'Thanks!' The men said in unison, grinning, and then they rushed over to a large group of people standing by the gateway. Josie knew that they were the twins' wives, grown-up children and young grandchildren. She watched them as they greeted each other enthusiastically, and set off around the show field to see the delights on offer.

Josie walked in the opposite direction because there was something specific at the show that she wanted to see. As well as classes for all types of animals, there were competitions for produce and crafts. Displays of flowers gave off a strong but pleasant odour as she passed them. Vegetables of massive proportions filled tabletops, with men standing proudly beside their crops. Then, there were tables full of eggs, butter, baking and preserves, followed by needlework and woodwork. She noticed a carved wooden figure of a horse that her father had modelled on Nutmeg, and she realised that her family must already be at the show. Josie walked by all of these with not much more than a glance until she came to the mineral and spar box section.

She inspected all of the exhibits in this category very closely and was impressed that there were several new pieces that she hadn't seen before — probably discovered within the last year. She wished she'd remembered to enter some of her specimens in the class, but with the rush of getting the sheep ready, it had slipped her mind.

A middle-aged, plump man approached her. 'Excuse me. I hope you don't mind me asking. Are you Miss Milburn?'

'Yes, I am. And you are?'

'Mr Glover. I'm a mineral dealer from Durham. I've heard you're a collector, and I'd like to give you my card. Please get in touch if there's ever anything you'd like. I have contacts all around the world.'

'Thank you, Mr Glover.' Josie took the business card that he held out for her, and asked, 'How did you know who I was?'

'Well, there aren't many ladies who collect minerals,

and when I saw you admiring that piece over there, I knew it must be you.'

'Yes, it's a good example, and it should easily win this class.'

The man laughed loudly. 'Perhaps I should have told you that I'm judging the mineral classes today! But you're right,' he said, winking at her. 'You've picked the winner!'

She noticed a magazine among the papers he'd placed on the table. The world 'Mineral' on the cover caught her attention.

Mr Glover saw what she was looking at and handed the magazine to her. 'It's a periodical from the United States of America. I finished reading it on the journey here this morning. Take it.'

Lifting it, she noted the name, 'The Mineral Collector', and when she flicked through the pages, she saw it was full of articles and advertisements.

'Thank you, that's very kind of you. I'm sure I'll enjoy reading it.'

'You're very welcome.' He tipped his hat as he turned to leave.

When Josie was alone, she felt as though she was being watched again. She decided to look for her family. As she walked amongst the crowd, someone pushed her from behind. Thinking it was one of her brothers fooling around, she stopped and turned quickly, ready to bump into him, but as she turned, she saw a face come into view. It wasn't Tommy or Matt. It wasn't a friendly face at all. The man who had pushed her was John Peart.

'What have we got here?' he said through gritted teeth. 'A little bastard all by herself.'

Josie instinctively stepped back, but he leaned down towards her, his face close to hers, his breath foul. She turned her face away.

In a low, threatening voice, he said, 'You set the law on me because you fell and bumped your head. I should have set them on you for tripping me up, you little bitch. I see you've managed to wheedle your way back to the farm. Well, I can promise you, you won't be there for long if I have anything to do with it.'

'What's going on here?'

Josie had never been so relieved to hear Tom's voice. John Peart seemed to shrink before her eyes as Tom stood over him. John narrowed his eyes at her, and hissed, 'You'll not always have someone watching over you.'

'That's enough,' said Tom, as he pushed John away. Josie didn't want anyone to know how frightened she was. Her hands were shaking, so she folded her arms and tucked them in as though they were cold.

'Watch out for him, love,' said Tom. 'He still bears a grudge about the farm.'

'I'll be fine,' she replied, sounding braver than she felt. 'I don't go out very often. The twins are at the farm most of the time, and Nelly is nearly always in the house with me.'

'It's time we got the sheep ready for the ring,' said Tom. He put his arm around her shoulder and led her back towards the animal pens.

An hour later, the judging was complete, and Josie was delighted with the results. In the class for Scottish Blackface rams, Tom's tup won, and Josie's was second in the line-up. In the sheep class, one of Ned Routledge's ewes took first place, and Josie's took second. Josie spotted the proud faces of Isaac and Jacob in the crowd as the judge presented the rosettes.

When the first day of the lamb sales arrived, Josie was a little apprehensive about returning to the mart because of what had happened the last time, but she wanted to see her first lambs sell at the auction. With the Rowell twins by her side and her stepfather and brothers there, she knew that she would be safe.

After a quick breakfast of bread and butter, with cheese and bramble jam, she went out into the yard where Isaac and Jacob were waiting with their sheepdogs. Jacob went down to the main road, so he could send the sheep up the road towards St John's Chapel. Isaac opened the field gate and sent his collie to round up the lambs and drive them down the lane. He and Josie walked briskly after the flock, and they were joined by Jacob at the main road.

When they approached the mart, Tommy had been looking out for them and was ready to steer the lambs towards the pens. Josie was relieved when her lambs were fastened up securely. Getting them to the sale had gone more smoothly than she thought possible.

Josie watched farmers and butchers milling around the pens, checking the stock, and then the auctioneer's voice rang out clearly as he started with the first lot of the day.

By the end of the sale, Josie had a massive grin on her face.

'Well done,' said Tom. 'You got a good price for your lambs.'

'Aye, I'm happy with it. I didn't get as much as you, though.'

'But it's just your first year. I told you it was worth entering the show. If you do well in the show, there'll always be plenty of buyers at the sales.'

'I know, and you were right,' she said. 'And thank you, I need all the help I can get.'

'You're doing alright, love.'

Chapter 27

Josie removed the warming pan from her bed, turned off the oil lamp and climbed into bed. She'd had a hard day, and within minutes of her head touching the pillow, she was drifting into a deep sleep.

Startled by a loud screech and lots of flapping, Josie sat bolt upright in bed; her heart was pounding as she tried to see what had caused the commotion that had woken her. She couldn't see anything in the darkness, but it sounded very much like there was a hen in her bedroom. Pulling back the quilt, she got out of bed and lit the lamp, to see an extraordinary sight. There was a large pile of soot in the fireplace and on the hearth. Everything in the room was coated in fine black dust, and a soot-covered hen was wandering around clucking loudly, looking lost but unharmed. Luckily, the fire had died down before Josie had gone to bed that evening. All Josie could surmise was that the chicken had come into her room through the chimney, clearing the flue of soot as it fell.

Josie slipped on a gown and went to Nelly's room. Knocking gently at the door, she said, 'Nelly! Are you awake?'

Nelly opened the door, looking very sleepy.

'Come and see what's happened,' said Josie.

Josie led the way to her bedroom and opened the door.

'What on earth has been going on in here?' asked Nelly as she looked around the room. 'There's no way a hen could have come down the chimney, bringin' all that soot with it, all by itself. Anyway, I locked them up last night, and they were all in the hen house. I counted them to make sure.'

'That's what I thought. Someone must have dropped it down the chimney to frighten me, and I have a good idea who it was,' said Josie.

'You can't sleep in here tonight. Not with all this muck.'

'The other rooms haven't had fires on in them for ages. They're freezing cold. I suppose I could sleep on the sofa downstairs.'

'I don't mind you sharing with me if you want? I always shared a bed with me sisters before I came here, so I don't mind if you don't.'

Josie was looking at the state of her room.

'Do you have a better idea?' asked Nelly. 'At least my room is warm and clean.'

'Aye, you're right,' said Josie. 'I'm too tired to make a start on cleaning this mess up tonight.'

The next morning Josie and Nelly rose early. As soon as they'd eaten breakfast, they went to Josie's room. When they opened the door, they just looked at each other — neither of them had realised the scale of the task that they faced. There was not a single thing in the room that was free of soot. Firstly, Josie took the hen to the coop, and then carried the mats outside and beat them, while Nelly scrubbed the floorboards. Nelly washed the windows, lamps, mirrors and ornaments while Josie took her minerals into the study, to clean carefully another day, and then removed the bed linen and took down the curtains and replaced them with clean ones before cleaning and polishing the furniture.

It was nightfall before they finished, and they sat by the fire in the kitchen to eat their supper.

'Are you going to tell PC Emerson?' asked Nelly.

'It could just have been bairns playing a prank.'

'I don't think so, miss. The roof's high on this house. I wouldn't want to climb up there in the dark with me hands empty, never mind carrying a hen.'

Josie knew that John Peart was responsible and she wasn't sure whether or not to tell the policeman. He'd gone to see John after the incident at the mart, and that hadn't helped. In fact, it may have incited him further. For now, she decided, she would let things lie.

A couple of days later, Jacob knocked at the back door of the farmhouse and opened the door.

'Morning, Josie,' he said.

'Good morning, Jacob. Is everything alright?'

'No, not really. It's the cows. They're not producing as much milk as they should. It's too early for them to be drying up.'

'Do they look well?' asked Josie.

'As far as I can see. There's only one thing I've noticed that's a bit odd. The cows are spending more time than usual at the water trough when we're bringing them in for milking.'

'So, they must be thirsty,' reasoned Josie. 'Where do they normally get their water?'

'There's a stream that runs through the pasture,' said Jacob. 'There should be plenty of water up there. It's rained quite a bit lately, but I'll go up an' check.'

'Yes, please. And let me know if you work out what's wrong.'

'Aye, I will.'

Later that day, Jacob and Isaac both came to the house.

'I've come with Jacob,' said Isaac, ''cos I don't trust him to tell you what's happened without him swearin' a bit, and I can't guarantee that I won't either.'

'What is it?' asked Josie fearfully.

'The stream at the top of the pasture has been dammed. There's no water running through it. Those cows could have been up there for days without any water. No wonder the poor beasts have been desperate for a drink when Jacob's brought them down for milking.'

'Why has it been dammed?' asked Josie. 'Has it been diverted onto someone else's land?'

'It's been diverted into an old mine shaft,' said Jacob. 'What a bloody waste of water!'

'I don't know who would do such a stupid thing,' said Isaac, shaking his head.

Nelly had been sitting quietly by the fire, mending clothes, listening to the conversation, and she said, 'Josie, did you tell them about the hen the other night?'

'What about the hen?' Isaac asked, looking directly at Josie.

When she told them what had happened in her bedroom, Isaac said, 'Why didn't you tell us, lass?'

'If John Peart is behind this, I'll do for him,' said Jacob, through gritted teeth,

'What we all need to do is keep an eye out,' said Isaac. 'Watch for anything out of the ordinary. To drop a hen down the chimney, somebody must have been hanging around waiting for you to go to bed. They had to put a ladder against the side of the house and then climb up onto the roof without being seen. To dam the stream and divert the water must have taken a while an' all. They must have been up there the best part of an hour. If you see anyone on this land, tell me.'

Turning to Josie, he asked, 'Have you told Tom about what's going on?'

'No.'

'You should,' said Isaac forcefully. 'He can let the rest

of The Felons know, and they'll keep a watch out an' all. That's what they're there for — to catch and prosecute people who do this kind of thing.'

'Aye, I know.'

'What about PC Emerson?'

'No, I've not mentioned it to him either.'

'Josie, this is getting serious,' said Isaac. 'He needs to know. I'll go and talk to him on me way home.'

'Thank you.'

Chapter 28

Springbank Farm
December 1896

Through the window, Josie watched large snowflakes
float slowly down to the icy ground. She wondered at the
beauty of the countryside in winter, and at the serenity of
the scene before her. It had been snowing for almost a
week now and, although she had a fear of winter storms,
she was prepared for the season ahead. There was food
in the cupboards, fuel in the stores, and all of her animals
had shelter.

Nelly knocked at the door and entered the parlour
carrying a hot cup of cocoa, which she placed on the table
beside Josie.

'Would you like anything else, miss?' she asked. 'I
made some oat biscuits this morning and a ginger cake.'

'No, thank you. I'm not very hungry.'

Josie noticed the frown on Nelly's face as the girl left
the room, and decided that she must try some of her
baking at lunchtime; Nelly tried so hard to please her.

Josie thought back to baking days at High House Farm where there'd always been plenty of hungry mouths waiting for food to come out of the oven. Often it had disappeared before it had even cooled; she missed her brothers.

Her mother came to the back door and removed her snow-covered cloak and hung it on a hook behind the door.

'It's cold out there today,' she said.

'Sit down, and I'll get you some tea. Unless you'd prefer cocoa?'

'A mug of cocoa would be lovely.'

Josie poured some milk into a pan and set it on the stove. 'I didn't expect to see you today,' she said.

'I wanted to ask you something. I've discussed this with Tom, and we'd both like you to come home for Christmas Day. Nelly will want to spend the day with her family, and we don't want you here by yourself. And the boys would love to see you.'

Josie hadn't given Christmas much thought with everything that had been going on recently. Nelly hadn't mentioned that she wanted to go home, but Josie was sure that her mother would be right. The twins would come to do the milking in the morning and the evening but were free to spend the rest of the day with their families. And she didn't want to be at the farm alone, not with everything that had happened recently.

'Thanks, I'd love to come over.'

After a warm drink, Mary donned her cloak and went back out into the wintry weather.

With little else to do, Josie's thoughts turned to Elliott, as they often did, and she decided that she would put pen to paper.

19th December 1896
High House Farm
Dearest Elliott

I hope that you are well and that you have overcome the problems in your mine by now.

I wanted to let you know that there was an earthquake in England on 17th December. It was stronger in the middle of the country, but we felt it here too. I have never experienced anything like it before. It happened early in the morning when most people were in their beds. I was woken by the jug rattling in the bowl on my dressing table. A mine near Cowshill had a rockfall as a result, but thankfully nobody was working at the time.

I hope Missouri does not suffer from earthquakes, although I suspect it does. I worry about you being in a strange place, where there are many dangers. I fear for your safety. Please be careful. I look forward to a time when you can come back to England, even it is only for a visit. It would be so good to see you again.

We have snow here now but it's not as bad as it often is. My family send season's greetings and

their good wishes for the coming year as do I.
Your dearest friend
Josie Milburn

Josie thoroughly enjoyed spending Christmas Day with her family at High House Farm. She left just before dark so that she could see her way home without a lantern. When she walked into the yard, the twins had finished milking and were taking the cows back to the pasture. Looking at the gateway, she couldn't see why it had caught her attention, and then she realised what was wrong. The gate was missing.

She waited until Isaac and Jacob came back down and said, 'What happened to the gate?'

'Good question,' said Isaac. 'It was there this morning, but it had gone by the time we came back this afternoon.'

'Aye,' said Jacob, shaking his head. 'It's not the only one that's missing either. There's a couple more gone too. The cows got into the meadow and have churned it all up. It's turned to mud down at the bottom.'

'Do you think someone stole the gates?' asked Josie.

'Aye, they've definitely been stolen,' said Isaac angrily. 'And they've taken the ones that'll cause us the most nuisance.'

'What can we do about it?'

'We'll hang a bit of rope across the gateways tonight – that'll keep the cows in — and tomorrow we'll have to start making some new gates.'

'Would you mind telling PC Emerson about this on your way home?' asked Josie.

'Aye, we will,' the twins said together.

'Thanks,' she said, and she then went inside where Nelly greeted her. While Nelly told her all about the homemade gifts that each of her brothers and sisters had received for Christmas, Josie worried about the pranks that somebody was playing on her, if they could be called pranks. That someone would go to such lengths to upset her on Christmas Day was disturbing. The cost of replacing hens and buying timber for the gates, the reduction in milk yield, and the time spent repairing watercourses and cleaning her bedroom were both costly and annoying. It had gone well beyond a joke, and she'd had enough of it.

Tom Milburn and PC Emerson met at Springbank Farm the following evening and hid in the shadows in the farmyard. It was a cold night, and after they'd been out for about an hour, Josie took out a mug of hot cocoa for each of them. While she was outside, a dog in the kennels barked.

'Go back inside, love,' whispered Tom.

'No,' she replied, 'if there's somebody about, I want to see who it is.'

'You're as stubborn as your mother.'

'She says I'm as stubborn as you!'

'Shush,' said PC Emerson. 'He'll not come near if he

hears us.'

Reprimanded, they stood in silence. The dog barked again; this time followed by a threatening growl. Josie listened intently for the slightest sound. A movement near the stable caught her eye, and she nudged Tom's arm and pointed in that direction. All three of them watched as a figure slunk into the stable. A horse whinnied. They all crept towards the building, blocking the doorway, and Tom lit a lantern.

Standing beside a side-saddle with a knife in his hand was John Peart, his eyes wide and his face ashen.

'Now, what do we have here?' said PC Emerson. 'Put the knife down.'

For a split second, John's eyes looked past them, and he gripped the knife in his hand. Josie could see that he was tempted to make a run for it, and brandishing a knife he might well have made it, but what good would that have done him. They'd seen who he was and what he'd been about to do. Sabotaging the girth on her saddle could have had disastrous consequences.

John threw the knife to the floor, cursing to himself, and then he held out his hands for the policeman to handcuff him. He'd been caught red-handed.

'I'll lock him up for tonight and take him down to the station in the morning,' said PC Emerson.

'Thanks, Robert,' said Tom.

PC Emerson took John Peart out of the stable, and as they passed Josie, John sneered at her, 'You'll not get away with this, you little bastard.'

Tom stood in front of John, and said, 'You ever do anything to our Josie again, I'll not bother to get the police involved next time. You think about that.'

Jacob moved forward and punched John in the face. Stepping back, he growled, 'And that's for what you did to me cows.'

'Did you see what he did?' John asked the policeman.

'I never saw a thing,' replied PC Emerson, as he led him away.

To Josie, Tom said, 'Now that we've got him, you don't need to worry anymore. Go back inside where it's warm, love. I'll go with Robert in case he needs a hand.'

Once she was back inside the house, Josie wished that Nelly had still been up to talk to, but she'd already gone to bed. She sat by the fire and stared into the flames.

Her mind was too active to sleep yet, so she picked up a copy of 'The Mineral Collector' magazine, to which she'd subscribed after the show, and flicked through the pages. A photograph of a distinguished-looking gentleman caught her eye, and she read the article that accompanied it:

> *'It is with great sadness that we announce the death of our notable founder, director, friend, geologist and distinguished mineral collector, Mr George Wiseman, who died at his home in New York at the age of 81 years. Mr Wiseman's collection of mineral specimens from around the*

world, many of which have been featured in this publication, is exceptional in its range and quality, far surpassing even those held by the most esteemed museums.

An auction of Mr Wiseman's collection will be held at the Grand Central Hotel, New York on Tuesday, June 22nd, 1897. This sale will offer a unique opportunity to purchase some rare and magnificent minerals, and it is expected to attract interest from collectors across the country and abroad.'

Josie lifted her head and stared into the flames once more, deep in thought. The advert had planted a seed in her mind, and by the next morning, it had grown into a fully formed question. Could she, Josie Milburn, a farm girl who'd always desired to see more of the world, go to a sale of minerals in New York?

Chapter 29

Now Josie understood what Elliott had meant when he'd said how good it felt to be on dry land after journeying across the Atlantic. The constant motion of the ship had not agreed with her, and for over a week it had unsettled her stomach and made her head hurt, but now that her feet were back on *terra firma*, she felt much better. The breeze coming off the ocean was refreshing, and as her head cleared, she was excited to be in a foreign country. She was standing on American soil.

Nelly stood by her side, holding a leather bag, her eyes wide as she took in the scene at the bustling harbour.

While Josie waited for her trunk, she watched people going about their daily work; men loading and offloading cargo in the docks. Passengers ready to embark clutched their tickets in their hands as they looked for their ship; those who had disembarked wondered where they should go. Some went to small boats that waited to take them across the bay, and others headed towards a long line of hansom cabs parked on the roadside.

She noticed several groups of people hugging, kissing and crying — friends and families parted and reunited — and for the first time since she'd left Weardale, she felt a whisper of isolation. But of course, that was her own doing; any one of her family would have accompanied her on the trip but, as always, she'd wanted to be independent and told them that she was perfectly capable of travelling to America alone. It had been her mother who'd insisted that Nelly accompany her, drumming into her that a lady never travelled without a maid.

She heard a deep voice shout, 'Miss Milburn. Miss Josephine Milburn.' A large man was standing over her trunk, and she went to him.

'I'm Josie Milburn.'

'I have your luggage here, ma'am.'

'Thank you,' she said. 'I'm staying in Manhattan. What's the best way to get there?'

'One of these boats will take you over, and then you'll need a cab to drive you to your hotel. Is it just the two of you?' he asked, nodding towards Nelly.

'Yes.'

'I'll carry your trunk for you, ma'am.'

Nobody had called Josie ma'am before, and the title made her feel older than her twenty-three years.

'Thank you,' she said. 'That's very kind.'

She was grateful for the porter's assistance. The trunk

was heavy and cumbersome, and even with Nelly's help, she would have struggled to carry it. When they reached one of the small boats moored in the harbour, the man hailed the captain, booked their fare and lifted the trunk on board. Josie thanked him and offered him a generous tip, which he accepted with a grin.

'Thank you, ma'am. Have a good day!' he said, before climbing out of the boat. She was grateful to her fellow passengers for telling her about the habit of tipping when she'd crossed the ocean, otherwise, she would have inadvertently offended many Americans during her visit.

After her long voyage, Josie was reluctant to step straight onto another boat, but she knew it wouldn't take long for them to reach Manhattan. She could see it in the distance. Nelly sat by her side, smiling, not seeming to mind being back on the water; in fact, she looked as though she was enjoying the whole experience.

Josie looked out over the bay, dominated by The Statue of Liberty. She was amazed by its size. She noticed the smell of fire, a smell that she would never forget, and her eyes scoured the coast for the source. They settled on a nearby island covered in charred wood, wisps of smoke showing that parts still smouldered. From that distance, it looked like the place was crawling with ants.

'What happened over there?' Josie asked one of the sailors, pointing at the island.

'That's Ellis Island, ma'am. The whole place burnt down a couple of days back. They've already started to rebuild it, and the ashes aren't even cold yet!'

Josie recognised the name, Ellis Island. It was often mentioned in the papers because it was where the immigrant ships docked.

The boat trip passed quickly, and it wasn't long before she disembarked at the other side of the bay — onto Manhattan Island.

A cab driver rushed towards her and said, 'Where to, ma'am?'

'The Hotel New Netherland, please.'

'Luggage?'

'I have a trunk. Would you mind helping me with it?'

'Not at all, ma'am.'

He recovered her luggage and carried it to his hansom cab that stood at the roadside, and he opened the door for her and Nelly to climb in.

Josie found the journey through the city fascinating. There were so many buildings; some spread out over areas as large as paddocks and others that looked almost as tall as the hills back home. There were so many people, so many shops and so many carriages. She'd never seen anything like it. The racket from the busy streets was unimaginable, and Josie wished she could shut out the noise.

The cab pulled up outside the hotel on Fifth Avenue. The driver opened the door and offered her a hand to help her out. Josie gave him a tip, and he looked very pleased with it.

A smartly dressed concierge came out of the hotel to greet her, and he quickly ushered her inside. They were followed by a porter who carried her trunk, and Nelly who had been very quiet since they'd arrived in Manhattan, taking in the new sights and sounds.

The hotel foyer was a large room with a high ceiling. It was elaborately decorated and immaculately clean. Josie checked in at the reception, and the porter showed her to her suite. He placed the trunk by the wardrobe and handed her the room key. She tipped him and then he left her and Nelly alone.

The suite was beautifully decorated with polished furniture, velvet curtains, delicate linens and fresh flowers. It comprised a sitting room, the master bedroom, a bathroom, a dressing room and a servant's room. Nelly said, 'It's grand, isn't it?'

'Yes, it certainly is,' replied Josie as she crossed the room to look out of the window. 'Nelly! Look at this.'

Nelly ran over to her, and they looked out across a vast expanse of mature trees — Central Park. The entrance road that they could see from their room teemed with horses and carriages, with dozens of people on foot at the edges.

Nelly laughed. 'It looks like a bee-hive! All those people buzzing about like busy little bees.'

To Josie, it reminded her of a show day in Weardale, when everyone came together, but she guessed that it would be bustling like this every day in New York.

By the time they'd unpacked, it was early evening. Josie had been invited to eat downstairs in the hotel dining room, and she wanted to look presentable on her first evening in the city, so she donned an evening dress and asked Nelly to help fix her hair. She felt regret at leaving Nelly alone to eat in the room, but Nelly assured her that she preferred it that way.

Josie and Nelly spent the next two days exploring the city. They walked for miles in Central Park, along pedestrian pathways through woodland, where they discovered a waterfall with a bronze statue of an angel next to a lake on which they took a boat ride. They browsed the fine shops in Manhattan in search of new clothes and gifts. Josie bought several new dresses, some hats and a beautiful pair of shoes with high heels. She'd laughed as she thought about how impractical they would be back home on the farm, where she always wore boots, but they were perfect for evenings in New York. Nelly treated herself to a new bonnet, which she wore with pride, and bought sweets to take home for her brothers and sisters.

Josie had been eager for the day of the mineral auction to arrive, and now that it had, she could hardly believe it. Up at the crack of dawn, she ate an early breakfast and then went to Nelly's room to wake her, but found the girl sitting on the floor next to a bowl, her bed strewn with empty sweet cartons.

'Oh, Nelly! Did you eat them all?'

Nelly nodded her head and groaned. 'My belly hurts. I think I'm going to be sick.'

'But it's the auction today!' Josie exclaimed.

'Sorry, miss. I can't go,' said Nelly, lifting the bowl and setting it on her lap.

'Will you be alright here if I go?'

'Yes,' said Nelly, looking very embarrassed. 'You've travelled halfway around the world for this sale. You can't miss it 'cos of me.'

After Josie dressed, she went to the foyer and asked the concierge to secure her a cab, and she was thankful when he returned almost immediately to accompany her outside. She couldn't wait to get to the auction and see the magnificent collection for herself. Her catalogue was dog-eared because she'd read the item descriptions so many times, imagining the beautiful pieces depicted in it, but that was not the same thing as seeing the specimens themselves.

The horse-drawn cab took her to the Grand Central Hotel where the auction was to be held at ten-thirty. It was just a few minutes after nine o'clock when Josie arrived, so she had plenty of time to look around before the sale was due to start. As she wandered around the display tables, she was reminded of the mineral exhibition at St John's Chapel where she'd first met Elliott. It seemed such a long time ago. Then she had been a care-free young woman who dreamed of a fulfilling life, and now she was a woman of independent means; which meant she could do what she wanted and go where she wanted, and she had nobody to answer to. This life is exactly what she had craved back then — but was it what she'd imagined it to be?

Despite everything, she realised that she still wasn't content with her life. How ungrateful that would sound if she ever gave voice to it! She was very fortunate in so many ways, and if her mother had been there, she would have said, 'Count your blessings, lass!' and she'd have been right. Josie knew she had no right to want more from life.

If she had wanted to share her life with a man, she wondered who would be interested in her now that the circumstances of her birth were common knowledge. An image of Charles Chapman came fleetingly to mind and with it a sense of unease.

A stunning piece of fluorite caught Josie's eye, and she thought how silly she was to be thinking about her troubles when she'd travelled to New York for a very specific purpose. She needed to check the specimens that she intended to purchase before the auction began. The particular piece that had captured her attention was a spectacular shade of purple, and the crystals were perfectly formed — it had to be from Weardale. She picked up the specimen's label and read that it was from Boltsburn Mine in Weardale, Durham and that it had been collected in 1877. It was so remarkable that she had to have it. She found the listing in the catalogue and drew a circle around the lot number. The other minerals she wanted were good, very good, in fact, but this one was by far the best.

People gradually moved away from the displays and headed towards the rows of chairs to take a seat before the auction began. Josie sat near the front on a chair at the end of a row, from where she would have a clear view of the auctioneer. She glanced around the room to see if there was anyone she recognised and then smiled to herself at how foolish that was when she was so far from home.

A red-faced man with white hair and bushy beard stood at the front of the room, with a gavel in his hand. He spoke with a loud and clear voice which was unmistakably English.

'Good morning, Ladies and Gentlemen. Thank you all for coming to this wonderful hotel this morning. The late Mr Wiseman would have been delighted that there is so much interest in his extensive mineral collection, which was his life's work. He travelled around the globe, collecting the best specimens that countries had to offer to put together this world-class collection that you see before you today. Now, without any further ado, the sale will commence.'

He reached for his copy of the catalogue, cleared his throat, and started the sale with lot number one.

The first specimen Josie wanted was lot number

fifteen, so she sat back in her chair and listened to the auctioneer. She was relieved when he spoke much more clearly, and a lot slower, than the auctioneer at the cattle mart in St John's Chapel. Bids came in from all over the room, and the final selling prices were high. She wasn't surprised by this. These were the *crème de la crème* of minerals, and buyers were willing to pay a premium price to own them.

She won lots fifteen and twenty-four and now the piece of fluorite that she had loved was about to be auctioned — lot number thirty-one. She shifted in her seat and clutched the catalogue in her hand.

'Here we have an exceptional piece of fluorite from Boltsburn Mine in Durham, England,' said the auctioneer. 'Where shall we start the bidding? Ten dollars. Anyone?'

The crowd gasped. That was the highest opening bid so far, but no offers were forthcoming.

'Five, then? Anywhere? It has to be worth that. Thank you, sir, at the back of the room.'

Josie held up her catalogue and waved it to catch the auctioneer's attention.

'Six, ma'am?'

Josie nodded.

'Seven? Thank you. Seven I have. The bid is with the gentleman.'

Josie held up the catalogue again, and said, 'Ten dollars.'

'Thank you! The lady at the front has the bid at ten dollars. Do we have any more?'

The auctioneer surveyed the crowd like a bird of prey, looking for the slightest movement in the room. And then his eyes widened, and he stood up straight, as he said, 'Twelve. Thank you! The bid is now with the gentleman at the back of the room and stands at twelve dollars.'

This was more than any of the other minerals had sold for and it was more than Josie had expected to pay. She looked around to see who was bidding against her and her heart skipped a beat. A young man wearing a dark, tailored suit stood in the doorway, the most handsome man that Josie had ever seen, and although his hair was longer and his skin tanned, she knew at once that he was Elliott Dawson.

His eyes met hers, and it was like time slowed down. He'd recognised her too and was staring at her, and then his face broke into a huge smile.

The auctioneer's voice droned on in the background, 'Ma'am, would you like to place another bid?'

The room was silent.

'Ma'am, are you alright?'

She turned back to the auctioneer. 'I'm sorry. No, I don't want to place another bid. Thank you.'

'Alright. Sold! This lot goes to the gentleman at the back of the room for twelve dollars. Your name, sir?'

'Elliott Dawson,' he said clearly.

'Thank you, Mr Dawson. Now, we move on to lot

number thirty-two, a superb example of azurite from Mexico....'

Josie stood up, and as she turned to walk to the back of the hall, she saw Elliott coming towards her. People in the room were watching them. As they met, Elliott reached for her hand and kissed it, looking deeply into her eyes.

'Josie...'

'Let's get out of here,' she suggested, suddenly feeling far too warm.

He placed his hand on the small of her back and led her out of the room, towards a sofa in the hotel foyer. He motioned for her to sit, which she did, and then he sat down next to her.

'Josie, what on earth are you doing in New York?' he asked, looking bewildered.

'The same as you, I expect,' she said, smiling. 'I'm here to buy minerals.'

'But how did you get here? Is there anyone with you?'

She noticed that he glanced down at her ring finger. He must think that I'm married, she thought.

'I'm not with anyone.'

'Really! You came to New York by yourself?'

She couldn't tell him that she had a maid. He would ask questions that she wasn't prepared to answer.

'I came with a friend,' she replied. Seeing his face harden, she quickly added, 'A female friend. She's not well today, so she stayed at the hotel.'

'I see.' His face softened, and he smiled the cheeky smile that Josie remembered so well from the early days that they'd spent together in Weardale. Her heart melted. 'I can't believe you're here,' he said.

'It's so good to see you again,' she said sincerely.

'Likewise! Would you like something to drink?'

'Do they have tea?'

'I'm sure they could make some.'

While Elliott went to order the tea, Josie wondered how she could explain her trip to America to attend a sale of minerals. She couldn't tell him the full story because she was afraid that he'd turn his back on her — and she couldn't face that again. She'd been heartbroken when he'd left her in England.

Elliott returned and said, 'They'll bring it over.'

'Thank you. That's one thing I've missed since I got here — a good cup of tea.'

'I didn't say it would be a good cup —'

They laughed.

'By the way,' he said, 'I intended to buy that piece of fluorite for you — as a gift. I was going to give it to you when I came home —'

At the mention of home, Josie could see that his eyes glazed over and she realised that the horror of the fire was still with him and that it would probably always be with him.

'I didn't think I'd be able to give it to you so soon.'

'Thank you,' she said. 'It's the best piece I've ever seen.'

'My father collected it. He sold it to a dealer for good money. I didn't know it was going to be in the sale today, but I would have recognised it anywhere.'

A maid brought over a tray and placed it on the table in front of them.

'Would you like me to pour, ma'am?'

'No, thank you. We can manage.'

Elliott took a coin from his pocket and handed it to the girl. She smiled and thanked him before leaving. Josie poured the tea into two china cups.

'So, how come you're here? I mean, it's expensive to travel,' asked Elliott.

That was the question that Josie had been dreading. She cleared her throat and said, 'I saw the auction advertised in a magazine, and I decided I'd like to go to it. Uncle Joe left me a bit of money when he died.'

'You haven't changed a bit,' Elliott laughed. 'You always knew what you wanted.'

She was relieved that he didn't ask about Joe's legacy, and she quickly changed the subject to divert his attention.

'So, how are your mines doing now?' she asked.

'Great! Better than I could have hoped. They're making good money already, and I'm looking to buy another. I wish you could see them —'

When he leaned forward to reach for his cup and saucer, his watch-chain came loose and hung down from his waistcoat. There it was. The fractured crystal. The other half of the whole. Elliott's crystal was mounted in gold and fitted to his watch strap, and he wore it close to his heart. She reached out and took hold of it, and as she did so, he closed his hand over hers and said, 'Can I take you to dinner tonight?'

Her heart somersaulted. Inwardly, she was thrilled that Elliott wanted to take her out. She waited until she thought her voice would sound normal before saying, 'That would be lovely, thank you. I'm staying at the Hotel New Netherland.'

'I'll be there at seven o'clock.'

He released her hand, and they supped their tea before going back into the auction room.

When Josie returned to her hotel suite that afternoon, she laid out on the dressing table the minerals that she'd purchased. They were stunning. She had taken the purple fluorite specimen at Elliott's insistence — she'd seen how much it meant to him and was touched that he wanted her to have it. It was the best piece that she'd ever seen and she would treasure it.

'Oh! You're back,' said Nelly, coming out of her room.

'Yes,' said Josie dreamily.

'Are you alright, miss?'

'Yes, I couldn't be better. How's your stomach?'

'If you mean, do I still have a bellyache, no, it's better now.'

'That's good. I'm going to take a bath, and then I'd like

you to help me dress. I'm going out for dinner tonight.'

'You're going out? In New York?'

'Don't look so shocked. I bumped into somebody I know from back home, and he'll be with me.'

After her bath, Josie stood in front of her wardrobe, wondering what would be appropriate to wear for dinner in New York. Picking out a green silk dress that she'd bought on her first shopping trip, she held it up against her — the colour complemented her eyes and her hair. She quickly put it on, followed by her new shoes. Nelly brushed her hair and tied it up neatly at the back of her head and curled the hair at the front, copying the hairstyle worn by fashionable ladies in the city.

Josie looked at her reflection in the mirror. Something was missing. For the finishing touch, she found her crystal pendant and swapped the gold chain for a ribbon in the same colour silk as her dress. As she tied it around her throat, Nelly stood back and stared at her. She said, 'You look like a princess.'

'Thank you,' said Josie, still looking in the mirror. She wouldn't go as far as a princess, but the woman looking back at her was hardly recognisable as the farm girl from Weardale.

At seven o'clock, Josie left her room to meet Elliott. He was waiting in the hotel foyer, and as she descended the staircase, his eyes followed her until she stood next to him. His eyes drifted up from the crystal to meet hers. He swallowed before saying, 'You look incredible!'

'Thank you,' she smiled. 'You look very smart too.'

Elliott was wearing a black evening suit and bow tie. His dark hair was shining, and his freshly-shaven face seemed to highlight his strong, angular jaw. She'd never seen him looking so attractive.

'Are you ready?' he asked.

'Yes, where are we going?'

'I reserved a table at The Waldorf.'

'Oh! I walked past it yesterday. It's a beautiful hotel.'

She took the arm he offered, and they went outside. Elliott hailed a cab.

When they arrived at The Waldorf, they were shown to their table by an immaculately dressed French waiter. As Elliott ordered their food and wine, Josie sat back and soaked up the atmosphere. The large room contained about thirty or forty tables that were comfortably spaced to give a certain amount of privacy to the guests, despite it being a public dining area. On each table stood a vase of fresh flowers. Around the room, there were wide columns and high-arched doorways draped with velvet, and the ornate ceiling with low-hanging candelabra was magnificent. A string quartet played in the corner of the room, adding to the relaxed, romantic mood.

'It's rather grand here, isn't it?' said Elliott.

'It's about as far away from Weardale as you could imagine.'

'That's true. But Weardale has its charms too.'

'Do you miss it?' she asked.

'Yes, sometimes.' He paused and then looked at her and said, 'I've missed you.'

'I've missed you too, Elliott. There's not a day gone by that I haven't thought of you.'

Why had she said that? She shouldn't be encouraging whatever it was that was happening here. Elliott was a handsome, self-made man. He wouldn't want her once he found out that she wasn't who he thought she was, that she was the love child of her mother and Joe Milburn.

She noticed that he was watching her intently, trying to work out what she was thinking, perhaps? She couldn't tell him what was on her mind, so she cleverly diverted the conversation away from home.

'Tell me more about Missouri.'

He got a faraway look in his eyes as he described Flat River, the small town where he lived, and the people he worked with, and the intricacies of the mineral veins that ran through his mines. She loved listening to him. He'd changed since he left Weardale. Not just his hair, or his tan, or his clothes. He was more confident.

After the waiter took away their plates, Elliott asked, 'How long are you staying in New York?'

'I haven't bought a ticket home yet, but there's a ship sailing this weekend.'

'You came all this way and didn't book a ticket home. Josie, only you would do that!' he laughed, and then his face straightened. 'Do you have to go back this weekend?

Could you stay longer?' he asked seriously.

'Why do you ask?'

'I was just thinking. Would you like to come to Missouri with me and see the place for yourself? I would love to show you around.'

'I — I don't know.'

'Don't worry about the cost. I'll buy your rail tickets and pay for a hotel room. Or you could stay at my place if you wanted?'

She thought it was sweet that he believed her hesitation was because she was concerned about the cost. If only he knew! What she was worried about was spending so much time with him travelling and at his new home, and then afterwards, having to leave him. Parting from him again would be impossible.

'What about my — my friend?' she asked. 'I couldn't leave her alone in the city.'

'She could come too.' He smiled his boyish smile.

Josie couldn't resist any longer. 'Yes, I'd love to see your mines.'

'That's great! Perhaps we could leave tomorrow?'

'Alright, tomorrow it is.'

'You should write home and tell your parents that you're staying longer. They'll be worried if you don't get back when they expect you to.'

'Yes, I will. They'll be so surprised to hear that I've met you in New York.'

After she'd agreed to go to Missouri, Josie wasn't sure

she'd made the right decision. The more time she spent with Elliott now would just make their final parting harder to bear. But she wanted to spend more time with him so much.

It was dark when they left the restaurant.

'Shall I stop a cab?' asked Elliott.

'No, we should walk. It's such a lovely evening.'

Josie took Elliott's arm, and they strolled back to Fifth Avenue, admiring the city at night. When they reached the hotel steps, Elliott moved towards her so that they were almost touching. She could feel the heat from his body.

'Goodnight, Josie. I'll see you tomorrow.'

Moving his hand slowly up her arm, he kissed her gently on her lips, and then whispered in her ear, 'Sleep well, my love.'

'Goodnight, Elliott,' she said, turning to go inside.

As she climbed the stairs to her room, she wondered how on earth she was supposed to sleep well when she couldn't get the image of Elliott out of her mind. He had reawakened all of her senses; she could still smell his masculine scent and feel his touch on her skin.

That night, Josie tossed and turned in bed. She'd had a wonderful evening, and she'd loved being in Elliott's company again. They'd talked like they had in the old days, the days before the fire, and she'd enjoyed every minute of it.

Chapter 30

New York City
June 1897

The next morning, Elliott ate breakfast at his hotel. He hadn't slept well, but he wasn't tired, he was excited. Since coming to America, he'd done well for himself. His knowledge of geology and mining had been the key to his success, and he was thankful to his late father for that.

He'd been so busy lately that he couldn't remember when he'd last written to Josie, but seeing her again yesterday had made him realise just how much he'd missed her, and what was missing from his life. The evening they'd spent together had reminded him of the strong feelings that they'd had for one another and the good times that they'd shared, and the promise that he'd made. He was ready to move on to the next stage in his life.

After breakfast, he made his way to Union Square and quickly found the shop he was looking for — Tiffanys. He entered the shop and was amazed by the beautiful jewellery on display.

An elderly gentleman approached him, and said, 'Good morning, sir. May I help you?'

'Good morning! Yes, I'm looking for a ring. A special ring.'

'Over here, sir. We have a wonderful selection of rings to choose from.'

The man led the way to a glass cabinet, which housed hundreds of gold rings, some plain bands and some set with gemstones. Elliott looked into the case. One particular ring stood out from the rest, a glistening diamond solitaire. He thought it would be perfect and he bought it.

Then, he walked to Fifth Avenue and entered the foyer of The Hotel New Netherland. A plump man was sitting behind the reception desk reading a newspaper, and he jumped to his feet when Elliott spoke.

'Good morning. I'm here to meet Miss Josephine Milburn. Could you let her know I've arrived?'

'Are you Mr Dawson?'

'Yes.'

'I'm sorry, sir. Miss Milburn checked out this morning. She left this for you,' he said as he handed Elliott the letter.

Elliott had a sinking feeling in his stomach. He ripped open the envelope and read Josie's words.

23rd June 1897
New York City

My Dearest Elliott

It was so good to see you again yesterday.

I'm sorry to leave without saying goodbye. I would have dearly loved to visit your new home and your mines, but I think it is for the best that I return to England.

I wish you all the very best for your future and I hope your business is a great success.

Your dear friend

Josie Milburn

'Do you know where she went?' pleaded Elliott.

'I'm sorry, sir. She didn't leave a forwarding address.'

Elliott ran out into the road and stopped suddenly, looking both ways. He didn't know where to begin to look for her. She'd said that there wasn't a ship sailing until the weekend so she must have checked into another hotel — to avoid seeing him! That thought hurt him deeply. He couldn't understand why she'd do that. Had he said something wrong? Or done something to upset her? Why had she agreed to go to Flat River with him one day and then changed her mind the next? Perhaps he should have made his intentions clear the night before, and proposed to her at the restaurant or on the walk back to her hotel.

A hansom cab went past, almost colliding with him. The driver shouted, 'Get off the road, you idiot! D'you wanna get killed?'

Elliott shrugged his shoulders. There was absolutely nothing he could do, so he wandered back to his hotel to collect his luggage. He checked out and then went directly to Grand Central Depot, where he bought a single ticket; he would be returning to Flat River alone.

On the train journey back to Missouri, Elliott's thoughts were in turmoil. He didn't understand why Josie had done what she had. Thinking back to the sale, he recalled his initial surprise at seeing her there, which had quickly been replaced by joy. The evening they'd spent together had been unbelievable. She'd looked beautiful — and she'd worn her half of their crystal around her neck. Damn it! That had to mean something. He'd been so thrilled when she'd agreed to visit his house and his mines. So, what had happened? Why had she run away from him?

After hours of deliberation, the only explanation that made sense to him was that she'd met somebody else in England and that she'd decided to return to him. Or perhaps the friend that she'd mentioned who had come to New York with her was her suitor, or fiancé, or even her husband. Whatever the reason, it didn't matter anymore. Her note and her sudden disappearance left no doubt whatsoever in his mind that she was no longer interested in him. She had wished him all the best for his future — his future in which she would play no part.

He dropped off to sleep several times on the rail journey, but each time he was woken by the same nightmare that had haunted him since the fire. The pitying looks from the other passengers told him that he'd been talking or crying out in his sleep.

When Elliott reached Flat River, he got off the train, dumped his bags at his house, and then went straight to his mine. He needed a distraction. As he wielded a pick-axe against the vein material, he decided that he'd had enough of women. He'd found his first love cheating on him. Over the years there'd been a few lasses that had almost thrown themselves at him, but he hadn't been interested in any of them. And then Josie Milburn had walked into his life. He had loved her wholeheartedly, and now she too had spurned him. Well, that was it. He was done with women. From now on, he would concentrate on his business. Mining would be his life.

'Elliott, is that you down there?' John Wilkinson's voice echoed through the mine.

'Aye, John. It's me.'

A few moments later, John joined him at the rock face and asked, 'When did you get back?'

'About an hour ago,' said Elliott, putting down the pick-axe and wiping the sweat off his brow.

'Was it worth the trip? Did you get anything in the sale?'

'It was alright, I suppose. I got a nice bit of spar that my father took out of Boltsburn,' said Elliott, his eyes lighting up at the thought of it. 'It was better than I remembered.'

'Good!'

'You'll never guess who I saw there.'

'Who?'

'Josie Milburn. The lass I was staying with before I came over here.'

'Really! The Josie that you named the vein after?'

'Aye,' said Elliott sadly.

'So why the long face?'

'Hmm, it didn't go well.'

'Sorry to hear that,' said John. After a moment's silence, he added, 'I hear she's done very well for herself.'

Elliott looked puzzled for a second, and then said, 'Oh! You mean the bit of money her uncle left her? She spent that on her trip to New York.'

'Bit of money!' John's laughter filled the mine.

'What's so funny?' asked Elliott.

'She didn't tell you, did she?'

'Tell me what?'

'While you were away, I got a letter from home. Me brother said everyone in the dale was talking about your Josie Milburn. Apparently, Joe Milburn left her everything when he died! There's all sorts of gossip goin' on about that!' John raised his eyebrows. 'But for whatever reason, there's no disputin' that she's a very rich woman. Anyway, I just popped in to make sure that it was you down here. I'm off to the pub. Fancy a pint?'

'No, thanks. I'm going to carry on here for a bit longer.'

'No bother,' said John. 'See you tomorrow.'

Elliott sat down on the floor of the mine and put his head in his hands. He'd read Josie's letters over and over again, and he'd noticed that she'd become distant around the time her uncle died, and he'd wondered if she'd been keeping something from him. But in New York, she'd seemed to be her usual self. So why hadn't she told him the truth about the money? And why had Joe left it to her? Having seen Joe and Josie together, he'd noticed Joe's eyes follow her around. Had he taken a fancy to his niece? Had he acted on it? It was almost two years since Elliott had left her in Weardale, and she was what now — nearly twenty-four? Most women were wed well before the age of twenty-four. Had he kept her waiting for too long?

He sat there on the floor of the mine until his candle burned down, trying to work out what was going on with Josie, and kicking himself for spending so long thinking about her when only hours earlier he'd resolved to forget all about her.

Chapter 31

Springbank Farm
July 1897

A young girl stood at the kitchen door, her hair matted and her clothes dirty. She sneezed, and then wiped her snotty nose on her sleeve.

'Miss,' she said in a croaky voice. 'I've come for our Nelly.'

Nelly was washing the breakfast dishes in the kitchen and, when she heard her sister's voice, she ran to the door.

'Amy! What's wrong?'

'Everybody's poorly. You've got to come home and look after us.'

Nelly looked at Josie.

'If they need you at home, you'd better go,' said Josie.

'But... will you manage here, miss?'

'I'll be fine. Don't worry about me.'

'Just a minute, Amy,' said Nelly, 'I'll go and get me things.'

While Nelly was upstairs, Josie asked the girl what was wrong with the family.

'I don't know,' replied Amy. 'Mother's in bed and won't get up. Our Billy, that's the baby, just cries all the time. The rest of the bairns have sore throats and a cough. I'm sorry, miss, I didn't know what else to do!'

'Has the doctor been to see them?'

'No, me father says he cannot afford the doctor. He's gone to work today, but I don't think he's well either.'

Nelly came back into the kitchen, carrying her small bundle of belongings.

'I'll come back as soon as I can,' she said to Josie.

'Don't worry about me. Your family need you more than I do. On your way home, call on Doctor Rutherford. Ask him to look in on them — and he's to send me the bill. Do you understand?'

'Thank you, miss. Thank you very much.'

Josie watched Nelly and her younger sister run down the farm track. She'd grown fond of Nelly, and she hoped that the doctor could help her family.

Feeling a little melancholy, Josie had a sudden urge to go outdoors. It was a beautiful day, and she decided that she would ride over to Rookhope. She asked Isaac to saddle Jet, and then she went into the garden to cut some beautiful pink roses.

Isaac met her in the yard and said, 'He should be good for you today. I've been exercising him every morning since he took off with you. He's much more settled now.'

'Thank you.'

Josie tied the flowers onto Jet's saddle and set off on her journey. Memories of the time she had spent with Elliott flooded her mind. When she passed the road leading to the ford at Westgate, she remembered the first day that she'd met him by the river — the first time he'd kissed her — and she smiled. As she climbed the steep bank out of Westgate, she thought about him hiding in the mines and coming to see her in the barn, and about lying on the moor with him that night looking up at the stars. Her skin tingled when she thought about his kisses and how he'd touched her. She longed for him still.

She followed the rail tracks up the Rookhope valley to Grove Rake mine, and she remembered that long afternoon she'd spent waiting for him and the fear she'd experienced when she overheard Tom and Joe talking about the police search for him. She rode down the road until she came to the place where Railway Cottages had stood. What little had been left of the houses had been demolished, and there was just a charred pile of stones and rubble in its place.

Continuing down the road, she reached the turning to Boltsburn and went to the mine entrance. All of this had started that day Elliott had taken her into the mine, the day the crystal had fractured. If that day had never happened, none of the dreadful things that had occurred afterwards would have happened either — Henderson's death, Elliott's arrest, the house fire, his mother's death, and Elliott's departure. It was all her fault for being selfish. If only she had listened to the age-old superstition. By going in that mine, she'd cursed them all, and she was so sorry for what she'd done. Tears rolled down her cheeks, and she wiped them away with her sleeve as she turned away.

There was one more place that she wanted to visit — the churchyard. She tethered Jet to the wrought iron gate and took the rose stems from his saddle. She walked over to where Mrs Dawson's body lay, being careful not to tread on the unmarked graves.

On Mrs Dawson's grave, there was a small posy of marigolds and they looked fresh. She wondered who could have left them there.

'I'm so very sorry, Mrs Dawson,' she said earnestly. 'It was my fault that you died. And I've lost Elliott because of what I did. That's a harsh punishment, but I deserve it, and I will have to live with it for the rest of my life.'

She placed the roses on the grassy mound and, with a tear in her eye, she returned to her horse and set off for home.

Elliott walked up the road to High House Farm, thinking that it hadn't changed at all; it was just as he remembered it. Tom and his sons were in the front field raking hay into pikes. Mary stood in front of the house, and she raised her hand to shield her eyes from the afternoon sun. She'd seen him. He heard her call out to Tom, who then looked in his direction and started walking down the field to meet him.

'Elliott! I thought it was you,' said Tom as he got closer to the gate.

'Aye, it's me. I'm back.'

'It's good to see you.' Tom shook his hand firmly. 'You're looking well. Very well. Come on up to the house.'

'Thank you.'

'You've chosen the right day to visit. It's baking day!' Tom laughed.

As they walked to the farmhouse, Elliott asked, 'How are you all?'

'Fine. And you lad, how are you?'

'I'm well, thank you,' said Elliott.

'Have you seen our Josie yet?'

'No, not yet.'

They went into the kitchen, and Mary greeted Elliott with a hug.

'Sit yourself down, and I'll make you a cup of tea,' she said. 'Unless you'd rather have a mug of ale?'

Tom replied, 'Make that two mugs of ale and get him a piece of that tatie cake. He's had a long trip — all the way from America.'

Turning back to Elliott, he asked, 'When did you get back, lad?'

'Yesterday. I'm staying at The Pack Horse at Stanhope.'

'You should have let us know you were coming,' shouted Mary from the pantry. 'You could have stayed here.'

'Thanks, but I left in a bit of a hurry. I didn't have time to write.'

Elliott reached into his jacket pocket and took out a bag of coins, which he handed to Tom and said, 'This is the money you lent me, repaid with interest. Thank you very much for helping me when I needed it.'

'You're very welcome, lad.'

'You know Josie doesn't live here anymore, don't you?' asked Mary, coming back into the kitchen and passing the ale to the men.

'Aye, so I've heard. I called at Springbank Farm on the way over, but Isaac said she'd gone out riding. I'll go and see her on the way back. You know, she's been writing to me all this time, and she never said she'd moved over there. Do you know why she didn't tell me?'

'There's a lot happened since you left,' said Mary, placing a large helping of pie in front of him. 'You should go and talk to her.'

Mary's words had made Elliott feel ill at ease, and his attention wavered when they caught up with each other's news. All the while, a question buzzed around in his head. What would Josie tell him that Mary couldn't?

He glanced at the long clock. He'd stayed longer than he'd intended. As he rose to leave, he said, 'I'll head over there now and see if Josie's back yet. Thanks for the drink and the pie. That's the best pie I've tasted in a long time.'

Elliott shook hands with Tom and kissed Mary on the

cheek and, as he turned towards the door, he noticed the smile that passed between them.

By the time Josie got home, the sun was very low in the sky, and the farmyard was eerily quiet. The Rowell twins had finished work for the day and gone home, so she dismounted and took Jet into the stable and removed his saddle and bridle. Taking a brush from a hook on the wall, Josie began to brush him down. While she worked, she thought about all the memories — good and bad — that her ride through Rookhope had unleashed, stirring up feelings that she'd hidden deep inside — particularly her feelings for Elliott. Despite everything that had happened, she still loved him dearly.

The sound of a horse's hoofbeats in the yard made her stop what she was doing, and she went to the door to see who was there. A well-dressed man was knocking at the back door of the house.

'I'm over here,' she called out in greeting. 'In the stable.'

The man turned to face her, and she saw that her visitor was Charles Chapman.

'Good evening!' he said.

She walked across the yard towards him feeling slightly confused. 'It's late for paying a visit. Is everything alright?' she asked anxiously.

He looked her over from head to toe.

'Everything is — perfect. And you're looking beautiful tonight, if I may say so?'

The compliment and the glint in his eye made Josie feel uncomfortable, and she instinctively stepped back. When he stepped forward and leaned towards her, she could smell alcohol on his breath.

'Aren't you going to invite me in?' he asked flirtatiously.

'I'm sorry, Charles, it's getting late, and I'm tired.'

'Just a quick nightcap? Surely, you'd appreciate some company this evening, when you're here all alone.'

Josie wondered how he knew she was alone. Nelly was still at her parents' house. The hairs on the back of her neck stood up. Desperately trying to look unperturbed, she said, 'I'm expecting company tonight.'

He hesitated for a split second, trying to work out if she was bluffing, and then he smiled.

'Nice try, but I won't be put off that easily. You've been leading me a merry dance, haven't you? Visiting my house, riding out with me, letting me hold you — and then you turned down my proposal. I know you're just playing hard to get. You want me as much as I want you!'

His eyes darkened as he looked at her.

Shaking her head, she said, 'You're wrong, Charles. I'm not playing hard to get. I don't want to marry you.'

'Ha!' he scoffed. 'I came here with good intentions, to seduce you honestly, and to charm you into marrying me. But there is another way.'

Suddenly his look and his stance felt threatening.

Josie rushed to the back door of the house, opened it, and went inside, but as she tried to close the door behind her, Charles put his foot in the gap and smiled maliciously.

'Please leave me alone!' she pleaded.

Josie slammed the door against his foot, but the action did not have the desired effect. He cursed loudly, but his foot remained where it was, preventing her from closing the door and locking him out. He continued to curse under his breath, and when he lifted his head, she could see that his face had turned red, and his eyes were angry. All she'd managed to do was infuriate him.

Using his shoulder, Charles pushed the door open and knocked Josie off her feet. She landed awkwardly on the flagstone floor. Before she could move, she saw him leering at her and then he was on top of her, clumsily running his hands up and down her body, feeling her through her clothes. She screamed at the top of her voice, but Charles placed a hand firmly over her mouth.

'Once my seed is in your womb, you'll beg me to marry you,' he growled.

She closed her eyes as if that would shut out what was happening, and she pushed against him with all her strength, but she couldn't move him. And then suddenly he was gone.

When she opened her eyes, she saw Charles sprawled on the floor a few yards away, and Elliott was standing over him, looking furious. As Charles attempted to get to his feet, Elliott punched him in the face, and in a low voice he growled, 'If you ever lay a hand on her again, I will kill you with my bare hands!'

Charles whimpered, placing his hand to the side of his face, and then he stumbled to his feet.

'Get out of here!' Elliott roared.

Charles staggered to the door, and moments later, she heard the sound of his horse leaving the yard. Elliott was above her now, looking down at her, his face full of concern.

Josie felt numb.

Elliott sat down on the floor next to her and gently lifted her onto his lap and held her. She snuggled into his chest, her heart beating rapidly and tears flowing down her face. There was no doubt in her mind that Charles would have raped her if Elliott hadn't intervened.

'You're safe now, Josie. You're safe, my love,' he whispered, over and over again.

She didn't know how long they sat like that, but she knew that she was safe in Elliott's arms, and the sound of his voice was comforting.

Charles's words were haunting her. If she had fallen pregnant to him in that manner, would she have married him? She was disgusted at the thought of being stuck in a loveless marriage to someone who would stop at nothing to get what he wanted. No, she would rather bring up a child alone than marry a man like him. And then Isaac's words came to mind, and she thought he had been right — Charles was losing his mind.

Josie shivered, and she felt Elliott's hold tighten. Thank

God, he had arrived when he did. But how could he be there? He was in America. Was she losing her mind too?

Carefully lifting Josie to her feet, Elliott held her against his chest and looked deeply into her eyes, and asked, 'Are you alright? He didn't...'

'I'm alright,' she replied with conviction. 'I'm just a bit shaky, that's all.'

She made her excuses so that she could tidy herself up, and when she came back downstairs, Elliott had made a pot of tea and laid out some food on the table.

'Sit down,' he said. 'You and me have a lot to talk about.'

Josie sat at the table and watched Elliott pace up and down in the kitchen. And then he stopped and stood next to her, leaning down with one hand on the table for support, he looked into her eyes. His voice was strained with pent-up emotion when he said, 'I don't know why you abandoned me in New York. I know you've been keeping things from me. And I've no idea why. And after what I've just witnessed here, I wonder how much more there is that you haven't told me. I want you to be straight with me, Josie. Can you do that?'

Josie nodded.

'Who was he?' asked Elliott through gritted teeth.

Josie swallowed audibly and looked down at the table. 'Charles Chapman,' she replied, and when Elliott silently waited for an explanation, she said, 'He asked me to marry him, and I turned him down. I didn't expect to see him again.'

When she looked at Elliott, she could see that he was struggling to stay calm.

'You never mentioned that you were seeing somebody. Is he the reason you left me in New York?'

'No!' She said firmly. 'I was never interested in Charles. I thought he was just being friendly, and I felt sorry for him. There was no more to it than that.'

'So, why did you run away from me in New York?'

Josie stood up and walked over to the window; it was completely dark outside. She needed a moment to clear her head. Turning back to Elliott, she said, 'There are things about me that you don't know, that you won't like, and I was frightened that if you found out about them, you wouldn't want anything more to do with me.'

'Oh, Josie,' he said, stepping towards her and taking her hand. 'Whatever it is, please tell me.'

This was the moment Josie had been avoiding for so long, and surprisingly she felt relieved that the time had come for her secret to be a secret from him no more. She needed to tell him so that at least she would know whether he still wanted her or not, but either way, she would be able to move on with her life.

'I told you that Uncle Joe left me some money when he died,' Josie said.

Elliott nodded.

'Well, that's true. What I didn't tell you was that Joe left me all of his money. He left me the house, the farm, the stock, everything.'

Elliott paused for a moment, and then asked, 'What about your brothers? Didn't he leave them anything?'

Turning to the window again because she didn't want to see his reaction to what she was about to say, she looked out at the night sky and said softly, 'No, he left it all to me. He left it to me because I was his only child.'

Josie paused for a second to give Elliott time to take in what she'd said, and then continued, 'My mother had me before she married Tom. Joe was my real father. I found out at his funeral.'

Elliott came up behind her and whispered in her ear, 'Is that the big secret that you couldn't tell me?'

She turned around and nodded, feeling calmer than she thought she should, but still a tear ran down her cheek.

'I was born out of wedlock, Elliott. I'm a bastard. You'll not want me now.'

He took her into his arms and said, 'If you think that would stop me from wanting you, you have no idea how much I love you.'

'Really?' she asked, surprised by his words.

'Oh, Josie!' Elliott held her tightly. 'I don't care who your parents are. It's you that I love. I'll even move back to Weardale if that's what it takes to be with you.' He pulled back and cupped her face in his hands, and he kissed her gently.

'You've had one hell of a day,' he said. 'Go up to bed

and get some rest. I'll stay down here tonight in case that man comes back.'

When she came downstairs the next morning, Josie found Elliott asleep on a chair in the kitchen. She went over to him and kissed him.

'That's a lovely way to be woken up,' he said sleepily. He pulled her onto his lap and kissed her again. Gazing into her eyes, he said, 'When we were in New York, there was something that I wanted to ask you.'

'Oh, what was that?'

He lifted her onto her feet and knelt on one knee in front of her.

'Josie Milburn, will you marry me?'

There was nothing she wanted more, and she guessed the smile on her face showed that. 'Yes,' she said excitedly, throwing her arms around his neck. 'Of course I'll marry you!'

Elliott rose to his feet and twirled Josie around in his arms.

'Thank you,' he said, kissing her fervently. Then he took the Tiffany box from his pocket and opened it slowly. He watched Josie's face as he revealed the engagement ring he'd bought in New York.

'It's beautiful!' she exclaimed.

He took the ring from the box and placed it on her finger.

Chapter 32

Elliott glanced in the shop windows as he walked down the front street at Stanhope. There was something that he needed, and he knew exactly where to get it — Richardson's General Dealers. When he entered the store, he was greeted by a friendly face.

'Good morning, Mr Dawson. Nice day, isn't it?'

'Aye, it is, Mr Richardson.'

Elliott stood beside the large counter and looked around at the variety of goods on display — groceries, household goods, hardware and haberdashery. There wasn't an inch of space wasted in the shop.

'What can I get you?' asked Mr Richardson.

'I need a necktie. A nice one for a wedding.'

'Oh, I love weddings. Who's getting married?'

'I am.'

Mr Richardson looked at him with a puzzled expression, and said, 'Congratulations! And may I ask who's the lucky woman?'

'Josie Milburn from Westgate.'

'Ah! I know the family well. Her mother comes in here oft enough. Now, let's see what we have over here.'

Mr Richardson walked away and disappeared to the far end of the shop, where Elliott could hear him opening and closing drawers. The shopkeeper came back with ties and cravats draped over his arm, and he placed them carefully on the counter.

A pale blue one caught Elliott's eye, and he picked it up.

'An excellent choice! The last person to buy this particular tie for his wedding was Mr Chapman. He and his wife were very happily married — until she died, that is.'

Elliott scowled; he didn't want to hear about Charles Chapman. The blue tie was quickly put down on the counter, and he chose a dark red one in its place. 'On second thoughts,' he said, 'I think I prefer this one.'

'This is the most expensive tie in the shop,' said Mr Richardson, raising his eyebrows.

'That's fine,' said Elliott, handing over a sovereign.

The shopkeeper smiled and put the coin in a drawer behind the counter. Then he said, 'Speaking of Mr Chapman, have you heard what's happened?'

Elliott shook his head.

As Mr Richardson carefully wrapped the tie in tissue paper and placed it in a paper bag, he started to tell Elliott the latest gossip about Charles Chapman and was soon in full flow. Whether or not Elliott wanted to hear it, he had to stay and listen or leave without his change.

When the shopkeeper had passed over the bag and a handful of coins, Elliott walked briskly out of the shop and ran back to his lodgings. He pushed past a few men who were standing in the doorway of the public house and shouted above the noise to the barman, 'Mr Dalton! Could I borrow a horse, please?'

'Aye, lad. Our Bessie's in the stable. Help yourself.'

'Thank you!'

Elliott rushed to the stable, tacked up the brown mare and set off for Westgate. He rode as fast as he could on the old animal; he wanted to tell Josie the news before she heard it from someone else.

When he reached the farm, he sighed. Josie was there, carrying a basket of eggs across the yard, and her whole face lit up when she saw him. She stopped and waited for him to dismount.

'Good morning,' she said. 'I wasn't expecting to see you until tonight.'

'Please can we go inside, Josie,' he said brusquely. 'There's something I need to tell you.'

Josie's face fell. 'What is it?' she asked.

'Not here.'

Elliott walked quickly into the house and held open the door for Josie, who marched past him and stood with her back to the table. She looked worried.

'There's a story going around Stanhope. It's about Charles Chapman. They're saying that he's in Durham prison.'

Elliott waited for the news to sink in.

'What for?' asked Josie.

'For not paying his debts. He owes a lot of money.'

Josie was shocked. She sat down at the table and put her hand to her mouth as she thought about her friendship, or relationship, or whatever it was she'd had with Charles. He had no money. Yet he'd always been well-dressed, and he rode a good horse. His family home was a large, old house with land, but it had been neglected. She'd thought that was because he was a bit eccentric, not because he didn't have the money to repair it. Thinking back to that day when she'd had tea with him at Stanhope, he'd let her pay for it without any argument; that had surprised her at the time. And then when they'd visited High Force waterfall, they hadn't stopped for refreshments despite the length of the journey. She'd put that down to his distress after she'd refused to marry him, but perhaps it had been because he couldn't afford to pay for a meal.

And now she understood his interest in her. He'd made himself known to her just after she'd inherited Joe's money. He'd befriended her and proposed to her, not because he had any feelings for her, but because he'd needed her money to pay off his debts! And then when she'd turned him down, he'd been so desperate that he was prepared to rape her to get her to marry him. The scoundrel deserved what he'd got.

Elliott had been watching Josie intently, and when he saw her lip begin to tremble, he stepped forward, and she rushed into his arms.

'Shush, it's alright. He can't hurt you now.'

After a few minutes, she stepped back and wiped her eyes on her sleeve.

'What about the children?' she asked. 'What'll happen to them?

'They're in the workhouse at Stanhope.'

'The poor bairns. What do you think will happen to them?'

'Mr Richardson seemed to think Chapman would be forced to sell his property to settle his debts before they let him out of prison. I should think he'll be able to buy a smaller house with what's left, and keep the children with him.'

'I hope he buys one a long way from here. I never want to lay eyes on him again.'

'By the way,' said Elliott, 'Do you know who Chapman's father-in-law is?'

'No. Should I?'

'John Peart.'

'John Peart from White Wells Farm?'

'Yes.'

'I had no idea,' said Josie, looking pensive. 'But come to think of it, I remember seeing Charles's wedding photograph and his wife looked a lot like Aunt Connie. They'd have been cousins.'

'Where did you see his wedding photo?'

'At his house. It was on the sideboard in the day room.'

'You went to his house?' Elliott asked incredulously.

'Yes, I did. Just once. But honestly, Elliott, Charles meant nothing to me.'

She reached out and took Elliott's hand, and he smiled at her.

'Aye, I know that,' he said gently.

'Do you think he wanted Springbank Farm because of the family connection?' she asked.

'It's possible, but I think it's more likely he just needed the money from it. It's no secret that Springbank Farm is one of the most profitable farms in the dale.'

'I wonder,' said Josie, 'if the two of them were in cahoots all along, with Charles trying to seduce me into marrying him and John trying to frighten me into taking a husband to protect me.'

'Now, that I would believe,' said Elliott. 'And now they're both locked up for their trouble.'

That evening, after they'd finished eating, Elliott turned to Josie and said, 'I'm so glad I came back to England to see you. When you left me in New York, I thought you didn't want me anymore — that you'd found someone else. Look, we're going to be married soon. No more secrets between us from now on. Promise?'

'I will promise,' said Josie, shifting uncomfortably in her seat, 'but before I do, there's something else I need to tell you.'

Elliott looked at her warily.

She said, 'It's about your company.'

He raised his eyebrows and said, 'The Dawson Mining Company?'

'Yes. Your investor, the person who made the anonymous investment —'

'What about him?'

'It wasn't a him. It was me.'

'You invested in my company!' he exclaimed.

'Are you angry?'

'No, I'm surprised, that's all.' He shook his head in bewilderment. 'Two thousand pounds. You have that much faith in me?'

'Yes, of course, I have! I knew you'd do well at mining, and I was right.'

Elliott laughed. 'So, we've been business partners all this time, and I had absolutely no idea.'

'Once we're married, my shares will pass to you. You'll own the company outright.'

'Josie, I don't know what to say. You're a remarkable woman.'

She rose from her seat and stood behind his chair. Putting her arms around his shoulders, and resting her head against his, she said, 'I know how much you want to go back to your business and I totally understand that,' and then she whispered in his ear, 'I want to go back with you.'

Elliott stood up quickly and gently placed his hands on either side of her head. He looked deeply into her eyes to see if she meant what she'd said.

'But what about the farm?' he asked.

'Matt could manage the farm for us. He's more than capable.'

Elliott nodded and took her into his arms. He lowered his brow to hers, and they stood together in silence for a moment, before he said, 'There's something that I should tell you, as well.'

Josie lifted her head to look at him. 'What is it?'

'After the tornado, I rented a new place, but I didn't tell you that I'd decided to build a house. The plot is on the edge of town, overlooking the river. After seeing how timber buildings fared in the storm, I used stone. It took longer to build, and it was more expensive, but it's much stronger. When I drew the plans, I had High House in mind, so it's similar to that — except the ceilings are higher!' Elliott laughed. 'The times I've bumped my head on those door frames! Anyway, I finished building it just before I went to New York. When I invited you to come to Missouri with me, it was because I wanted to show you the house.'

'It sounds wonderful,' she said sincerely.

Holding her more firmly, Elliott said, 'I built it for you, Josie.'

Chapter 33

High House Farm
September 1897

The day dawned clear and bright, and Josie woke early to the sound of songbirds in the garden. She dressed quickly and walked over to High House Farm.

'By, you're keen,' said Tom, beaming, when Josie came into the kitchen.

Josie returned his grin.

'Your mother's already got the water on for your bath,' said Tom.

'She must have been up earlier than me,' laughed Josie.

'To be honest, I don't think she slept a wink. She's as excited as you are about today.'

'Where is she now?'

'Up in your room, getting everything ready.'

'I need to see Matt first. Do you know where he is?'

'Aye, he's gone out to do the milking,' replied Tom. 'You'll find him in the byre.'

Josie went out to the cow byre where she heard the

rhythmic splash of milk filling a bucket. Matt was sitting on a small stool beside a shorthorn cow.

'Morning, Matt.'

Looking up at her in surprise, he asked, 'Shouldn't you be getting ready?'

'There's something I need to ask you, and I mightn't get the chance later on.'

'What is it?' he asked.

'If I went away, would you manage Springbank Farm for me?'

'While you're on your honeymoon?' asked Matt. 'Surely the twins could see to things for a couple of weeks.'

'No, it's not for our honeymoon. I'm going back to America with Elliott, and I want to know if you'll manage the farm for us.'

'Oh! Of course, I would, if that's what you want. Aye, I'd love to.'

'That's great! Nelly could stay on and keep house for you.'

She noticed Matt's eyes twinkle, and his mouth curled up at the sides.

'What's so funny?' she asked.

'There's something you should know,' he said. 'I've been seeing Nelly Green for over a year now, and I'm going to ask her to marry me. If she stays on at Springbank Farm, it won't be as my housekeeper; she'll be my wife.'

Josie smiled broadly and hugged her brother, which

caused the milk to squirt on the stone floor. They laughed together.

'I'm so pleased for you,' she said, wondering how she hadn't known that Nelly and her brother had been seeing each other all that time. She had never suspected a thing.

Since Nelly had started at Springbank Farm, Josie had become very fond of her and had missed her while she had been away, caring for her family. Thankfully, they had all recovered from whooping cough, even the baby, and Nelly had returned to the farm.

'Heh! You'd better go. I'm surprised Mother hasn't come down here looking for you.'

Josie went back to the house and ran up the stairs to her old room. Her mother was laying out a beautiful white dress on the bed.

'There you are!' said Mary, hugging her daughter. 'Eeh, I wish you'd stayed here last night, lass. There's so much to do. Tommy's filling the tub for you. Go and have a bath first, and I'll make breakfast, that way your hair will have time to dry while you're eating. And then I'll do your hair before you get dressed.'

'I see you've got everything under control,' laughed Josie. 'Thank you.'

Josie followed her mother's plan, and it didn't seem long before she was back in her room, dressed in her finery, and looking in the mirror at her reflection.

Her shiny, dark hair was pulled back from her glowing face and tied in an elaborate knot at the back of her head.

Her eyes shone brightly. She wore a white lace bridal gown with puffed shoulders, a tiny waist, and a tiered skirt that trailed to the floor. She hardly recognised herself.

Josie stood still as Mary carefully placed a small tiara on her head and fastened the veil in place before she stood back to admire her daughter.

'You look beautiful,' she said with a tear in her eye. 'Just as a bride should on her wedding day.'

'Thanks, Mother,' said Josie. 'I couldn't have done it without you.'

Mary smiled, and then she said, as though she had just remembered, 'Something old, something new, something borrowed, something blue.'

'Well, the dress is new,' said Josie. 'And I borrowed your hairpins. I'm wearing blue garters...'

'What about something old?'

'My fluorite pendant,' said Josie, lifting her hand to touch the crystal.

'But that's not old. It can't be two years since you had it made.'

'Ah, but the crystal itself is probably the oldest thing in this house.'

Mary rolled her eyes but accepted that her daughter was probably right. She looked Josie up and down and said. 'You're ready. Let's get you to that chapel.'

When they arrived at the Wesleyan Methodist Chapel at Westgate, the family went inside, leaving Josie and

Tom standing outside the door.

'Are you sure this is what you want, love?' Tom asked her quietly. 'It's not too late to change your mind.'

'I want this more than anything.'

'That's what I hoped you'd say,' said Tom, 'and I hope you'll be as happy together as me and your mother have been.'

They heard the wheezy sound of the organ starting up, and then the Wedding March began. Tom opened the door and held out his arm to Josie. As they walked up the aisle, she noticed that the chapel was full, even the balcony, and then she saw Elliott waiting for her at the altar; he looked so handsome in his grey, tailored suit. When she was standing by his side, he looked down at her and smiled his cheeky smile that she loved so much.

The minister began the marriage service, and it was over before she knew it. Elliott kissed her in front of everyone, and not caring that the room was full of family, friends and neighbours, she reached up and put her arms around his neck and kissed him back.

The minister coughed loudly, which made the congregation burst into laughter. The couple moved apart, grinning at each other.

'Come on, Mrs Dawson. We need to go to your parents' place,' said Elliott, and then he whispered in her ear, 'And then I'll take you home and have you all to myself.'

Heat coursed through her body and she blushed furiously. Elliott winked at her. Then he took her hand

and led her out of the chapel, to smiles and words of congratulation from the guests.

Elliott stopped briefly outside the chapel to throw coins for the children, and then the wedding party made their way to High House Farm for the wedding breakfast.

When they eventually returned to Springbank Farm, Elliott picked up Josie and carried her over the threshold, but rather than put her down inside the door, he continued straight up the stairs to their bedroom, much to Josie's amusement.

Josie took off her necklace and put it down on the dressing table. Elliott took out his pocket watch and placed it next to the pendant — the two crystals side by side.

'They were always meant to be together,' said Josie wistfully.

He took her hands in his and looked at her lovingly.

'Just like us,' he said. 'We were always meant to be together, too. We've waited so long for this night.'

Josie turned her back to him so that he could unbutton her dress, and she slipped out of it. Then she turned around and walked into his arms. He kissed her with a passion that she hadn't felt since that night long ago on the fells.

Epilogue

High House Farm
September 1898

Knocking at the door of the house she'd once called home felt strange to Josie, but she'd been away for so long now that she didn't feel comfortable just walking in as she would have done in the past. She heard someone bustling around inside, and then the door opened wide.

'Josie!' exclaimed Mary, and then she turned around and shouted, 'Tom, it's our Josie. She's here!'

Mary opened her arms and Josie hugged her mother, and as soon as they parted, she felt Tom's strong arms around her.

'It's good to see you, love,' he said huskily.

'Come in, lass,' said Mary. 'We can't have you standing out here on the doorstep, can we? Why didn't you tell us you were coming? Are you here on your own?'

'Let the lass get into the house before you start bombarding her with questions. She'll tell us in her own good time why she's come back. Get the lass a cup of tea.'

'It's so good to see you both,' said Josie. 'And I'd love a cup of tea.'

She went inside and sat at the kitchen table. Her mother put the kettle on the stove and spooned tea into a teapot, and then carried three empty cups over to the table. Tom sat by her side.

'So, how's that man of yours?' asked Tom.

'He's well.'

'That's good. Did he travel back with you?'

Josie shook her head and said, 'He insisted that I came home myself.'

She noticed the look of concern that passed between Tom and Mary.

Mary joined them at the table and filled the cups from the teapot, before asking, 'How long are you staying?'

'I'm not sure. For a while. I hope Matt and Nelly won't mind if I stay at Springbank Farm.'

'They'll be pleased to have you,' said her mother. 'And the house is so big that they'll hardly know you're there.'

'I was sorry to miss the wedding,' said Josie.

Mary smiled and said, 'Ah! It was a lovely day, and they looked so happy together.'

Tom looked at Mary, and she shut up. They sat in silence, waiting for their daughter to explain why she'd returned from America without her husband.

'Don't look at me like that,' said Josie. 'I didn't want to come home without him.'

'You haven't said why you've come back yet,' said Tom.

'Is everything alright between the two of you?'

'We had an argument before I left. Elliott wanted me to leave right away, and I wanted to wait until he could travel back with me.'

'Why the rush?' asked Mary. 'Why didn't he want you to wait for him?'

'Because I'm expecting.'

'Aw, love. That's great news,' said Tom. 'Did you hear that, Mary? We're going to be grandparents.'

'You should be thrilled, Josie,' said Mary, smiling warmly. 'There's nothing in this world better than being a mother.'

'I'm happy about the baby, I am, but I wish I hadn't had to leave Elliott over there. He didn't want me to have the baby in Flat River. He wanted me to be here with you. And the crossings can get quite rough in winter, so he wanted me to travel home now.'

'What's so important in America that he let his pregnant wife travel all that way on her own?' said Tom crossly. 'That's what I want to know.'

'It's not his fault. Not really. The Dawson Mining Company has done very well, and a large company has made an offer for it. He wants to stay there until the sale goes through and then he'll come back. I hope he gets here before the baby's born.'

'When are you due?' asked Mary.

'Around Christmas time.'

'So, if he's selling his company, what does he intend to

do for a living?' asked Tom.

'He's made quite a name for himself over there because the leases he took out were on the best bits of the veins. The company has asked if he'll do some prospecting for them.'

'In America?' asked Mary.

'Aye, in America. And other countries as well. Just for a month or so at a time.'

'That's not a very steady job for a man with a family,' said Tom.

'With what he's been offered for the company,' said Josie, 'and what the farm makes, he doesn't need to worry about providing for us. If he does this prospecting work, it'll be because he wants to do it, not for the money. And I'm keen for him to do it because I want to go with him. I'd love to travel more and see other places.'

Mary looked proudly at her daughter, and said, 'Who'd have thought it, eh? Our Josie, gallivanting around the world.'

Author's Historical Note

Weardale is renowned around the world for its minerals, especially fluorite which is known locally as spar, but also for quartz, galena, calcite and other less common minerals. Weardale specimens can be found in the national collections of many countries.

Miners removed mineral specimens and sold them to dealers, who then sold them to collectors, and the mine owners turned a blind eye to the practice. The miners also collected *bonny bits* for themselves, using larger pieces to decorate gardens and wall tops, and smaller pieces to make spar boxes.

A *Grand Mineralogical Exhibition* was held at St John's Chapel in December 1895. In *Fractured Crystal*, I moved the event forward to July to fit the story. Years later, The Friends of Killhope reinstated the *Grand Mineralogical Exhibition* and hosted the event annually in Weardale for many years.

The minerals were a by-product of the lead industry. Middlehope, Boltsburn and Grove Rake were actual lead mining sites at the time of the story. The Grove Rake headframe is the last surviving headframe in County Durham. It was saved from demolition in 2018. However, this structure was not on the site at the time of the story.

The Rookhope arch and the flue holes on the opposite side of the road are all that remain of Redburn smelt mill today.

While researching the name for the small gaps in drystone walls that allow sheep to pass between fields, I discovered many names are used in different parts of the country. In Rookhope they are known as bool holes. I was unable to find another reference to that name, although bool hole is used in Cumbria for the hole in the ceiling above cattle sheds, used to throw down hay. In other parts of England, these gaps are called hogg holes, hogget holes, sheep creeps and lunky holes. In general, smoot holes are smaller gaps intended for hares and rabbits to pass through, and sometimes they incorporated traps. However, in Weardale, the term smoot hole is used for sheep-sized holes too, so I used smoot hole in the story.

Many Weardale families emigrated to America in the nineteenth century and wrote to their loved ones back home. There is a fantastic set of letters at Killhope Museum, written by members of the Graham family who lived at Killhope. They give a wonderful insight into the lives of people at that time. Some Weardale families went to Missouri, which had a booming lead mining industry in the late-nineteenth century, dominated by the St Joseph Mining Company at Flat River.

The tornado that hit St Louis and the surrounding area on 27th May 1896 was devastating. It is described as the costliest and the third most deadly tornado in US history, with at least 255 fatalities and over 1,000 injured. The damage was estimated at over $10 million, and more than 5,000 people lost their homes.

The Mineral Collector was an annual periodical published in New York. Volume One was published in 1895. It was intended to be read by collectors, students and dealers. However, the mineral auction and the collector, George Wiseman, in *Fractured Crystal* are fictional.

An immigration station was opened on Ellis Island in New York Harbour in 1892 to process and health check immigrants. All of the timber buildings were burnt down within two hours on 15th June 1897, destroying immigration records from 1855 to that date. Luckily, there were no fatalities. The source of the fire was unknown.

Also by Margaret Manchester

The Lead Miner's Daughter
Amazon #1 International Bestseller

It is 1872 when Mary Watson, a lead miner's daughter, leaves her childhood home to work at Springbank Farm. She soon meets a handsome neighbour, Joe Milburn, and becomes infatuated with him, but is he the right man for her?

Mary's story is woven into a background of rural life and crime in the remote valley of Weardale. Not one but two murders shock the small community.

Find yourself in the farmhouse kitchen with the Peart family, walking on the wide open fells, seeking shelter underground and solving crimes with PC Emerson as this intriguing story unfolds.

Will the culprits be brought to justice? Will Mary find true love?

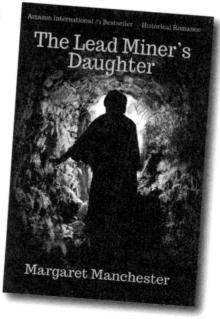

Carved in Stone

Amazon #1 UK Bestseller

Northern England 1881. Sent away during her brother's trial, Phyllis Forster returns home after a seven-year absence to find Weardale and its people have changed. They've turned against the Forster family, and she desperately wants to win back their respect. Can trust and harmony be restored in this rural community?

At 28 years old, she has almost given up hope of love and marriage, and throws herself into the management of the family estate, until two very different men come into her life.

Ben, troubled by the past and full of anger and distrust, is a shepherd who shuns the company of others, until his new boss arrives at Burnside Hall.

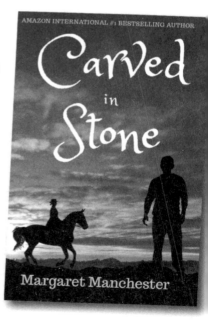

Timothy, the new vicar, is preoccupied with the ancient past, but he takes a keen interest in Phyllis.

Will she settle for just a husband? Or will she defy convention and follow her heart?